Sons of Potenza

John Rosa

DEDICATION

For Julie
You are my inspiration, my love, my life.

CONTENTS

Dedication   i

1   Prelude   1

2   Book I   Pg 17

3   Book II   Pg 55

4   Book III   Pg 153

This is a work of fiction. Any reference to historical events, real people or real places are used fictitiously.

PRELUDE

It was a modest house, certainly not one befitting the ruler of organized crime in the Rocky Mountain region. But Charlie Salardino loved it anyway.

Located off West 35th Avenue and Vallejo Street in North Denver, Salardino had moved into the three-bedroom bungalow with his beloved wife Gina just before Christmas the previous year. A small artificial Christmas tree Gina purchased at the Montgomery Ward department store off South Broadway Boulevard was the first thing the Salardinos put up in the front sitting room, decorated with gold glass bulbs, shiny silver garland and twinkling lights you could see from the sidewalk out front.

The tree was carefully packed away with the other Christmas decorations in the detached two-car garage now, replaced by an upright piano and an oversized chair that Charlie would sit in to play his mandolin. The sitting room also featured a nice cherry wood coffee table Gina had purchased the same day as the Christmas tree, along with an ornate three-person sofa, adorned with small red and yellow roses on cream-colored cushions.

The sofa was protected by a clear plastic cover that would only come off for the most important guests – guests that only Gina deemed worthy. Charlie always chuckled to himself about that because the only person that Gina would find worthy was the Pope himself, and there was little chance his Holiness was visiting, at least not while Charlie was the most powerful mob boss in Denver.

Charlie had argued with Gina that the plastic cover was silly -- "Why have a couch if no one can sit on it?" -- but she had dug her heels in and wouldn't budge. It was the Sicilian in her, and one of the reasons he loved her so fiercely even after close to 30 years of marriage. They had wed on the steps

"

of a small church in their hometown of Taormina when he was only 17 and she was barely 15, before they had made the voyage over to America, and his love for the most beautiful girl in the village had never wavered. He had never strayed during that time, even with the abundant opportunities that running Colorado's largest prostitution ring had offered him. People mocked him about this, calling him "Saint Charlie" – they all had gumars and found it harmless – but always behind his back and only to a point. One thing you did not disrespect was Charlie's love for Gina.

Charlie Salardino was old school, a real "Mustache Pete." He had made his bones back in Sicily when he was just a teenager, and then he came to the States to help a distant cousin, Big Jim Colosimo, run Chicago in the early part of the century. Colosimo controlled Chicago's South Side and had more than a hundred brothels spread throughout the area. But Big Jim had limited vision, and when prohibition took effect in 1919, he declined to take advantage of the opportunity the illegal liquor trade offered.

Salardino didn't suffer from this myopic view, and so he sided with another distant cousin, Johnny Torrio, and an up-and-coming Al Capone, to take out Colosimo and seize control of the South Side. They expanded their power during the ensuing "Beer Wars," and Salardino became a trusted lieutenant. After Torrio retired and Capone took control, the new boss of Chicago sent Charlie out West to run the bootlegging operation in the Rocky Mountain territory.

When Salardino arrived in Colorado in the mid 1920s, the area's underworld was run by the Carlino brothers in Pueblo, 120 miles south of Denver. Salardino initially worked with the Carlinos, but eventually broke free to run racketeering and bootlegging in Denver, and often found himself at odds with his former associates in the Steel City.

In May of 1931, Sam Carlino was mowed down by a spray of gunfire in the kitchen of his North Denver home. A couple months later, Pete Carlino was found with three bullet holes in him under a bridge southwest of Pueblo.

Detectives questioned Salardino about the murders but could never tie him to either death. Salardino, who owned a car dealership, a couple of restaurants and a grocery store, insisted he was a legitimate businessman and had nothing to do with that life. He loudly proclaimed to any newspaper reporter that would listen that he was being discriminated against because he was an Italian, even more so one from Sicily.

With the death of the Carlino brothers, however, Charlie Salardino did in fact become the acting boss of the Rocky Mountains. When prohibition was lifted in 1933, Salardino changed his focus from bootlegging to gambling, loansharking and prostitution, and over the next decade he consolidated operations throughout the Front Range, running things in Denver while keeping the Pueblo faction under his thumb. And he made sure to keep his friends in the Midwest happy, sending regular tributes back to The Outfit in

Chicago.

Salardino wasn't above using violence to retain power – police estimated that 30 murders tied to organized crime took place in Denver and Pueblo in the decade after the deaths of the Carlino brothers. But Charlie also knew that violence often cut into profits, so he preferred a more peaceful existence. Disputes in the family were handled diplomatically, and everyone was making money.

In fact, for the past two years, there hadn't been a single murder in the Denver metro area that police attributed to mob activity. Salardino had settled into a comfortable existence, content with the money he was bringing in and the power he held in the region. He knew that some in his organization were growing restless and wanted to expand the gambling and bookmaking arms of the family and the reach it had throughout the West. There were also grumblings about getting into the growing narcotics industry, but Charlie really didn't want the headache, or the attention from law enforcement. He figured if everyone was making money, there shouldn't be an issue.

Despite being the man in charge, Charlie didn't ask for a lot himself, accepting a smaller percentage of tribute than most bosses across the country. He wasn't worried about his status in the hierarchy of things, or his perception in the public. Hence, the small bungalow house when he could have easily afforded one of the many mansions that were popping up in the Capitol Hill area. Charlie preferred to lead from the shadows. He was content with his station in life, especially if Gina was safe and happy.

Things had settled into a comfortable rhythm, so occasionally, Charlie afforded himself a day off from business, unheard of in his line of work. One couldn't imagine Lucky Luciano blowing off business concerns to take a stroll along the New Jersey boardwalk, or Joe Profaci going for a picnic in Central Park. But, as he got older, Charlie started to appreciate a slower pace to life. Denver wasn't Chicago, or New York, or even Kansas City for that matter. He believed he could afford to take a day of leisure occasionally. That Saturday was one such day for Charlie, as he planned on relaxing and playing his mandolin before taking Gina to the city for dinner and a movie later that evening.

Gina was out that afternoon, visiting her mother who they had put up in a house just four blocks away, and Charlie had just sat down to play the mandolin when the front bell rang. Charlie wasn't expecting anyone, so the bell caught him by surprise. Usually Charlie's bodyguard, his nephew Danny Villecco, would be close by and would go answer the door for him, but Danny had also taken the day off to visit his father at the prison in Canon City.

Charlie didn't have either of the pistols he normally carried on him. They were in the garage, on the workbench he had used to clean and oil them earlier this morning, steps away from the boxed Christmas tree.

Charlie cursed himself for being careless. He didn't think anyone had it out for him right now, but someone of his standing always had enemies. He shouldn't have let Danny go away without some kind of other backup in place; a man with Salardino's stature couldn't afford to be caught without some sort of protection.

The bell rang again, followed by three strong raps on the door. Charlie carefully set down the mandolin and walked over to the front window, slightly parting the lace curtains to see if he could determine who was on his front porch.

Charlie relaxed a bit when he saw it was Gaetano Scaglia and Sam Pelligrino at his door, two of his lieutenants. He wasn't sure what they were doing there, but at least it was two people he knew, if not necessarily trusted.

"Give me a second. I was in the back," Charlie called out, straightening the drapes before making his way to the entryway.

Charlie opened the door and nodded to his visitors. "Tano. Pilgram. To what do I owe the honor?"

"What took so long? You in the pishadoo?" Tano laughed. He was always a smart ass, and Charlie didn't appreciate the disrespect. Built like a fireplug, Gaetano 'Tano' Scaglia envisioned himself as Denver's version of Benjamin Siegel. Just 28, Tano was already something of a local celebrity, always dressed to the nines in $300 suits and available to any reporter or camera in the area. Tano was dark and handsome, if you overlooked his nose. A former amateur boxer with terrible lateral movement, Tano's nose had been broken so many times it now resembled a question mark on his wide, Cupid-like face, earning him the hated nickname Smush by his enemies.

But Tano was a valuable lieutenant, overseeing Denver's gambling and loansharking operations along with his two brothers Giacamo and Giuseppe. Their father, Raffaele, was a long-time associate of Salardino, serving as Charlie's underboss for many years. Their partnership began during prohibition and continued through the decade afterward, but Raffaele had recently taken a step back with his sons filling the void.

Gaetano Scaglia was as tough as they came. Even though he was pretty much a stationary target in the ring, Tano rarely lost. He was methodical, stalking his opponent around the squared circle, absorbing blow after blow until he eventually cornered his opponent and ended the fight by knocking them out of the ring. They could hammer his face over and over, but Tano never went down and would eventually catch them with a shot of his own that weakened their knees and took the fight right out of them.

Outside of the ring, Tano never lost, no matter how many rounds it took. He'd beat you down with fists, feet, pipes, bats – whatever he needed to break your legs and your spirit. He was the best collector in Salardino's organization, and his reputation was growing throughout the region.

Sam Pelligrino, meanwhile, was something completely different. He was a straight up killer. The Outfit had loaned him to Salardino during the Carlino Brothers conflict to help Charlie consolidate power, and Pelligrino was probably responsible for half of those 30 murders the cops attributed to the war between Denver and Pueblo. While he was good with a pistol, Sam preferred up close work and was lethal with a blade and a garrote.

Following Salardino's takeover of the Rocky Mountain region, Pelligrino decided he liked the thin mountain air better than the hustle of Chicago and elected to stay in Colorado. It didn't hurt that there was a $25,000 bounty on his head back East, but that didn't bother Pelligrino as much as it probably should have. Huge for a Sicilian at over six feet tall and close to 300 pounds, Pelligrino was the most feared man in the western portion of the country.

"You going to invite us in? It's cold out here," Tano asked, a big smile across his smushed face. Pelligrino, as usual, was silent.

Salardino hesitated, still a little unnerved by the unexpected visit. He finally relented and stepped aside, allowing the two men into his home and steering them toward the sitting room.

"I don't have a lot of time. I'm taking Gina into the city for dinner and a movie tonight, and I need to start getting ready," Charlie said while picking up the mandolin and sitting down on his chair, anxious to get his visitors out of his home as quickly as possible.

Pelligrino delicately sat on the edge of the plastic covered couch while Scaglia took a seat on the piano bench.

"What's with the plastic cover?" Tano asked, nodding toward the couch.

"Gina doesn't want any undesirables to sit on her couch. The plastic protects it from getting stained."

"Did you hear that, Sam? You better sit somewhere else," Tano laughed. "You're definitely an undesirable, a real gavone." Pelligrino didn't move.

"Is Gina here?" Tano looked around the room, trying to find a trace of Charlie's wife.

"She's at her mothers, but she should be on her way back."

"You're pretty good with that thing, aren't you?" Tano pointed at the mandolin. "Would you play us something? I love that old dago music."

The request rubbed Charlie the wrong way. Why was Tano asking him to play something? Charlie wasn't there to entertain them. Salardino was the boss of the family and should be treated with the respect that commanded, not someone who performed on demand.

Salardino ignored the request. "What do you need? I don't have a whole lot of time." Charlie was trying to keep the annoyance out of his voice but failing.

"We want to talk to you about an organizational change," Tano's smile left his face. "At the top."

Charlie glanced over at Pelligrino and noticed that he had pulled a handgun with a suppressor on the end out of his jacket pocket and had it leveled at him.

"What is this?" Charlie asked, looking from Tano to Pelligrino and back to Tano again. Salardino, who was known for being calm and cool under pressure, didn't feel calm and cool at that moment. He could feel the fear rising in his gut. "What kind of comedy is this?"

"No one's laughing, Charlie," Tano said, his grim face showing no emotion.

"Does Jack know what you are doing?"

Giacomo "Jack" Scaglia was the oldest and unquestionably the smartest of the three Scaglia brothers. He was also Salardino's underboss, Jack assuming the role his father had held before taking a step back, and Charlie knew Tano wouldn't make a move like this without his go ahead.

"Oh yeah, Jack knows," Tano said, that smug smile that Salardino had grown to hate coming back to his face. "In fact, it was his idea."

Charlie broke out in a cold sweat, and he could taste the bile rising in his stomach. He wasn't going to take Gina to the movies tonight, or on any other night. He was cashing in. And Charlie knew it was his own fault. It was his complacency that had led to this moment. Jack Scaglia had been suggesting for months ways to expand their empire, but Charlie had fought against it, not wanting to go through another bloody war. Salardino was perfectly happy with the life he had forged and the money he was bringing in. His mistake was thinking others were also content.

He knew Jack and the Scaglia brothers were ambitious; Charlie just underestimated how ambitious they really were. Charlie couldn't help but think back to his own cousin, Big Jim Colisimo, and the lack of ambition and vision that had led to his demise. The irony was not lost on him.

"You don't have to do this, Gaetano," Salardino said, using his formal name. "I'll step aside and let Jack take over. He can run things. I'll just be his consigliere."

"We already have one in our father," Tano said, taking his own pistol out of his coat pocket, slowly screwing a long black suppressor on the end. "You know that won't work."

"This is about Central City, isn't it," Charlie asked, the whole time his mind racing to see if he could find a way out of this situation.

"I don't know. You would have to ask Jack; he's the smart one. I'm just the good looking one."

Salardino looked over at Pelligrino, whose eyes had never left Charlie since he had sat down on the plastic covered couch. "You got nothing to say here, Sam? Wait'll they figure out what's going on with you. You think Jack will put up with that?" That caused Pelligrino, who had been sitting as still as a monument on a hill, to flinch ever so slightly. But whatever it was that bothered him passed quickly.

"What is he talking about, Pilgrim?" Tano asked, turning to look at

Pelligrino. "What are you up to?"

Pelligrino finally spoke, his voice barely above a whisper. "He's just trying to save himself."

That seemed to satisfy Tano, who nodded thoughtfully before turning his attention back to Charlie.

"You sure you don't want to play something?" Tano pointed his weapon toward the mandolin Salardino was holding. "Your Swan Song, so to speak?"

Charlie started going through his options in his head. He wasn't strong or fast enough to overtake Tano and Pelligrino physically, and he had left his pistols in the garage. He had lied about Gina being on her way back; he didn't expect her for another couple of hours at the earliest. He could offer them money, or more power, but he knew that would be futile. If Jack Scaglia was behind this, then he had already explored all the angles and Tano and Pilgrim would know that their best course of action was to continue down the current path. The decision had been made – Charlie Salardino was in the way and needed to be removed.

Playing something might not be a bad idea, he thought. It would give him some time to think things through, see if he could find a solution to get out of this situation. Charlie nodded his head and began plucking a few notes on the instrument, working his way into an old Sicilian song with a sad melody. He played for a little over a minute, with Tano nodding along to the rhythm. "Bella," Tano said, and he seemed to relax, dropping his gun hand just a bit.

Salardino took that opportunity to swing the mandolin at Tano's face, aiming for his grotesque nose. The instrument splintered into dozens of pieces and Tano Scaglia let out a surprised yell. Still quick for his age, Charlie lunged at Tano, going for the younger man's throat. But at the same time Pelligrino fired, his bullet catching Charlie in the left shoulder.

Salardino took a couple of uneasy steps before collapsing heavily onto the plastic covered couch.

Charlie looked down at the blood rapidly spreading from his shoulder to his chest. "Damn." He looked at Pelligrino incredulously. "You shot me."

Charlie put his hands to his wound, trying to staunch the bleeding. "You really shot me," he repeated. He ripped open his shirt, displacing several buttons and exposing his undershirt, which was now stained a bright crimson color. Surprisingly, Charlie didn't feel a lot of pain – just a burning sensation, like someone had stuck a hot poker in his shoulder.

Charlie Salardino didn't feel the next shot at all.

Tano had risen by now, blood flowing from his nose. "You mother-fucking-mutt." Tano put the suppressed end of his pistol on Salardino's forehead before firing a shot that sent a fine pink mist into the air and blood and brains onto the family pictures that adorned the back wall behind the plastic-covered couch.

The light faded from the eyes of Denver's mob boss, as quickly as the flame of a candle being snuffed out, and he slid off the sofa onto the floor. He was already obviously dead, but Tano and Pelligrino stood over Charlie Salardino and emptied their pistols into his body.

When they were done, Gaetano Scaglia looked around the room at the mess they had made. Smoke swirled from the barrels of their guns, and the coppery smell of blood and cordite was heavy in the air. There was blood and bone everywhere, including bright red streaks on the plastic covering the couch.

"Would you look at that?" Tano said, nodding toward the plastic cover. Blood was dripping off it, but the cushions underneath were still pristine. "That plastic cover worked." Pelligrino nodded, grunting in agreement. "Gina will be so happy."

BOOK I

SATURDAY, JUNE 11, 1960

CHAPTER 1

Jimmy Donato cursed under his breath as he came to a stop at Colfax and York Street and softly banged his hands on the big steering wheel of his 1957 Chevy Bel Air. It was a beautiful Saturday afternoon in Downtown Denver, and there was very little that could spoil Jimmy's good mood that day. But he had spent the last 10 minutes circling the same five-block radius of Colfax Avenue looking for a parking spot near Hollywood Don's Rock n' Roll record shop without any luck.

Jimmy traveled to this stretch of the "longest commercial street in America" every Saturday to buy a new record from Hollywood Don's and a new shirt from Henri's Clothier, which was three doors down from the record shop. Like every Saturday, Jimmy's younger cousin, "Little John" Johnny Donato, was with him. But unlike most Saturday's, there wasn't a parking space to be found on this glorious afternoon.

"Dammit, every housewife in the state must be down here today," Jimmy said, easing forward as the light at the intersection turned green. "I'm about to say screw it and just head back."

Instead, Jimmy took a right on Vine Street and circled around one more time. After getting back on Colfax, Jimmy stopped in the middle of the road in front of Don's and put the Bel Air into park.

"Slide over and drive. I'll run in and get my stuff while you circle around," Jimmy said.

At 15, Johnny was six years younger than Jimmy and wouldn't have his license for another couple of months. But Johnny was the best driver that Jimmy knew, already dominating the races at the short track out by the family farm, and Johnny loved the Bel Air almost as much Jimmy did, having helped soup it up in their free time.

"There's always a ton of cops out by the Capitol. What if they see me?" Johnny asked.

"Just don't get caught," Jimmy said, hopping out as an old man in a 1930s-era Ford pickup behind them laid on his horn. "I'll be quick. I just need 15, 20 minutes."

Johnny slid over and got behind the wheel, chirping the tires as he took off east down Colfax. Jimmy worked his way between the bumpers of a couple of parked cars before going in the front door of Hollywood Don's.

This was Jimmy's happy place. A half-dozen teenagers were flipping through the rows and rows of records in bins, posters of rock n' roll stars covering the walls and he was greeted by the sounds of "Cathy's Clown" by the Everly Brothers coming over the store's loudspeakers.

"Jimmy, there you are. I didn't think you were going to make it." Don Simkins, the namesake of the shop was behind the glass counter just inside the entrance, finishing off a sale of an Elvis Presley record to a couple of girls in bright poodle skirts. A tall, thin man in his late 30s, Don had thick, black horn-rimmed glasses and jet-black hair swept back in a pompadour style framing a pleasant face.

"You know I wouldn't miss it," Jimmy said, shaking Don's hand as he sidled up to the counter. "What do you have for me this week?"

"There's a new Dion and the Belmonts, a Roy Orbison, and you still haven't picked up the latest Sam Cooke."

"Ah, yeah. I heard that's a good one."

"Are you going to see your girl this weekend? The girls can't resist Sam Cooke."

"I'm headed over to The Scotchman as soon as I'm done here."

"Wait, I've got something I want you to hear." Simkins turned around and took an album out of a cardboard box that was on a shelf behind the counter. There were a couple of record players on the shelf as well, one stacked high with 45s – where the "Cathy's Clown" single had been replaced by "Sea Cruise" by Frankie Ford – and one set up to play 33 1/3 long play records. Don took a vinyl disc out of a cover, careful to only touch the edges of the album, and put it on the turntable, gently setting the needle down. He then switched over the public address system from the table playing the 45s, and the hiss of the new record came over the speakers.

Suddenly, an upbeat guitar filled the store. And then an easily recognizable voice took over.

"Bo Diddley's a gunslinger
Bo Diddley's a gunslinger
Yeah, ah-ha
Yeah, ah-ha"

Don was bobbing his head, a huge grin covering his face. "It just came in.

I haven't even heard it yet."

Jimmy picked up the record sleeve which featured the musician decked out in Western clothes standing in a corral with a guitar at his feet. Jimmy bobbed his head for a few seconds along with the music and smiled.

"I like it."

"I do, too." Don came back and joined Jimmy at the counter. The two discussed new records for the next few minutes, all the while with Bo Diddley playing in the background, before Jimmy remembered his under-aged cousin was circling around outside waiting for him to make his purchase.

"Shoot, I've got to get going. I'll just take the new Bo Diddley."

Jimmy paid $3.23 for the record and hustled out of the record store, telling Don he'd see him next week, before quickly heading toward Henri's Clothier down the street.

Henri's was divided into three sections, a front room off the entrance that had racks of shirts and pants along two walls, along with shelving down the middle that led to a display case with a cash register on top of it. Off to the right was another room up a small incline that featured dressing rooms, an area with mirrors on three sides where measurements were taken, and more racks and shelving. The racks in this room all featured suit jackets and sports coats, along with winter coats, lightweight jackets and raincoats. There was also a wall of dress shoes and an area for boxers, undershirts, socks and belts.

Both of those main front rooms were decorated in a deep, dark mahogany and exuded class and wealth.

Behind the counter there was an entrance to another, larger room, that spanned the width of both front areas. In this room there was worktables, sewing machines and yards of every type and color of fabric you could imagine. This room was mostly unfinished, but this was where Henri Deshambeau, the shop's owner, designed and manufactured his custom wares.

When Jimmy entered the store there was no one in the front room, but he could hear voices coming from the area where measurements were taken. Jimmy walked back that way and saw Mr. Deshambeau measuring the arm length of a small but distinguished looking man who appeared to be in his mid 40s. There was another, larger man sitting in a hard-back chair off to the side. He had a blank, unreadable face and took in Jimmy with dark, cold eyes.

"Ah, young Mr. Donato. I was wondering if you were coming in today," said Deshambeau, a short, squat man with a heavy French accent. "I must finish up with Mr. Scaglia here, so if you wouldn't mind waiting in the other room. I pulled a couple of shirts you might like and put them under the counter if you want to go check them out."

"Sure thing Mr. Deshambeau, no problem."

"Thank you, James." With Deshambeau it was always James or Mr. Donato, never Jimmy.

Jimmy made his way back to the front room, but he could see the man getting measured looking at him in the reflection in the mirror. Jimmy recognized that man as "Black" Jack Scaglia. Jack Scaglia was in the local papers a lot and was said to be the head of Denver's biggest organized crime family. The other scary man was most likely Anthony "The Ram" Carpineto, Scaglia's bodyguard.

Growing up in a large Italian family, Jimmy was obviously aware of the mob and, even though his immediate family appeared to be completely legit, there was always rumors about involvement on the fringes with various cousins and uncles. His great-aunt Nettie ran a saloon off of Broadway that got its start during the height of prohibition, getting liquor first from the Carlino brothers and then later the Scaglias. Nettie's was also known to host barbooth game most nights, a dice game that Jimmy would occasionally take part in, and the Scaglias were rumored to get a piece of it.

The Donatos and the Scaglias were from the same city in southern Italy, Potenza, and Jimmy had heard the families used to be friendly in the old country, although they had gone down separate paths once they reached America.

Even so, Jimmy was a little unnerved by coming face to face with reputed mobsters, more so with The Ram than with Jack Scaglia, who presented more like a college professor than a career criminal. Jimmy knew enough, however, to understand that while Carpineto might look scary, Scaglia was the one that was truly frightening.

Jimmy looked behind the counter and found a stack of shirts that had been set aside for him. He was partial to Original Penguin polo shirts by Munsingwear, so Mr. Deshambeau would pull out two or three for Jimmy to choose from each Saturday. This week's selection had a pale-yellow version, along with a standard black and a light blue.

Jimmy set the yellow one aside, and then busied himself looking through a new batch of button downed collared shirts with French cuffs that had just been set out. After a couple of minutes, Deshambeau, Scaglia and Carpineto made their way to the counter.

"I should be able to have that for you by the end of next week Mr. Scaglia," Deshambeau said, putting a little notebook he had taken the measurements down in next to the register.

"Thanks Henri. You're the best," Scaglia said, shaking the tailor's hand. "I always appreciate the work you do."

Scaglia then turned to Jimmy. "Donato. The Donatos that own the greenhouses?"

"That's right, sir."

"It's ironic, running into you here. I was just having a conversation with my father the other day, and he brought up your family. Did you know, our families are both from Potenza? Your dad's grandpa and my granddad Danilo were chums back in the old country.”

“I had heard that, sir.”

“It’s strange our families aren’t close now. I wonder why that is?”

“I’m not sure, sir.”

Scaglia nodded, taking a moment to size Jimmy up. Jimmy was a good-looking kid with dark hair cut short. He was several inches taller than Scaglia and decent sized – not too big but definitely not skinny. His clothes were nice without looking expensive, a simple collared shirt and crisp blue jeans.

Jimmy took Scaglia in as well. His dark hair with a touch of salt-and-pepper was freshly barbered, and he had dark eyes and a slightly dimpled chin. He had a Roman nose, but it was proportionate to his face. Jimmy thought Scaglia could have passed for a politician or a college professor, a handsome man who exuded a sense of importance.

Scaglia nodded again, and then patted Jimmy on his cheek. “Tell your father and your Uncle I said hello. Tell them to come by my restaurant and I will treat them to dinner some night.” He turned to Carpineto, who handed him a sharp looking Fedora he placed on his head. “Let’s get going Anthony.”

They started heading out the door but before they got there, Scaglia turned back.

“Hey Henri. Let young Mr. Donato pick out a couple of shirts and pants and put them on my tab.”

“Yes, Mr. Scaglia,” Deshambeau said.

Jimmy started to protest, “You don’t have to do that, sir.”

“I know I don’t have to do it,” Scaglia said, with a smile. “I want to. Just accept thc gift, kid.”

With that, Black Jack Scaglia and Anthony The Ram Carpineto walked out the door.

CHAPTER 2

Johnny slid behind the wheel, watched his older cousin maneuver onto the sidewalk in front of Don's Record shop and then put his foot into the accelerator, lighting up the wheels on the Bel Air.

Johnny loved this car, having spent the better part of six months helping his cousin fix it up. Jimmy had been able to pick it up cheap a couple of years earlier, shortly after turning 19, when the original owner lost control of it while drag racing, careening off a dirt road and taking out 50 yards of barb-wired fence before slamming into a big cottonwood tree behind the Donato family farm in Adams County.

Johnny was still amazed at the wheeling and dealing that Jimmy had done to end up with the car. The original owner was Dick Carey, the young shop teacher and varsity basketball coach of the high school Jimmy had recently graduated from, who was fortunate to escape the crash with only a concussion. That outcome was much better than the fate of his young female passenger, who definitely wasn't Coach Carey's wife and may have been the senior captain of the pom pom squad at that very same high school, Jodi Drake. She suffered a couple of broken ribs and a ton of broken glass was embedded in her scalp. The emergency room nurse couldn't tell if the glass came from the shattered windshield or the bottle of whiskey she had been sharing with the driver, but it wasn't a good look for either of them.

Not to mention the car, a 2-door coup, was in really bad shape, the entire passenger side trashed, the suspension bent and the transmission dropped in a ditch a good 25 feet behind where the vehicle finally came to rest.

Jimmy had a soft spot for Coach Carey, having played back-up small forward his senior year on a team that won league and advanced to the state regional tournament. That was Coach Carey's first year at the school, having joined the Falcons after a stint as a starting point guard at Western State College in Gunnison. He installed a motion offense and a "point your guns" defensive philosophy that immediately took the high school from a mediocre program to one that lost only four games all season.

Jimmy also felt bad because he had been driving the car, a 1950s Oldsmobile, that had been racing against Coach Carey when he lost control and left the road. But in the immediate aftermath of the crash, Jimmy saw an opportunity to not only help out the coach, but also to get his hands on a sweet ride. Jimmy had his cousin, Joey Carabetta, who had been watching the race along with Johnny at the unofficial finish line a quarter mile away from the starting point, take Coach Carey and Jodi Drake to the local emergency room in the Oldsmobile while he had Johnny go to the farm and get a tractor that could tow the wrecked coup into a nearby garage on the property.

Jimmy immediately started spinning a tale that saved Coach Carey's reputation, and probably his marriage, and got Jimmy the pink slip to the Bel Air. Jimmy took blame for the crash, saying he had changed the oil in the car as a favor to the coach, who allowed him to take the car for a drive around the property when he was done working on it, the coach tagging along in the back seat. Jimmy was trying to get Jodi to go out with him, and in an attempt to impress her, put his foot into the gas of the Bel Air, reaching a high rate of speed in a short amount of time. Unfortunately, they were unaware that the fence along the back of the property was in a state of disrepair after a recent storm, and several of the farms' pigs had gotten out of their pen and through the damaged fence, and were crossing the road when Jimmy came upon them. Jimmy obviously swerved to miss the hogs, and the car caught a rut on the side of the road and he ended up slamming into the cottonwood.

It was a preposterous story, but Carey's wife, a young, innocent girl that was pregnant with the couple's first child, bought it. Or at least wanted to believe it. Carey's insurance agent, who was a distant cousin of the Donatos, also signed off on it, placing the blame on the storm and the pigs, so a payment went out to the Donatos to repair the damage to the fence, and another for $1,500 to Coach Carey to cover the cost of repairing the Bel Air. Coach Carey agreed to give the settlement to Jimmy in exchange for $250, the Oldsmobile and for Jimmy taking the blame.

The car went for $2,000 brand new, so Jimmy knew what a steal he had. He was able to use the money from the insurance settlement to repair the car and soup it up any way he wanted. The original engine, a V-8 with a four-barrel carburetor, put out a respectable 180 horsepower, but that wasn't enough. Jimmy wanted the bigger 283 V-8 that upped the horses to 220. There was also an engine with mechanical fuel injection that put out 283 horsepower, but that was currently out of his price range.

Luckily, Johnny was one of the best mechanics around despite being so young. They scoured the local swap meets and junk yards, picking up what they needed to build their own engine and carburetor, and ended up with something that put out around 250 horsepower.

They also did all the body work to get the car back to its initial shape, and then Johnny painted it Viper Red. They added chrome sway bars and control arms in addition to the other trim, and ended up with a ride that was the envy of everyone when they cruised the streets of Denver.

Although the car was Jimmy's, Johnny felt a sense of ownership as well. Honestly, he did about 90 percent of the work - Jimmy was more of an idea man, while Johnny was the one that had more practical skills.

Johnny headed east on Colfax, not too worried about anyone noticing a 15-year-old behind the wheel of a car he didn't have any business driving. The Little John moniker, which he was given because he was named after his dad, was ironic at best. Already almost 6-foot tall and thick across the chest, Johnny looked and carried himself older than he was. And he had been driving vehicles on the family farm from the time he could see above the dash (actually, longer than that because he used to sit on apple crates to see past the steering wheel) and was widely considered the best driver in the family.

Johnny quickly found himself near Denver's Civic Center Park and the Colorado State Capitol. Built in the 1890s, the Capitol looked similar to the United States Capitol and had a distinctive gold-plated dome that sparkled under the brilliant June afternoon sun. Johnny loved that building, and slowed down so he could admire it and the surrounding grounds around it. There were plenty of families out at the park that day, enjoying picnics in the sunshine and kids trying to fly kites against the magnificent blue sky.

While Johnny was busy admiring the scene, he failed to notice the big, red-headed police officer directing traffic around the Capitol. But the officer definitely noticed the shiny red Bel Air.

Officer Dean Fitzpatrick eyed the car and grimaced. He had been patrolling Colfax for more than a decade and he had no time for young punks and troublemakers. And those two dagos who rode around in that car were troublemakers in Fitzpatrick's eyes, especially the older one with his scheming ways. The younger one seemed kind of dense, a typical dumb wop, but the older one was too clever by half. The kid, Jimmy was his name, hung around a neighborhood bar that Fitzpatrick frequented, and had taken quite a substantial sum of money off him during a barbooth game a couple of months back. Fitzpatrick was sure he had cheated, but the owner of the bar was the kid's aunt, or cousin or something, and sided with the thieving spaghetti bender.

Fitzpatrick ran into Jimmy again a couple of days later, this time while he was on foot patrol near an ice cream parlor a couple blocks south of the Capitol. As Fitzpatrick walked by, he eyed Jimmy at the counter, drinking a milkshake with a pretty young girl and big kid that looked a lot like a younger version of Jimmy.

Seeing Jimmy Donato in there, grinning with a pretty girl hanging on his every word, quickly brought back up the anger Fitzpatrick felt towards him, believing in his heart there was no way that young punk could beat him at dice.

Officer Fitzpatrick tightened up his belt, and then strode into the ice cream parlor, the bells above the front door jingling as he went in.

"Good day to you, Andrew," Fitzpatrick said, tipping his hat to the owner who was working behind the counter. Fitzpatrick took a quick look around the room. Besides Jimmy Donato and his group at the counter, there were patrons in three of six booths that lined the far wall, enjoying their sweet treats while a Tony Bennett song played in the background. "Having any issues today," Fitzpatrick asked the shop owner as his attention returned to Donato, whose back was turned to the officer, his eyes focused on the dark-haired beauty next to him.

"No, officer Fitzpatrick. Everything is good today," Andrew answered while cleaning a spot on the counter with a dish cloth.

"No trouble from even this guy?" Fitzpatrick said as he poked Jimmy lightly in the back with his nightstick. "He looks like trouble to me."

Jimmy quickly spun on his stool, the anger on his face announcing that he was ready to confront whoever was poking him. Seeing Officer Fitzpatrick in front of him, however, Jimmy's scowl quickly turned to a big grin, his eyes lighting up with recognition.

"Fitz!" Jimmy exclaimed, using the nickname that Fitzpatrick wasn't particularly fond of, because that's what everyone had called his deadbeat father as well. "It's good to see you. I didn't recognize you in uniform. You look good." Jimmy leaned forward, the grin still on his face. "Very intimidating, I might add."

Fitzpatrick didn't expect this kind of reaction from the kid. He was expecting, or hoping for, anger so maybe he could escalate the situation and deliver the bum a beating. Fitzpatrick enjoyed beating troublemakers, and he was good at it. And this kid deserved a beating. But here the kid was, grinning like they were old friends. Just the sight of Jimmy, in a smart looking green collared shirt with a penguin on the crest and remnants of a strawberry shake mustache on his mouth, pissed Fitzpatrick off.

"Are you causing trouble today, Jimmy? I won't put up with any mischief on my beat."

"No, no mischief Officer, I promise" Jimmy said, wiping his mouth with the back of his hand. "I'm just enjoying some ice cream with my girl, Connie, and my little cousin Johnny."

"Why don't you join us? It's a hot day out and you look like you could use some ice cream," the girl said. She was stunning, with a bob haircut and big brown eyes with flecks of green in them. Fitzpatrick, a lifelong bachelor who had to pay for any companionship he enjoyed, was immediately jealous that a worthless punk like Donato had a girl like that.

"Yeah, that's a good idea, Officer Fitzpatrick. Join us. I'll even pay."

Jimmy leaned forward conspiratorially, whispering to Fitzpatrick. "I did really well at a game of chance recently and have a little extra money."

It took all the restraint Fitzpatrick had to not stove in the side of the dumb little wop's head right then. He tightened his grip around his night stick, his face turning a shade of red that looked unhealthy.

Fitzpatrick observed that the rest of the patrons had stopped eating their ice cream, noticing the tense scene that was playing out on at the counter.

Instead of hitting the kid with his nightstick, Fitzpatrick pointed it at him, the end of it grazing Jimmy's chin.

"You best watch yourself, Donato. I know you cheated me, and I'll get my money back from you, one way or another."

"Wanna bet?" Jimmy said, eliciting a groan from Connie but causing Johnny to chuckle loudly.

Fitzgerald turned his attention to Johnny now, crowding him at the counter.

"You think that's funny, dough boy? Why don't you come down to Nettie's with your cousin there, and I can teach you a lesson as well?"

"I would love to," Johnny said, backing away from the officer, "but I'm only 15."

Connie, who had risen from her stool, tried to get between Fitzpatrick and Johnny. She put both hands on Fitzpatrick's chest, lightly pushing him back. "Come on, officer Fitzpatrick. There's no need for you to get upset. We're just trying to beat the heat, having some ice cream."

Her touch, as light as it was, sent bolts of electricity through the big Irishman. She smelled of flowers and vanilla ice cream, and Fitzpatrick was worried he might fall as his knees temporarily turned to rubber.

Fitzpatrick turned away from her, regaining a modicum of composure. The other customers in the store were looking at him, and some appeared to be laughing a bit at him. This pissed Fitzpatrick off even more.

"I'll be seeing you around Donato," Fitzpatrick barked before storming out the parlor's front door.

In many ways that incident was even more disturbing to Fitzpatrick than the loss of the money playing dice. He vowed that day, as he returned to his foot patrol, that he would make Jimmy Donato pay, not only for taking his money but also for making him look foolish in front of the girl, the store owner and the other customers.

Over the next few weeks, Fitzpatrick returned to Nettie's on a semi-regular basis, but that only led to him losing more money at barbooth as Jimmy seemed to be keeping away from the saloon. He found out what kind of car Donato drove, and had his buddies who patrolled the streets pull the kid over whenever they came across him. But the kid was careful never to be caught speeding, and the car was in impeccable condition. The younger cousin always seemed to be with Donato, but there was nothing illegal about that. The only thing they were able to do was give him a warning for having a pair of novelty fuzzy dice hanging from the rear-view mirror as it might impair the ability to see the road properly.

It had been several weeks since Fitzpatrick had seen any trace of Jimmy Donato, until today when the bright red Bel Air came cruising by the Capitol.

Curiously, it looked like there was only one of them in the car today, and it looked like it was the younger one. The younger one, who was only 15.

Only 15. Not old enough to drive.

It took Fitzpatrick a second to realize what was going on. He was about 20 yards away from the northwest intersection where the car was slowly passing the Capitol when Fitzpatrick started blowing his whistle and yelling for the car to stop.

All of the yelling and whistle-blowing seemed to shake the driver out of his daze and he looked directly at Fitzpatrick running towards him, recognition coming across his face. Officer Fitzpatrick was still a good 10 yards away when the driver started laughing, shoved his left arm through the open window with his middle finger sticking high in the air, before he shot through the intersection, sending a couple of slow-moving pedestrians diving out of the way.

Fitzpatrick stopped and gave one long, loud blast of his whistle before spitting it out of his mouth, half-collapsing with his hands on his knees while trying to catch his breath with his face turning a similar shade of red as his hair.

"Goddamn dagos," he cursed. Knowing there was no way of catching the delinquent now. But that doesn't mean they had won. Eventually he'd catch up with Jimmy Donato and his younger cousin – and he would get the last laugh.

CHAPTER 3

Johnny Donato saw the big dumb Irish cop spot him and panicked a little bit. This was going to get him in trouble for sure. Driving underage wasn't that horrible, but Johnny was sure that the cop would trump something up, because he had proven in the past to have a hard-on for him and Jimmy for some reason. Johnny wasn't sure why, probably just because they were young and Italian.

The first thing that raced through Johnny's mind was how much trouble he was going to be in with his Pops, and how many weekends he'd be grounded. But when he took another glance at the cop, he realized how hard a time the fat Mick was having running the half block to get to him. Johnny took a quick look in front of him – two younger guys were still in the crosswalk, but they'd be able to get out of the way easy enough – turned and laughed at the cop and then put his foot into it. He probably shouldn't have laughed at the officer, or flipped him off, but he couldn't help it.

The Bel Air sped through the intersection – the two pedestrians easily jumped out of the way – and Johnny was two blocks away before he even bothered to look back. It appeared that the Irish cop never even made it to intersection.

"Lay off the potatoes, fatso," Johnny laughed. It would be easy enough to circle around while avoiding the Capitol – the area around it was laid out as a grid of one-way streets that allowed you to run parallel with Colfax without actually going on it. Johnny took a left and went north about six blocks before heading back west.

By the time Johnny had circled around and got back on Colfax a block west of Don's Record Shop, Jimmy was coming out of Henri's with a couple of packages under his arms. A spot had opened up in front of the shop, and Johnny slid in and put the car in park. He scooted over to the passenger side as Jimmy made his way into the driver's seat, putting his packages in the back.

"How'd it go?" Jimmy asked.

"Great. Ran across our favorite Irish cop by the Capitol. He tried to get me to stop, but I flipped him off and sped away."

Jimmy looked at his younger cousin and laughed. "Seriously?" Johnny was usually very quiet, so to be so brazen, especially to a police officer, was out of character a bit.

"Seriously. I bet he's pissed, so we should probably try to avoid him for a while."

"Ok." Jimmy had put the car into drive and eased back into traffic. "You want to go get a soda?"

"Jimmy, why do you even ask? We do the same thing every Saturday. You come down here, buy a record and a shirt, and then we go get a soda so you can flirt with Connie. If I didn't want to do that, I wouldn't have come with you."

"Geez, don't get sore. I was just asking."

"I'm not sore. I'm just saying you don't have to ask."

Jimmy laughed and reached over and ruffled his cousin's hair. Although they both had siblings of their own, the two Donato cousins were closer than brothers.

The entire Donato clan was close; Rocco Donato was the first to emigrate to America, coming over from Potenza, Italy in 1886, going to work for an uncle on a vegetable farm in Brighton, a small city northeast of Denver in Adams County. Once established, Rocco sent for his wife, Lucia DeNiro, and they raised five children: Josephine, James, Antonette, Anny and John.

James, the oldest son, was born in 1890, and when he was old enough, he joined his father truck farming out of Brighton and nearby Welby. In 1914 James married Asunta Sciara, a pretty, dark-haired girl who was born on the boat coming over from Italy in 1895. James' younger brother, John, would marry Asunta's younger sister, Clara, a couple of years later as well.

James and Asunta, or Suzy, had three children – Anthony, Lucille and John – and bought 20 acres of land near 66th Avenue and York Street in Adams County. Things were going good for the Donato clan, until James dropped dead of a heart attack at the age of 38 in 1928.

Suzy was a notoriously hard worker, and even though James' death derailed some of their plans, she was able to keep the family afloat. She did have to sell off about half of the York Street land in the late 1940s, but that presented an opportunity for a different path for the Donato family moving forward.

As part of that land deal, Suzy took ownership a greenhouse off of 32nd Avenue and Federal Street in Denver that featured 25,000 square feet of growing area and a retail shop. Suzy ran the greenhouse with her youngest son, John. They originally grew several different crops there, but John, who had served in the Air Force during World War II, slowly converted it over to an all-carnation business. Colorado's climate was ideal for growing carnations, and by the mid 1950s it was a solid, money-making crop.

Seeing the success that his mother and his younger brother was having growing carnations, Anthony, the eldest son who had continued truck farming originally, also decided to go into the carnation business and built a greenhouse on the York Street property in 1955.

The Donatos were part of a group of about a dozen Italian families that immigrated to Colorado and then went into the floral business following the end of the Great Depression. The largest contingent, by far, settled in Adams County, which is made up of close 1,200 miles of land north of Denver. For the most part, the families all got along with one another and were willing to help each other out when called upon. There was a lot of marriages that connected the various families to one another, including Anthony Donato marrying the daughter of Joe Carabetta, a grower based in Wheat Ridge, and the Italians quickly became a powerful entity in Colorado's floral industry.

Colorado's brisk climate and abundance of sunny days was ideal for growing vegetables and cut flowers, and once an irrigation ditch to bring water from the Platte River into Denver was built in the early 1870s, the greenhouse industry in the state took off. By the turn of the century, approximately 400,000 square feet of growing area was dedicated to cut flowers in the region.

Carnations quickly became the crop of choice as growers found the flower thrived in Colorado's high-altitude climate that featured warm, sunny days and cool, crisp nights. Many of the early growers had Dutch or English backgrounds and most sold their wares in shops next to the greenhouses where the flowers were grown. The few retail shops and groceries that sold flowers throughout the metro area would get their inventory delivered in horse-drawn covered carriages, which utilized charcoal heaters in the wagons to avoid freezing in the winter.

Local realtor John A. Valentine would help expand Colorado grower's reach, opening Park Floral Company in east Denver in 1879. Valentine would become a national leader in the floral industry, becoming one of the first to take customer orders over the wire, shipping arrangements to cities outside of his immediate area. Valentine is also credited, along with William Penn of Boston, with coming up with the phrase "Say it With Flowers," which was prominently used by the industry for more than a century. At a national meeting of the Florist TransWorld Delivery Association in New York in 1910, Valentine drew up the first set of rules and regulations concerning the expected conduct of the organization's members. Many of these regulations were later adopted into the Constitution and By-Laws of the FTDA.

Even more so than Valentine, Swedish immigrant Anders Lindgren was instrumental in establishing Colorado as a national power in the floral industry in the United States. In August of 1925, Lindgren founded Colorado

Wholesale Florists in the basement of the Wyn Hotel. Within a couple of years, he incorporated several other local growers and began marketing Colorado's flowers out of state. Lindgren had strict quality standards for the flowers he sold, and he standardized prices throughout the region.

Lindgren was known as a savvy businessman and a fierce negotiator. Rival florists popped up here and there, but they all eventually failed, either being incorporated by CWF or going bankrupt, or worse. Rumors were rampant that the money Lindgren used to stake his company didn't all come from legitimate means. It was well known he became wealthy during prohibition, and his methods were seen as cutthroat. While other florists disappeared, Lindgren's company continued to grow, and he had to move to bigger facilities on three occasions to accommodate that growth. By the start of the 1940s, CWF had a stranglehold on the market in the Rocky Mountains. Most of the Italian families delivered their products to Colorado Wholesale, and by the summer of 1960s, many served on the company's various boards and committees.

John Donato, Johnny's dad, and Anthony Donato, Jimmy's father, were both on the board of directors of CWF. Although there was nothing official or on paper, they were the de facto leaders of the group of Italian growers in the company. For a long time, the Italians were content with their arrangement with CWF, but lately there was a growing sentiment in the group to break free and form their own company. While CWFs profits continued to grow, and Anders Lindgren became wealthier and wealthier, the share the growers received remained stagnant. Expenses continued to rise, but compensation didn't.

With support from most of the Italian growers, the Donatos had quietly started making plans to break out on their own.

There were plenty of details to be worked out. CWF had deals in place to provide flowers to many retailers in the metro Denver area and had agreements on the Western Slope and the Eastern plains. Lindgren and CWF also shipped to several neighboring states including Wyoming, Kansas and Nebraska.

Plus, Lindgren wouldn't look kindly on losing about a quarter of his growers to a start-up that would be a rival. There weren't any contracts that bound the Italian growers to CWF – they were more like independent contractors who got paid for goods and services delivered. But he would no doubt feel like the Italians were breaking a long-standing agreement.

There were other logistics to work out as well. The Italian growers would need a large space to use as a storage and distribution center, and if they could sign agreements with retailers, they would need vehicles to transport their goods. They figured there was enough Italian grocers throughout the metro area and the rest of Colorado they could convince to make deals with them to sustain the new company at first until they could expand their reach, but they would take a hit financially until they were better established.

John and Anthony Donato would take another blow to their income as they would lose the small salary they received for being on the board of directors, which also included a bit of profit sharing. They were the only Italians associated with CWF that received a piece of the profit, even though it was miniscule, and this was one of the reasons the rest wanted to break free. While he made sure the growers made enough to survive, Lindgren was also a pragmatist, and kept most of the profit to himself. He had become extremely wealthy and owned a three-story mansion in the Capitol Hill area, just down the street from the Governor's Mansion.

There had been negotiations to try to convince Lindgren to offer things like stock options and profit sharing, but he had been resistant so far. He knew the growers didn't have many other options and, if he was being honest, he didn't consider the Italians smart enough to go out on their own. Lindgren thought they were good, hard workers, but they weren't very bright. As long as he continued to give them a living, he wasn't too concerned about their wants and needs.

After the most recent proposal was shot down at the latest board of directors meeting in March, the movement amongst the Italians to break free gained momentum, and the Donatos had come on board with the idea.

In fact, a group of the growers was expected to meet with John and Anthony Donato to discuss things the next day after the Sunday lunch at the Donato farm. Jimmy, who helped run his father's greenhouse, was expected to attend. He knew his dad and his Uncle John were anxious about the meeting as the Italian growers were growing impatient and were ready to make a break from CWF. At only 21 years of age, Jimmy understood what happened over the next six months would probably shape the direction his life took well into the next decade or more.

But that was for tomorrow. Right now, Jimmy was focused on getting across town to 49th and Federal and the Scotchman drive-in, where his girlfriend Connie Triola was one of the car hops. The Scotchman was a typical drive-in, featuring burgers, fries, shakes and flavored sodas. It was also a place where you could show off your car, and there were very few cars around as nice as Jimmy's '57 Bel Air.

It was just after dusk when Jimmy pulled into the parking lot, and the place was already completely full, with all of the prime spots taken up. There were just over two dozen parking spots available, and cars would circle for hours waiting for one to open up. The Scotchman was part of a cruising loop that was popular with Denver's youth that started downtown on 16th Street and headed into North Denver and then to Federal Boulevard. Kids would do the loop endlessly on summer nights, wanting to see and be seen. And no night was complete without getting a burger and a drink from the Scotchman.

Jimmy was usually a late arrival to the festivities, but that was on purpose, so he could be seen rolling in in his beautiful Bel Air. Jimmy's cousin, Joey "Cars" Carabetta, would get there earlier in the afternoon and hold a spot up front for him. As soon as he saw the Bel Air pull in, Joey jumped in his beat up 1953 Buick Roadmaster and backed out, allowing Jimmy to slide in while Joey Cars found a parking spot on a street a couple of blocks over.

Jimmy rolled down his window, turned up his radio (which, like the majority of the rest of the cars, was tuned to 950 KIMN and was currently playing "All Shook Up" by Elvis Presley) and opened his door. Before he could even get completely out of the car, Connie ran up and threw her arms around him.

"Jimmy!" she screamed, planting kisses on his forehead and neck. "What took you so long?"

Connie was a pretty young girl with short, dark curls and a mischievous look in her eyes. She had graduated from high school a year after Jimmy and was studying to be a beautician during the week and worked at the Scotchman at nights and on the weekend.

Seeing Johnny, Connie said "Oh, you brought the baby." She reached over and tousled his hair. "Hi Little John."

"Stuff it, Connie." Connie loved to tease Johnny about how young he was, but it didn't really bother him even if he acted like it did. Actually, he loved the attention, because the other car hops would also tease him. And it was well known that the Scotchman only hired the cutest girls to be car hops, their signature kilts highlighting their long legs.

"What do you guys want to eat?" Connie asked, with Jimmy ordering a Hot Kookie – a cinnamon Coke – and a Mr. Horrible Burger; Johnny a strawberry Sloppy Malt and a chili dog. Joey returned as Connie went to go retrieve the food, and Jimmy surveyed the rest of the parking lot.

"There's a lot of nice cars here tonight," Joey said and Jimmy agreed as he took a look around. There was a couple of Ford Thunderbirds including a really nice '55 in inspiration yellow; a '53 Hudson Hornet, a '59 Cadillac Coupe deVille and, what Johnny thought was the nicest of them all, a '57 Chevy Corvette convertible painted Inca Silver and White.

The Corvette also caught Jimmy's eye, and he asked Joey, "Who's car is that? I haven't seen it before."

Joey took a look while scooping up the last of his fries out of a paper basket he had been carrying around. "Oh, that is a nice ride. That's Clyde Scaglia's car."

"Who?" Johnny asked

"Clyde Scaglia. You know, Black Jack Scaglia's kid? The football star at DU."

"Really? I just ran into his dad today at Henri's. He was getting measured for a suit."

Joey looked at him incredulously. "You ran into Black Jack Scaglia and survived? Man, Jimmy, you must have a horseshoe up your ass."

"Knock it off Joey. He seemed nice. He said his granddad and great grandpa Rocco were friends back in Potenza." Jimmy eyed the young man standing next to the Corvette. He was strongly built, wearing a Denver University letter sweater. His hair was straw colored and swept to one side. There was another man in a DU letter sweater with him, along with three coeds hanging on his every word.

"If he's Black Jack's kid, why does he have the yellow hair?"

"His mom was a blonde showgirl back in the day. A real looker. What'd ya expect? Black Jack is a big deal. He runs Denver."

"How do you know so much about it, Joey?"

Joey was long and lean, with rope-like muscles coursing through his back and arms. His hair always seemed greasy, even after a fresh shower. He was tough as shoe leather, taking second place at the state wrestling tournament his senior year at 145 pounds. He was also a lot sharper than he looked, and he was completely loyal to his cousins, especially Jimmy, who was the same age.

Joey shrugged his shoulders. "That stuff fascinates me. It's hard for us Italians to get ahead in America. Guys like Black Jack and his brothers found a way to become important people."

"Why do they call him Black Jack?" Johnny asked.

"Because he runs all the gambling houses and poker games around here," Jimmy said.

"That's not the only reason why," Joey said, slurping down the last of his chocolate malt. "It's also because he likes the coloreds."

"What?"

"People say he's got a soft spot for black people. He became friends with a couple when he was in the joint, and then he beat the hell out of couple of yokels that were harassing some down by his parent's restaurant after he got out. It quickly became known you don't fuck with them just to fuck with them when he was around.

"They also say that he likes the dark meat, if you know what I mean." Joey took a flask out of his back pocket, took a slug and tried to hand it to Jimmy, who waved him off.

"The dark meat?" Johnny asked.

"He likes black women. Rumor has It that he's had more than one black gumar. Remember Laughing Sam?"

"Who?"

"Laughing Sam? The big fat guy they found down by the train tracks on Larimer with a bullet in his head about six years ago? They say he earned that bullet because he was going around claiming that Black Jack Scaglia had a little black bastard with one of his gumars."

"No shit? Man, that's crazy," Jimmy said.

"One thing I can tell you if you ever run into him again, though, is don't call him Black Jack to his face. He hates that name. You'll end up on the train tracks next to Laughing Sam."

"Huh, I didn't know that," Jimmy said, laughing while grabbing Joey in a headlock. "You better be careful what rumors you're spreading Joey Cars, or you'll be the one next to Laughing Sam."

CHAPTER 4

After things wound down at the Scotchman, Jimmy took little John home and then he and Joey Cars headed over to Colfax east of the Capitol and his Aunt Annette's saloon, Nettie's Place. Nettie had opened the joint around 1915, just in time for Colorado to become one of the first states to outlaw booze ahead of the nationwide act of prohibition. Nettie's had survived, thanks in part to help from the Carlino brothers, and later Charlie Salardino and the Scaglias, and was now a well-established neighborhood bar that catered to a group of local regulars. Nettie was still a fixture at the bar, even in her late 60s, but it was her daughter, Simona who ran the place.

No one knew who Simona's father was, well, at least Nettie wasn't talking, and that was okay with Simona, an uncommonly beautiful woman with a fiery attitude that was a characteristic of all the Donato women. She was as big of an attraction as the bar's drinks, which were always heavy and free flowing.

Jimmy and Joey warmly greeted Aunt Nettie, who was seated on her usual stool at the end of the bar, and Simona, who had a pair of draft beers waiting for the young men at the only free spots at the bar. After catching up with her cousins she went back to the far end of the bar and resumed chatting with a large dark man in an expensive suit, their heads coming together in an intimate manner.

Jimmy and Joey spun around on their stools to take in the rest of the bar, which was about half full at this time of night. There was a spirited barbooth game going on along the back wall of the bar, with about a dozen men gathered around a long table throwing dice.

"Are you going to play tonight?" Joey asked Jimmy as he took a handful of assorted nuts out of a small dish on the bar.

"I don't know. Probably," Jimmy said as he swung back around, taking a drink of his beer. Jimmy was a really good barbooth player, almost always coming out ahead when he did play. He hadn't played in a while; unlike most players he didn't always have the urge to play. He would be perfectly fine just having a drink or two and avoiding the dice altogether. He just followed his gut and some nights it told him to play, others it said to stay away.

Right now, his gut was telling him to wait, so Jimmy and Joey were having a conversation about the different cars they had seen at the Scotchman, in particular the Scaglia kid's Corvette. Jimmy was telling Joey how much he liked the car when someone came up behind him and gave him a hard, two-handed shove in the back, causing him to spill his beer and stumble off of the stool.

"There you are, you dirty little dago." It was officer Dean Fitzpatrick, off-duty and obviously half in the bag, wearing an ill-fitting blue sports coat. Joey started to get up but the big Irish cop put a beefy forearm into him, pinning him against the bar.

"I've been waiting for you all night. Where's that other dumb wop, the dense one?"

"Who, Johnny? He's at home, he's not old enough to be in the bar," Jimmy said as he started to dust himself off and get up from the floor.

"That's right, he's not old enough to be here. He's not even old enough to drive, yet I saw his greasy ass tooling around the capitol this afternoon in your fancy car, didn't I?"

Before Jimmy could answer Nettie came up and smacked Fitzpatrick with her walking stick, causing him to let Joey loose and take a step back from Jimmy.

"What d'ya think you're doing?" Nettie said, poking Fitzpatrick with the end of her stick. "You leave those boys alone."

"You watch yourself, mom," Fitzpatrick pointed a finger at Nettie. "I'm sure I can find plenty of reasons to shut down this shithole."

"Hey now, there's no need for that," Simona said from behind the bar. "What is your issue with my cousins, Dean?"

Jimmy knew exactly what the officer's "issue" was. Many of the nights that Jimmy did play barbooth, officer Fitzpatrick was the one that came out on the short end of things. For the past six months it seemed like every time Jimmy threw dice, he would go home with a good chunk of Fitzpatrick's bankroll. In fact, the last time they played Fitzpatrick claimed that Jimmy was cheating, using loaded dice. Fitzpatrick, who was even drunker that night, ended up taking a swing at him, which Jimmy easily sidestepped, sending the officer crashing to the floor and earning the Irishman an exit out the back door.

"This little fuck (he pronounced it fook) knows what he did," Fitzpatrick said, spittle coming out with each word as his faced turned redder than normal. "He's been cheating me for months in here, then he had his little boyfriend harass me on patrol this afternoon. I'm going to take him to jail and impound that fancy car of his, by God. But first he's going to learn a lesson."

Fitzpatrick cocked back his arm, preparing to slap Jimmy when the man who had been talking to Simona at the end of the bar grabbed him by the wrist.

"I wouldn't do that if I was you, Dean."

Fitzpatrick looked at the man and fear immediately crossed his face.

"Smush? What're you doing here?"

Gaetano Scaglia squeezed Fitzpatrick's wrist even harder, turning his hand a translucent shade of pale.

"What did you call me?" Fitzpatrick knew he fucked up, that Tano Scaglia hated that name. Hated it so much that the rumor was he had plastic surgery done on the nose a few years back. Fitzpatrick looked into the heavy cupid face in front of him and didn't think the nose looked that bad. The bad thing was the anger behind those dark eyes.

"Sorry, Tano. Mr. Scaglia. I didn't know you were here."

"Well, I am," Tano said, finally releasing the cop's wrist. "You leave these boys alone."

"They're a couple of lowlifes," Fitzpatrick spat. "They need to be taught a lesson."

"No, they're friends of mine," Tano said stone-faced. "Maybe it's you that needs to be taught a lesson, Fitzpatrick."

Fitzpatrick stared at Tano Scaglia for a second, and then slowly shook his head. "No. No, I'm fine. I was just going home."

"That's good. Maybe go home and get the vig you owe me for your barbooth bets," Tano said. "And from now on, you leave these boys alone. The other one too, Johnny? You understand that?"

Fitzpatrick nodded his head and turned, heading toward the door.

"I want to hear you say it," Tano said.

Fitzpatrick turned around, and slowly nodded again. "I'm going to leave these boys alone from now on."

"Good. Now get the fuck out of here."

SUNDAY, JUNE 12, 1960

CHAPTER 1

Sundays were always Johnny Donato's favorite day of the week.

The smell of his mom's sauce cooking in the kitchen would greet him as he woke up; the aroma of the tomato sauce simmering on the stove filled their split-level ranch house and served as a make-shift alarm clock. He would quickly throw on his robe and bound up to the kitchen where his mom, Millie, would be putting the finishing touches on the sauce that would cook for the next few hours and his dad was sipping his coffee while reading the Sunday paper. There would be a couple of different pastries, some fruit and biscotti laid out on the table.

His mom would hand him a small cup of coffee and his dad would shuffle over the Sunday funnies from the paper and Johnny would sit down and dunk biscotti in his drink while reading about the latest exploits of Alley Oop and Dick Tracey. When his dad was done with the sports page, he would hand it over and Johnny would read about last night's baseball game. The Denver Bears were in first place in the American Association and had a good chance at winning the pennant this year. Bobo Osborne, Johnny's favorite player, was battling Joe Macko of the Houston Buffs for the home run crown in AAA that season and he checked every morning to see if Bobo remained in the lead.

Johnny loved this time alone with his mom and dad. His sister Isabella, who was six years younger, would be up soon while his brother Dominic, four years his junior, would sleep until he was awoken just in time to get dressed before heading to church. But right now, it was just Johnny and his mom and dad and Frank Sinatra playing on the Victrola in the other room.

Besides this morning ritual, Sundays also meant a trip to church before a big family lunch with all the aunts and uncles and cousins. The setting of these lunches would alternate between the original Donato farm near Brighton and the property on York Street, where today's feast was going to be held.

Fifteen minutes after Johnny had sat down, his little sister Bella made her way into the kitchen, clutching a stuffed rabbit and rubbing her eyes. Johnny got up and got her a glass of milk and a bowl of Trix, kissing her on the forehead. He would read her the funnies while she ate her breakfast. Little Lulu and Archie were her favorites, and she would laugh and laugh at the punchlines.

Meanwhile, Big John would move on to the business section and Millie would start browning the meatballs and sausages that she would combine with the sauce for added flavor.

That was Johnny's signal to go take his shower and put on his Sunday best. His dad insisted the family dress up for church, which meant a suit and tie for the boys and a dress for Bella. Johnny would do this process quickly so he could go with his father to check on the greenhouses before collecting the family for church. There were no off days when you ran a greenhouse; it was a 24-hour, 365-day a year job.

Johnny was in and out of the shower in less than five minutes and had on the suit his parents had purchased from Ted's last Christmas almost as quickly. He slipped on his Brooks Brothers shoes that he polished every week until they had a high shine on them, racing back to the kitchen just as his dad was pulling on his fedora and heading out the door.

Big John and Little John Donato climbed in the family car, a 1941 Packard 110 Woody Station Wagon, and rolled down the gravel driveway, waving at Granny Suzy who lived next door and was out watering the flowers on her front porch. Granny Suzy's house was the middle of the three Donato homes on the property, a small, two-bedroom ranch. Uncle Anthony, Jimmy's dad, and his family lived in a two-story colonial on the eastern-most portion of the property. It was quiet in front of his house, but Johnny knew they would be getting ready to head to church and Uncle Anthony was most likely checking on his greenhouse, which was located at the rear of the York Street property, as well.

As they hit the road and headed towards the Federal Street greenhouse, Big John clicked on the radio. As were most radios in the Denver area, it was tuned to KIMN which was currently playing "Save the Last Dance for Me" by The Drifters.

Johnny listened to the music for a minute, but there was something gnawing at him.

"Hey Pop, can I ask you a question?"

"Sure, Johnny. What's on your mind?"

"Do you know Jack Scaglia?"

Big John took a sideways glance over at his oldest son, taking him in. Little John Donato was about as good a kid as a father could want. Only 15 years old, he was already as big as his dad, tall and strong. He was loyal to his family, doting on his younger brother and sister and devoted to his mother and father. He was a hard worker, never complaining about the jobs he was given no matter how tedious or time-consuming.

Little John was quiet, so some people thought he was not the smartest kid. But Big John knew that was not the case. His son took things in and calmly analyzed the situation, and he was actually highly intelligent. He could take apart and rebuild a tractor engine by the time he was 12 years old. He was also very likeable and Big John could not recall a time when his son had lost his temper. It was a trait that many of the Donato men shared; they remained unflappable in most tense situations. They were not as fiery and as quick to fly off the handle as their Sicilian cousins.

The question about Jack Scaglia had taken him a little by surprise, however. The Donatos and the Scaglias were both from the same city in Italy, Potenza, so most people assumed they were connected. Big John's grandfather, Rocco, and the Scaglia patriarch, Danilo, had grown up together back in Potenza and were said to be great friends. But the two families didn't interact once they became older, and he wasn't sure why. There was a disconnect between the two friends at some point, but no one really talked about it. And Rocco had been dead for several decades at this point, so there was no asking him.

And there was the whole shadow of "The Mob" and "Mafia" that hung around the Scaglias. There was no question that the Scaglias ran organized crime in Denver and the surrounding area, and they were something of celebrities around town. Jimmy Cagney movies and the Kefauver hearings of the previous decade had captured the imagination of most Americans and they tended to romanticize aspects of the lifestyle. They also tended to believe that anyone that had Italian heritage was connected in some way, and there was plenty of Italians who liked to play that up.

But Big John Donato had no illusions about what the Scaglias were and how they had rose to the position they were in. He wasn't a choir boy – he knew that many Italians were oppressed once they got to the new country and he didn't hold it against those who did what they had to for their families to survive, even if it meant cutting corners or breaking laws. But he also understood that the Scaglias and others like them took advantage of the weaker and less fortunate, often times their own countrymen. They weren't above using fear and intimidation, and often violence, to get what they wanted.

For the most part the Donatos had always tried to do the right thing and had gotten what they had through hard work.

"Why do you ask, Johnny?"

"Jimmy ran into Jack Scaglia this weekend when he was out buying his shirt. Scaglia told him that his granddad and Great Grandpa Rocco used to be friends back in Italy."

"That's true. They grew up together, and both came over to this country about the same time. I've met them a few times – mostly at St. Rocco's Feast – but I don't really know them well."

"Did you know he's in the Mafia?"

Big John took his eyes off the road and looked at his son. "Who told you that?"

"Joey Cars."

Big John laughed. "That figures. Look, I don't know if that's true or not. I know there's rumors that not all of the Scaglia's money comes from legal means, but I doubt that they're hooked up with the mafia families in New York. I heard that the if there is any mafia in this area, it's down in Pueblo."

Little John took that in and thought about it for a second. "But he's a bad guy, right?"

By this time, they had reached the greenhouse and Big John parked the car but he didn't get out. Instead, he turned to his son and seemed to come to a decision.

"That's not an easy question to answer. He definitely does some things that are considered outside of society's norms. You have to understand that not all things are black and white. When our people came over, there wasn't a whole lot of opportunities for Italians and people suffered. So, there were a lot of people who broke rules, just to get by. A lot more people than you probably realize. Did they do some bad things? Definitely. Does that make them bad people? Not necessarily.

"Our family was fortunate. Grandpa Rocco had a place to land when he came over and he was able to grow the farm through hard work. But that wasn't the case for everyone. So, they did what they had to do to survive. I know Jack and his brothers made most of their money during Prohibition, which was just the government trying to take away something that everyone wanted. So, I don't hold that against them. Shoot, your Uncle Sonny had a still of his own in one of the old barns at the farm where he made moonshine out of sugar beets. And Uncle Paskey never stopped making his dago red wine even when it was illegal."

The thought of Uncle Paskey Ditolla stomping his grapes in his backyard made Johnny smile.

"And honestly, Jack Scaglia does a lot for his community. A lot of times when someone can't get a loan from the bank, Jack will help them out. If you're in danger of getting your heat or water turned off, it's known you can go to him and he will help you keep them on. And the neighborhood where he lives is the safest in the city."

Johnny nodded. "So, the stories about him aren't true?"

"I didn't say that. He does things that I wouldn't do. He can be a dangerous man and you want to be careful around him. Jack Scaglia may help you out one week, but he wouldn't hesitate to give you a beating the next. He may help you out, but he's always looking to see how that benefits him. There's a lot of angles to dealing with someone like Scaglia.

"Like I said, it's a complicated question."

Big John seemed to get lost in his own thoughts at the moment, looking out the vehicle's big windshield at the front of his shop. Johnny had noticed his father had seemed particularly stressed recently. He was always a serious man, but he was quick with a smile and always made time to interact with his children, whether it was playing tea with Bella, or shooting baskets with Dom and Johnny. But he had seemed to be preoccupied lately, and was having a lot of late-night conversations with his brother Anthony and Grandma Suzy.

"Are you Ok, Pop?" Johnny asked him, putting his hand on his father's forearm.

Big John looked at his son and collected himself, smiling before starting to answer. "Yes, I'm fine. I just have a lot on my mind.

"Look, Johnny. You're old enough to know the truth about things. You know the move we're talking about doing with the other Italian florists? Leaving CWF?"

Johnny had been listening to the discussions for months. It was impossible not to – it was about the only thing Big John and his brother Anthony talked about these days. "Sure, you're thinking about going out on your own."

"Yes, but it's not just me and Grandma Suzy and Uncle Anthony that would be leaving. There's a good-sized group of other growers who want to break free, and they're looking at me and Uncle Anthony to lead them. So, I have more than just our family to think about. All of these other growers, if we make a move, I'm responsible for their families now as well."

Johnny quietly whistled. "That's a lot of responsibilities."

"It is. And in order to do this, and do it so that all of our families can survive, I may have to do something that I'm not totally comfortable with."

Johnny looked at his dad with a new appreciation of what he had been going through. His dad was the most decent person he knew and always put other's needs ahead of his own. So, Johnny could imagine how this was weighing on him. "What is it Pop?"

Big John shook his head slightly and squeezed his son's arm.

"We're going to have a meeting this afternoon, after Sunday pasta, and I want you to stay for it. Moving forward, I want you to be by my side for all of this. You're my partner in this – the family business is going to go to you if something happens to me. You have to run it to take care of your mother and your brother and sister. And Granny Suzy. Understand?"

This kind of floored Johnny. He had been working at the greenhouse for years, and always just assumed it was expected he would take a bigger role as he grew older. But this was the first time the future was spoken about out loud. He suddenly felt like he had a lot more responsibilities, just like his dad. And, after what he had just been told, he felt a responsibility for those other growers' families as well.

"Yeah, Pop. Whatever you need."

"Good." Big John lovingly tapped his son on the cheek. "Now, come on. Let's go make sure the greenhouse will survive the rest of the day or we won't have the future to worry about anyway."

CHAPTER 2

They got back home just in time to pick up the rest of the family and make it to morning mass at The Nativity of the Blessed Mother Catholic Church, the local parish frequented by most of the Italians in the area.

Located on an acre of land near the South Platte River in Welby, Nativity was built by local immigrants for just over $1,000 in 1912. Originally a simple red brick church, it had grown as the surrounding community had grown throughout the years, adding a school in the early 20s and a gymnasium and small cafeteria in the 1950s. The actual church was expanded in the 1940s with an entrance and a bell tower added and the rectory was moved from a room behind the altar to a two-story home on the northwest corner of the property. Beautiful stained-glass windows depicting the stations of the cross lined the walls and large marble statues of Jesus and Mary's husband, Saint Joseph, flanked the altar, which was always adorned with fresh cut flowers donated by the Donato greenhouses. Directly behind the altar, above the Tabernacle, was a 12-foot marble statue of Mary, the Blessed Virgin and namesake of the parish, herself.

It was a beautiful parish, one that the surrounding Italian community took great pride in. Like most of their neighbors, the Donatos never missed a Sunday service and, while Little John Donato's mind would often wonder during the mass, he appreciated the tradition it provided. At this point in his life, he could recite the entire mass, besides the homily, verbatim, and there was something comforting about that. While attending religious classes in preparation for confirmation, Father Aldo Lepore told Little John's class that you could walk into a Catholic mass anywhere in the world, in any language, and you should be able to follow along. That stuck with Little John and was strangely reassuring.

This Sunday's gospel was The Parable of the Unmerciful Servant from Matthew 18:21-35.

Then Peter came to Jesus and asked, "Lord, how many times shall I forgive my brother or sister who sins against me? Up to seven times?"

Jesus answered, "I tell you, not seven times, but seventy-seven times.

"Therefore, the kingdom of heaven is like a king who wanted to settle accounts with his servants. As he began the settlement, a man who owed him ten thousand bags of gold was brought to him. Since he was not able to pay, the master ordered that he and his wife and his children and all that he had be sold to repay the debt.

"At this the servant fell on his knees before him. 'Be patient with me,' he begged, 'and I will pay back everything.' The servant's master took pity on him, canceled the debt and let him go.

"But when that servant went out, he found one of his fellow servants who owed him a hundred silver coins. He grabbed him and began to choke him. 'Pay back what you owe me!' he demanded.

"His fellow servant fell to his knees and begged him, 'Be patient with me, and I will pay it back.'

"But he refused. Instead, he went off and had the man thrown into prison until he could pay the debt. When the other servants saw what had happened, they were outraged and went and told their master everything that had happened.

"Then the master called the servant in. 'You wicked servant,' he said, 'I canceled all that debt of yours because you begged me to. Shouldn't you have had mercy on your fellow servant just as I had on you?' In anger his master handed him over to the jailers to be tortured, until he should pay back all he owed.

"This is how my heavenly Father will treat each of you unless you forgive your brother or sister from your heart."

Following the reading, Father Lepore made his way to the lectern to deliver his homily. He was wearing his green chasubles which represented a time of hope. A slight man, Father Lepore had immigrated from Naples about six years earlier, shortly after being ordained in a ceremony at the Vatican. Still in his early 30s, Lepore had wavy black hair and soft, almost feminine features. The older women in the parish doted on him, while the younger girls wondered how seriously he took his vows of chastity. The men, meanwhile, figured he was a finook, and preferred the church's other priest, the stern Lorenzo Ramazzotti, who had been with the parish since the beginning but was approaching 90 years old. Ramazzotti, who believed whole heartedly in the wrathful God from the Old Testament and was known to loudly berate people while taking their confession, was now almost completely blind and only said mass once a week, on Saturday afternoon.

Despite being small in stature, Father Lepore had a booming voice that filled the chapel when he spoke. He took a prolonged moment to look over his flock before starting his remarks.

"For the past couple of weeks, we have been discussing the parables of Jesus, simple stories he told his followers to illustrate deeper, moral lessons. This week's parable is one that I think many may struggle with because it's about forgiveness, and not just forgiveness for a single slight, but forgiveness over and over again. And, we all know how Italians love to hold a grudge."

This brought a smattering of nervous laughter from the pews, and Father Lepore smiled to himself. There were plenty of stereotypes about Italians that were untrue, but he knew that their penchant for holding a grudge was accurate.

"I know it's true. Back in my hometown of Casandrino, my granny Giulia held a grudge against another local woman, Sofia, for more than 80 years. Every time they came across each other, my granny would give her the evil eye and flash the mano cornuta at her before spitting on the ground. And Sofia would do the same. These were women who lived well into their 90s. I can remember asking granny Giulia why she did this, and she couldn't even remember. It was something that had happened back when they were both young girls, and the anger had lasted their entire lives. They couldn't forgive each other, even when they couldn't remember why they were angry with one another in the first place."

Again, this brought some nervous laughter.

"But today's gospel tells us that isn't how Jesus wants us to live our lives. When Peter asks him, Jesus says to forgive your brother or sister not once, not even seven times, but 77 times."

While Father Lepore went on about the parable for another several minutes, Johnny's mind began to wander, and he started to think about how this lesson related to his own father. Johnny didn't know exactly what it was, but his father was on the verge of doing something he wasn't comfortable with. Johnny knew his father was an honorable man, a man of the highest character. What line was he willing to cross to make this move successful? And could he forgive himself?

CHAPTER 3

As soon as they got back from mass, the Donato clan continued preparing for the Sunday feast.

Big John, Uncle Anthony, Johnny, Dominic and their younger cousins Michael and Peter hauled out the tents and long tables from the storage garage and set them up between the cottonwood trees in Granny Suzy's backyard. Milly returned to her kitchen to get the sauce simmering again and check on the meat, while Granny Suzy and Mary Ann would start boiling the water in large pots on Granny Suzy's stove.

They retrieved the rolls of dough, which they had made the day before and left to dry overnight, out of the cooler and started running it through the pasta maker. Granny Suzy had two of them that she clamped on opposite ends of the big butcher block table in her kitchen, with Big John manning one of them and Anthony manning the other. In the past, they would flatten the batches of dough with a rolling pin, but the pasta maker had a roller attachment that did the job quicker. Johnny always helped his dad do this, and usually Jimmy worked with his dad on the other machine. But Jimmy, who had gotten his own apartment in Thornton last summer, hadn't arrived yet, so Michael was helping Uncle Anthony on this particular day.

Johnny took a roll of dough, covered it in a generous amount of flour, and then fed it into the roller part of the machine while Big John ran the hand crank. They would send the same piece of dough through the roller two or three times until it was properly flattened. Once they were through flattening the dough, Big John and Anthony would switch the hand crank to the pasta cutter attachment. They had several different cutters – Fettucine, Angel Hair or thin, and Spaghetti. Today they were making thicker noodles with the Spaghetti cutter, which was Johnny's favorite. He took the flattened dough, added more flour and then fed it into the cutter while his dad ran the crank, catching the noodles as they came out the other side. It was surprisingly hard work, and Big John and Uncle Anthony had well-muscled forearms and biceps from years of doing the process.

Once there were enough noodles cut, they were immediately put in the boiling water in the pots, and didn't take long to cook. When Granny Suzy determined the noodles had reached the proper tenderness, the pots were drained and the pasta was distributed on several large platters. Milly's red sauce was added to the majority of the dishes, but there were also a couple platters of noodles mixed with just butter and grated parmesan cheese.

Meanwhile, the rest of the family had arrived and were seated out in the yard at the long tables covered in red-checked table clothes. There were crusty loaves of bread and bottles of olive oil and balsamic vinegar on each table, along with several jugs of dago red wine and pitchers of ice water. There were also bottles of Royal Crown Cola and Hires Root Beer chilling in steel tubs filled with ice.

More than two dozen family members and friends had shown up for today's feast including Suzy's daughter Lucille Ditolla and her family, which included husband Paskey (who supplied the wine) and their five children. There was also a group of Carabettas, including Joey, his parents and his five siblings. Jimmy and Connie Triola arrived just as the platters of pasta were being brought out. Johnny and Dominic helped their mom Milly bring out the bowls of meat that included sausage, meatballs, oxtails and braciole, thin slices of fried veal stuffed with parmesan cheese and bread crumbs, tied with string into a roll and then marinated in the sauce.

There was a definite pecking order to where people sat, with Granny Suzy at the head of the middle table, surrounded by her three children and their spouses. The table to her right held the adult cousins, while the children took up the table on the left. Jimmy was at the head of that table, surrounded by Connie, Johnny and Joey Cars. The younger kids filled out the rest of that table.

It was a loud affair, with everyone trying to be heard over everyone else. Granny Suzy didn't allow any business to be spoken of during the feast, so the conversations were joyful and lighthearted. The latest recordings by Elvis, Frank Sinatra and Dean Martin were big topics, as was the Denver Broncos, a new professional football team that was going to start playing in the fall.

They took their time eating, enjoying the food and the company. When most people seemed to be done with the main meal, plates of cannoli and cups of espresso were brought out. When that was done, everyone pitched in to haul the dirty dishes into Granny Suzy's kitchen, washing and drying everything in less than 15 minutes.

After the cleanup was completed, more wine would be poured and Paskey would break out his mandolin, playing along while Granny Suzy sang old Italian songs. The women gathered at one of the tables to share stories, while a good portion of the men broke into raucous game of morra, bursting into cheers when someone guessed correctly.

The youngest children started playing a game of hide-and-seek in the yard while Dominic and a few of the older kids tossed a baseball around. Usually Jimmy, Johnny and Joey Cars would make their way to the garage to tinker with Jimmy's Bel Air or to take a look at the 1928 Cadillac that Big John and Johnny were slowly restoring. But today they stayed close because they were all expected to take part in the discussion about the future of CWF and the Italian growers that was going to take place a little later that afternoon. As the eldest son in each family, it was expected that they would follow their fathers into the family business.

"Connie, when the other growers get here, you're going to have to find something to do," Jimmy told his girlfriend, who responded with an exasperated look.

"Why can't I listen in? What am I supposed to do, go play dolls with your little sister?"

This brought a laugh from Johnny, who said "Who's the baby now?" He got a punch in the arm from Connie for his comment.

"Look, most days it wouldn't be a big deal, and if it was just our families it wouldn't be an issue at all. But other growers are going to be here, and they're going to discuss business that they don't want shared with others. It's just the way it is." Jimmy put his arm around Connie's shoulders and gave her a kiss on the top of her head. "Go find my mom and Aunt Millie. I'm sure they're going to play cards or something."

"Really?" Connie asked.

"Really. I'm sorry, that's the way it has to be."

Connie sighed loudly and gave Jimmy a hurt look, but then got up and put her hands on her hips.

"Just remember this when you're not getting any tonight," Connie said and started to walk away.

That brought uproarious laughter from Johnny and Joey, who raised his glass of wine and said "Good for you, Connie. You tell him."

Jimmy nodded his head and smirked, and as soon as Connie was out of earshot, said "I'm still getting some tonight."

CHAPTER 4

Pete Villano was the first to arrive, followed shortly by Abe Notary out of Golden and the Mortozzi brothers, Frank and Louie, from Littleton. Sal Ligrani and Mike Mauro came together, as did Jerry Pachello and Clyde Minella.

Ted Losasso, the oldest of the attendees at 77, was the last to arrive and he was helped to one end of the table by his son Enzo and grandson Tony.

When everyone was settled and the glasses of wine and cups of coffee were poured and platters of biscotti and ricotta cookies were distributed, the meeting started. Suzy Donato, the only woman at the proceeding, sat at the head of the table, flanked by her son's Anthony and John. Although they made decisions equally, Anthony deferred to his younger brother John, who was better at public speaking, to lead the meeting.

John stood and cleared his throat, bringing the meeting to order.

"Gentleman, I want to thank you for joining us today, many from long distances." John introduced each attendee individually, thanking them again for making the trip. "We have important decisions to make today, decisions that will shape the futures of our families for generations to come." Big John looked over at his son, Johnny, who wasn't sitting at the main table but was just off to the side along with Jimmy and Joey Cars. "Make no mistake, these greenhouses are part of our families, as much as a child or a sibling. I work my greenhouse with my mother, Asunta, and my wife, Mildred, and one day it will be run by my son, Johnny. My brother Anthony has another that he runs with his wife and his son, Jimmy. These are not office jobs that you go to in the morning and leave behind when you walk out at closing time."

John walked behind his mother and squeezed her shoulder. None of the others spoke. Some were sipping their wine, or smoking cigars. These were all good men, family men. And they were being taken advantage of, not being able to fully enjoy the fruits of their hard labor. They could only take so much and had reached a breaking point. They all hung on John Donato's words. They knew him to be a good man, an honest man, and they trusted him to lead them out of this situation.

"And we are at a crossroads. We've all been able to carve out a living working with Anders Lindgren and Colorado Wholesale Florists, and in some cases a really good living. But recently it's become apparent that our options are limited at CWF. Anders controls what we grow and how much we grow, and how big a portion of the profits we get. For the past several years, are portions have remained the same while The Big Swede takes more and more."

This brought grumbles from the collected group, and Clyde Minella shouted out "It's not right!"

John nodded, before continuing. "So, we have been having discussions for quite a while now about breaking free and going out on our own. And I think most of us agree that is what we need to do, otherwise you wouldn't be here today." The group nodded in agreement.

"But I want to remind you, before we make this move, there are plenty of risks involved in doing this. Lindgren won't be happy about this, and he will fight us every step of the way. Right now, CWF has distribution agreements in place with a lot of the retail centers around the state, and they have capital and equipment that we don't have. It may take us a while to get back to a level playing field, and it will hurt us in our wallets until we get to that point.

"But, once we get there, we will be in control, and our money-making potential will be a lot greater than it would be under Lindgren."

"How long do you think it will take before we are back to a level playing field," Abe Notary asked.

John Donato shook his head. "I don't know. It could be three, maybe four years." This brought groans for the group. "It could be even longer, and who knows? We may never get there.

"We have to decide if that risk is worth it to get out from under this pezzonovante Lindgren."

There was more talk amongst the men, and John let it go on for a couple of minutes. People were starting to get heated. He looked over at Joe Carabetta first, and then his brother Anthony, who nodded.

John raised his hands and said "Friends. Paisans," quieting the talk.

"Listen. We may have a solution that could ease the pain and quicken the transition to where we see greater profits much earlier." This perked everyone up and the group went silent. "But, it's not without its risks as well."

John motioned over at Joe Carabetta. "You all know Joe Carabetta, my brother Anthony's father-in-law who runs Carabetta Floral out of Wheat Ridge? Joe was recently speaking to a friend of his and was telling him about our troubles with Lindgren and CWF, and this friend may have a solution for us. Joe?"

Joe stood up, looking very much like a typical Italian farmer. Just a shade under 5-foot-6, Joe had snow white hair and wore suspenders over a plaid shirt. He was soft spoken, but his voice had a little bit of grit to it after a lifetime of smoking hand rolled cigarettes. He was born in the old country, coming to the states while he was still in short pants.

"So, I was playing bocce with some of the fellas over at the Sons of Potenza a couple of weeks back, and I was telling them about our situation here with CWF. Well, the next week when I went back, this one fella came to me and says 'I talked to my son about your situation, and he thinks he may be able to help out.' So, I says, 'Yeah?' and he says 'Yeah.' So, the next day, I went and talked to his son, told him our problems, and he says, 'Yeah, I can help you out.'"

John Donato couldn't help but chuckle at Joe Carabetta's speech, delivered in broken English. He knew Joe was uncomfortable being the center of attention, so John was surprised he even got that out of Joe.

"What does that even mean?" Jerry Pachello asked.

"It means he can help us out. I don't know?" Joe Carrabetta threw his hands up in frustration and sat down again as he was peppered with questions.

John Donato again put up his hands to calm everyone down. "What it means is Joe's friend's son has a big empty warehouse we can use as the distribution center. It even has a big cooler, so we wouldn't have to install that. And he has delivery trucks we can lease, and he thinks he can help us get inroads in with a lot of the local grocers and other retail shops. And he has access to other distribution hubs, even out of state."

This brought cross talk and nods of agreement from the gathered group. Pete Villano, a fit, tan and tall man in his early 50s, stood up and spoke. "That's tremendous. So, what's the issue?"

Big John paused, looking at first at his mom and brother, and then over at his son, before continuing.

"Joe's friend? Ralph Scaglia. His son that offered to help? Jack Scaglia."

47

BOOK II

TUESDAY, JUNE 14, 1960, MORNING

CHAPTER 1

Danilo's Italian Restaurant was located on the first floor of a triangular shaped, two-story brick building on the southeast corner of 38th and Tejon in North Denver. The building originally housed a meat market and a drug store, but in 1947 Jack Scaglia, who already owned a nightclub and a grocery a little further south on Tejon, bought the building for $22,000 and opened up the restaurant, which was named after his paternal grandfather, for his father and mother to operate.

Danilo's quickly became one of the hottest restaurants in the Denver metro area and was considered by many to have the finest Italian food north of Pueblo. Jack's father Raffaele was semi-retired, and could always be found on a stool at the far end of the long mahogany bar that ran along the north wall, while his mother, Pietrina, ran the kitchen, overseeing the recipes on the menu which featured constantly changing specials depending on what cuts of meat or seafood they could get that week.

Pietrina ran a tight, efficient kitchen that was mostly staffed by family members and friends, and she kept the place impeccable. It was said that the floors were so clean at Danilo's that one could eat off of them, although Pietrina would be quick to throw you out if you tried.

While the main floor was open to the public, the basement and the second level were off limits to "civilians."

At first glance the basement was used as a storage area, complete with a giant freezer that took up most of the area. But upon closer inspection, one could tell that there was no way that the freezer took up the amount of space that it should. Under even more scrutiny, one would see a reinforced steel door with a peep slot in a back corner that led to Denver's most exclusive gambling den, complete with poker and blackjack tables, roulette wheels and slot machines.

The top floor featured more storage, several offices including Jack's large corner suite that looked out toward the state capital, and another poker room that was home to the even more exclusive executive game, reserved for high rollers and only held about once a month.

When Anthony Carpineto drove Jack's big Buick to the front door that following Wednesday morning, there was a half-dozen neighborhood kids milling around, as was typical. They were always waiting for Jack, who would hand out hard candy from his pockets and peel off dollar bills from his cash roll to give to each one of them before sending them on their way.

As Carpineto drove the car around to the back parking lot, Jack Scaglia entered the front door and was immediately hit by the cool conditioned air. He had paid for top-of-the-line units for both the main and top floors, and they put them to good use. In the morning it was almost uncomfortably cool in the building, but that was so it could keep up as the kitchen heated up and the sun continued to beat down during the day.

Jack found his father, Raffaele, in his usual perch at the end of the bar, sipping an espresso and listening to the news on a radio behind the bar. He could already smell the sauce cooking in the back and heard his mother, Pietrina, singing along to Italian standards and laughing with her sister Mamie in the kitchen.

Jack went behind the bar and got himself an espresso from the machine they had imported from Italy. He went around and kissed his father on the top of his head before sitting down on a stool next to him at the end of the bar.

"How's it going, Papa?" Jack asked.

"Bueno. Bueno, figlio," Raffaele answered, patting his sons' hand. "How are you this wonderful morning?"

"Bueno. Anything interesting in the paper?" Jack nodded toward the Rocky Mountain News that his father had in front of him.

"This is yesterday's paper. I was just reading about the Floyd Patterson fight. You know he knocked that Swede out for more than 10 minutes?" Raffaele loved boxing. "I wish I could have seen that. Although I made a pretty good payday on that fight. I had a bill down on Patterson."

"I always thought Gaetano could have been a champion," Raffaele said, pushing a plate of biscotti over towards Jack to share. "Your brother was a hell of a fighter."

"He couldn't move. He was like a sitting target. Tano could throw a vicious punch, but he couldn't avoid getting hit. Those professional fighters would've beat his face to a pulp," Jack said.

Raffaele laughed. "You're right, he couldn't move. Those moolies would have made his nose even uglier than it was."

They both knew Tano was sensitive about his nose. It had taken a beating when he was younger, earning him the nickname Smush. As soon as Tano had enough money squared away he had his nose fixed by a plastic surgeon, although he never would admit it.

"One other thing," Raffaele said, pointing at an article in the paper. "It looks like that new football league has signed a TV deal. The American Football League? We have to make sure we get them on the book. It's going to be huge around here, especially with the Broncos in town."

"It's taken care of papa. I've been talking to our friends in Chicago, and they're going to feed us the line. Lefty is already all over it and has insiders already in place."

"Good, bueno. I'm thinking of getting season tickets to the Broncos. I bet Clyde would like to go."

"He would."

"Can you look into it for me?" Jack nodded; another task added to the list of things he had to do.

"How is Clyde? And little Angie?"

"They're all good. Growing fast. Clyde's got his own place, over by the university. He said the football team should be really good this season, they should compete for the league title. And Angie will be a senior in high school this year. She's really smart. Looking at colleges on the west coast. She wants to study fashion."

That brought a smile to Raffaele's face. He doted on his grandchildren. "And Frances? You guys doing well."

Frances, or Frannie, was Jack's wife of more than 20 years. A former fashion model and chorus girl, Jack had first seen her at a downtown department store and was immediately struck by her beauty. But Jack felt it was "not proper" to approach a lady in public, so instead he arranged a meeting through a mutual acquaintance. They were married less than two years later and, although Jack had strayed from time to time, he still loved her. Their relationship wasn't always easy – he felt she drank too much and took too many pills; she thought he needed to keep his pants on, especially around the moolinyans, who she felt were less than human – but they were devoted to their children and their family.

"She's good, too. I think she's planning on coming to help with the lunch rush later," Jack said. "Have you heard from Joe?"

"Ehh," his dad said, a small look of disgust flashing across his face. "He's still out in California, hanging out with that producer, working on his tan. He's like a Hollywood fanook, your brother."

"C'mon Papa. Don't be that way," Jack said. His youngest brother, Joe, had led a troubled existence for the past decade or so. Always a nervous sort, he had developed an addiction to narcotics in his mid-20s and was facing a long prison sentence after being arrested with a half-pound of heroin in 1948.

Jack had worked with a friendly judge to get it reduced to a healthy fine and time served, and the family had shipped Joe off to a rehab facility in Monterey, California. While in rehab Joe met a man, Al Franco, who produced stag movies, and they became fast friends. When Joe was finished with rehab, he decided to stay in California and went to work with Franco. The rehab didn't stick, and Raffaele Scaglia was less than happy with his youngest son.

"Let's not talk about Joe," Raffaele said. "Do you have a busy day?"

"I do, Papa. I have a couple of meetings. In fact, your friend Joe Carabetta and the Donato brothers are coming by in a little bit."

"Ahh, good," Raffaele smiled. "Are you going to help them out? Remember, Joe is my friend, and these are good people."

"I know Papa. I'll help them out if I can."

"I trust you will do right by them," Raffaele said, patting his son's hand. Now in his mid 60s, Jack knew his dad had been slipping recently. There was a time when Raffaele Scaglia was one of the sharpest minds around, always two steps ahead of his adversaries and the law. But those days were in the past. He was more forgetful and needed a walking stick to get around, sipping on anisette from morning to night to dull the constant pain from a decades old hip injury he sustained while helping Jack during the Salardino conflict. There was a history of dementia in Raffaele's maternal side of the family — the Lombardis — and Jack was afraid that was what the future held for his father. But Raffaele's eyes were clear right now, and he wanted his words to be heard.

"Look Jack. They're good people, the Donatos. My dad Danilo, the namesake of this restaurant we are sitting in," Raffaele gestured around the dining room, "owes a debt to their grandfather Rocco from back in the old country. So, I want you to take that into consideration when you negotiate with them. Do you know what I'm saying?"

Jack nodded at his father. He knew what he was saying. He wanted their partnership to be legitimate.

"I hear you, Papa. I'll see what I can do." Jack touched his father's cheek lovingly. "Do you want to sit in?"

"No," Rafaelle shook his head. "I'll make Joe wait down here with me and play pinochle. See if I can get some scharole off of him."

"Ha," Jack laughed. "You do that. You know, one day you'll need to tell us what this big misterioso is between the Donatos and Papa."

Rafaelle nodded. "I will. But not today."

CHAPTER 2

Jack Scaglia eased into the leather chair behind his large, cherry-wood executive desk with the multiple drawers and brass pulls, and looked out the east-facing windows toward downtown Denver and the gold-domed Colorado capital building. It was a magnificent view – some say the best this part of North Denver offered.

Anthony Carpineto came in the office and sat another espresso in front of Scaglia, asking "You need anything else, Boss?"

"No, Anthony, I'm good. Grazzi."

"Ok. Reggie is scheduled to be here around 10:30, and then you have the Donatos at noon. Let me know if you need anything." Anthony headed over to his own office, a much smaller room across from the executive poker area and next to the top of the stairs, which was the only accessway to the top floor. No one could get up the stairs, and to Jack, without getting by The Ram.

Jack took a sip of his espresso – he had paid to have the machine imported over from the old country when they opened the restaurant, and he often thought it was the best money he had spent – and clicked on the small transistor radio on the corner of his desk. The sounds of Dean Martin singing "Only Forever" came over the airwaves and Jack smiled. Although he loved Frank Sinatra as much as anyone, Scaglia preferred Dino.

Jack's meeting with Reggie Jefferson was still more than 20 minutes away, so it gave him some time to reflect on what his father said and his journey to get where he was, which was as the unquestioned head of the mob in the Rocky Mountains.

It really was an unlikely journey when he thought about it. His paternal grandparents, Danilo and Angeline Scaglia, were from Potenza and were part of the immigration boom of the 1880s, sailing from Naples to New York City. After a short stay in Buffalo, the Scaglia's made their way west, setting in Denver around 1890.

Danilo and Angeline quickly had three children, a daughter named Katrina and sons Raffaele and Mario. Danilo found work as a laborer with the Denver & Rio Grande Western Railroad and made a decent living, able to provide a comfortable life for his wife and children.

Raffaele and Mario followed their father into the railroad business, with Raffaele quickly showing an adeptness for management, making his way to the position of foreman by the time he was in his early 20s. Raffaele married Pietrina Molinaro around 1905 and they had seven children in quick succession – Mamie, Corinne (who died at six months old), Giacomo, Genevieve, Gaetano and, finally, Giuseppe, who was a surprise six years after Tano.

Raffaele continued to do well at the railroad, but his feelings towards the business soured when Danilo passed away after contracting pneumonia while working outdoors during the winter, and then his uncle Mario was killed in a freak accident when his legs were severed above the knees after slipping on wet tracks during a switch over in 1912.

Raffaele took the small settlement for the bachelor Mario's death and bought a horse and wagon and went into the fruit and vegetable peddling business. He would deliver to homes all around town, including to the wealthy families that lived in the big brick houses on Capitol Hill.

While he was doing fine peddling fruit and vegetables, Raffaele found an even more profitable venture when Colorado become one of the first states to vote for Prohibition in 1916, a full four years ahead of the nation as a whole – selling moonshine.

Raffaele would sell liquor to customers along his vegetable route as well as to speakeasies and underground bars in the Bottoms and lower Downtown areas. And, when they were old enough, he would use Jack and Tano as his "runners."

Even in those early days, Jack showed a knack for exploiting situations to his advantage. When he would go with Raffaele to pick up the booze they would sell to their customers, Jack would observe where the bootleggers had the liquor hidden. Later, he would go back with his cousin Paulie Molinaro and steal a couple of bottles. While the bootleggers would sell their bottles for $2 a pop or more, Jack and Paulie would come and undercut them, selling their stolen bottles for $1 each.

One time, when Jack was 16, they came across a garage in North Denver that was being used for storage, and they were able to steal a half-dozen five-gallon kegs. Jack and Paulie made a good payday selling those kegs to local speakeasies, but it also brought them unwanted attention from the Carlino brothers.

The Carlinos had just survived a bloody war with the Danna family for control of liquor out of southern Colorado, and they had been using the garage that Jack and Paulie had come across to store their booze in the Denver area. After the theft was discovered, the Carlinos set out to make an example of whoever had stolen from them.

When Raffaele Scaglia heard about this, he feared for his eldest son's life. The Carlinos had turned southern Colorado into the wild west in their war with the Dannas, the bodies of their enemies lining the streets of Pueblo and Trinidad. They weren't known for showing good judgement or restraint, and it was safe to assume that the lives of Jack and Paulie meant nothing to them. Knowing this, Raffaele went to Charlie Salardino, who had been recently installed by the Capone mob to look over their interests in the Denver area and who provided the booze that Raffaele sold along his route. Raffaele told Salardino what happened and pleaded for him to intervene on Jack's behalf.

Salardino, who didn't particularly like or respect the Carlinos, did like the little vegetable peddler in front of him, and saw an opportunity to gain a strong ally in the days and years to come. Raffaele Scaglia was small time, but he was shrewd, and he had three young sons who were loyal to their father. Salardino had his own plans, and they didn't include the Carlinos long-term. He agreed to step in for Raffaele, but there would have to be a price to pay, which amounted to an extra 10 percent of everything the elder Scaglia made pushing booze. And, Jack and Paulie would have to take a beating.

The Carlino crew caught up with Jack and Paulie two days later coming out of a soda shop on Larimer Street. There was four of them, strong young men armed with rubber hoses and wood bats. Jack took the initial hit, getting smacked across his back as he stepped out of the storefront. He took a good two dozen blows, but they were mostly to his thighs and upper back, not anything too substantial.

Paulie Molinaro had it much worse. The first shot was to the front of his skull, cracking his right orbital bone and sending him to his knees. The men then proceeded to reign down more than 100 blows on Paulie, laughing and taunting him the entire time.

Jack laid in the gutter, hearing the beating his cousin was taking, the guttural noises Paulie made while the men pounded on him. Paulie sounded like an animal, making noises that humans should never make, begging for someone to help him, until he finally fell unconscious. When they were done, one of the men, who appeared to be the ringleader, unzipped his pants and pissed on Paulie, saying "Maybe next time you'll think before you steal from the Carlinos."

That same man then went over and grabbed Jack's chin in his gloved left hand, bringing his face close to Jack's. His breath smelled of cinnamon schnaps and he had a port-wine birthmark over the left side of his face. The man told Jack, "Lucky for you, you got a guardian angel, kid." He then spit in Jack's face before giving him a back-handed slap with his right hand. Jack crumpled into the gutter again and the man kicked him in the ribs. "C'mon,

Ernie. Let's go," another man said, and the crew walked around the corner to a waiting sedan.

Jack would never forget that face, with the port-wine birthmark. Lying in the gutter, holding his battered ribs after he wiped the man's spittle from his face, he vowed that he would get his revenge one day.

Jack found out later that it wasn't by chance that he had gotten off easier than Paulie – that was another thing his father had negotiated with Charlie Salardino. Jack did feel guilty about what happened to his cousin, but not too guilty. He was glad it wasn't him. The Carlino crew really did a number on the 15-year-old Paulie, breaking five ribs, his left femur and all of the fingers on both of his hands. He had a collapsed lung and had lost more than a dozen teeth and the vision in his right eye was never the same. He would be bedridden for more than two months, and his days running the streets were over.

Jack, on the other hand, was back helping Raffaele three days later. They never spoke about the incident, but Jack understood what his father had sacrificed to keep him safe. Raffaele was a prideful man, and it had to be hard for him to beg for his son's life, and maybe equally as hard to give up a bigger piece of his action. After struggling so long, the Scaglia's were finally making some headway thanks to Raffaele's hard work. They had moved to a bigger apartment that had running water and an indoor toilet, and Raffaele had been talking to Charlie Salardino about putting some money on the street. But that would have to wait, because Jack had been impetuous and ripped off the wrong people.

Jack decided then and there he would make it up to his father and his family and from that point forward there was no one who hustled as hard as Jack Scaglia on the streets of Denver.

CHAPTER 3

Once Gaetano was old enough, Jack started taking him out and showing him the ropes on how to be a good "runner" on Raffaele's routes. Jack would still ransack booze filled garages they would come across, but only after making sure who owned the stash.

There was an Irishman, Glenn McGregor, who had a shed filled with bonded whiskey off of 38th and Pecos. Jack and Gaetano took the whole stash, netting more than $12 a bottle. And Raffaele did the right thing, giving a portion to Salardino and using another portion to pay off the local police.

When McGregor started making noise about finding "those dago hoodlums" that ripped him off, instead of going to war, the Scaglia's went into business with him. McGregor had a pipeline to bonded whiskey out of Canada, which was highly sought after those days. McGregor had a small crew made up of Irish, Germans and Swedes, and they were successful enough that they could use the help of the Italians, even if they didn't particularly like them, to expand their empire. The McGregor clan was a particularly vicious group, leaving a trail of broken bones and lifeless bodies in Boulder County. One of the most vicious members of this group was a young Swedish immigrant Anders Lindgren, who was said to be as ambitious as he was brutal.

Meanwhile, Raffaele Scaglia got his hands on a couple of Ford transportation trucks and outfitted them with overloaded springs to hide that they were hauling heavy cargo in the back. Through Charlie Salardino's connections in Chicago, they partnered with Al Capone's mob to move the liquor from Canada to Iowa, and then from there to various points throughout the Midwest and the Rocky Mountain region.

At its height, the Salardino/Scaglia bootlegging operation had more than two dozen transport trucks running whiskey from Canada, moonshine from Iowa and even bourbon from Mexico. They supplied close to 100 different establishments with booze in the Denver area alone, with one of their biggest paydays being the Policeman's Ball held every year around Christmas time. The Denver Post estimated bootleggers in the metro area were bringing in more than $100,000 a week; in truth, it was probably closer to $250,000.

While Salardino and the Scaglia's ran things in Denver, the Carlino brothers had taken control of Southern Colorado by virtue of wiping out most of the Danna family during the early part of 1926. With the southern part of the state secure, Pete and Sam Carlino started looking to expand their empire north to Colorado Springs and Denver. That was fine with Charlie Salardino at first – there was enough demand for everyone to have a piece. But eventually the Carlino's reckless ways and outright greed started to wear on Charlie. It didn't help that Pete Carlino bought a mansion on Federal Boulevard in the Highland neighborhood, establishing Denver as the base of his operations.

Things reached a breaking point when, in July of 1930, a prohibition agent who happened to be a decorated World War I veteran, was murdered in the southern town of Aguilar, Colorado, after he had made a number of bootlegging arrests in the area. The assassination of the agent, Dale Frances Kearney, brought a ton of heat down by the feds, crippling operations for an extended period of time while they hunted for the killers. That forced the Carlinos to focus more on their operation in Denver as things suffered in the south.

As part of his plan to have a bigger piece of the pie in Denver, Pete Carlino arranged to hold a "Bootlegger Convention" during the early part of 1931 at a roadhouse in Wheat Ridge. Carlino hoped to establish working relationships with the other bootlegging families in the state, define territories, as well as agree on standard prices for the liquor and to set up a collective fund that all would contribute to, which would be used for bail money, attorney fees and as a sort of "mob widow" rescue fund.

Unfortunately for Pete Carlino, he didn't know that the feds had been successful in placing an undercover agent within his ranks in the aftermath of the Kearney killing.

That agent, Lawrence Baldesareli, was presented as a professional gunman out of Chicago, and quickly rose to the position of Sam Carlino's bodyguard and main driver. Baldesareli alerted the authorities about the convention and, just as it got underway, it was raided by 23 armed police officers as the attendees sat down for a chicken dinner. Close to 30 suspected bootleggers were arrested that evening, including Pete and Sam Carlino, along with seven other Carlino associates.

Surprisingly, not included among those arrested were Charlie Salardino or any members of the Scaglia family. They had their own informants among local law enforcement and were tipped off to the raid the day before and stayed far away.

Despite the number of arrests, the raid didn't produce any real lasting results. For one thing, the bootleggers had smartly kept the convention "dry" and there was no illegal booze or weapons found on the premises. Because of that, actual charges were hard to come by outside of vagrancy, which both Carlino brothers were hit with. The authorities used the arrests as an opportunity to question the suspects about the local liquor operations, but most of the men arrested remained tight lipped. The police did hold the men for several days, but eventually let them all go without sentencing.

In the following days and months, the Carlino brothers' behavior continued to become more erratic; Pete Carlino was convinced there were out-of-town assassins on the hunt for him, so he made plans to go to Omaha with Baldesareli to hide out and collect money and guns. But before he did that, he made arrangements to firebomb his Denver home to collect the insurance money. Baldesareli again tipped off the authorities beforehand, but they failed to act, so just before midnight on March 16, 1931, Pete Carlino's Denver home exploded in a blast that was so powerful the roof was lifted completely off the frame of the house, bricks were hurled blocks away and the structure crumbled to its foundation. Neighboring homes had all of their windows blown out and several sustained structural damage as the shockwave from the explosion was felt as far as six blocks away.

The explosion outraged the public as local papers said the motive was gang related, even though the authorities knew better. The following day they raided Sam Carlino's home, looking for clues into the blast. Sam wasn't at home and Pete was in the wind, and truth be told the authorities weren't looking for the duo that hard. Both the police chief, Robert Reed, and the mayor, Benjamin Stapleton, were considered corrupt. Still, in the days following the explosion, acting on information supplied by Baldesareli, the police arrested three Carlino associates that were involved in the bombing. They eventually caught up to Sam in a car on 12th and Champa Street in Denver and arrested him and Baldesareli, who had just returned after dropping off Pete in Omaha as planned. During the arrest, the police came across a slip of paper with an address on it. When they search the property at the address, they discovered a weapons cache that contained a loaded Browning Automatic Rifle, a loaded automatic shotgun, a loaded .22 pistol and 125 rounds of ammunition.

While Sam Carlino was detained, Baldesareli was only charged with carrying a concealed weapon, a minor offense, and was back on the streets after paying a $25 fine. That, combined with how quickly the authorities tracked down the three men who had actually carried out the firebombing of Pete's home, raised suspicion of Baldesareli amongst the Carlino crew.

Sam Carlino arranged for his release after securing a $5,000 bond, and by the end of the month, the other three men suspected in the bombing were also bailed out.

A couple of weeks later, on a Saturday, Sam was due in court to face charges surrounding the explosion. Lawrence Baldesareli, who was living in the Mayflower Hotel on 17th and Grant Street in downtown Denver at the time, was supposed to pick up Carlino from his home and take him to the court appearance. Baldesareli retrieved his car from a nearby garage, and then parked in front of the Mayflower, needing to get something from his hotel room before picking up Sam. As Baldesareli exited the car, he was greeted by a shotgun blast from a red convertible Ford that was passing by. Baldesareli was hit on the left side of his upper body, slugs ripping into his arm. The undercover agent dove for cover, making it into the hotel lobby as a second blast missed him entirely as the Ford sped off.

Although he wasn't seriously injured, the authorities understood that Baldesareli's cover was blown and his time undercover in the Carlino mob was over. Armed guards were placed outside of his hospital room, and the Denver Post ran a story in that evening's paper, detailing Baldesareli's time in one of Colorado's deadliest crime families.

Although Sam Carlino was cleared in the firebombing of his brother's house, the actions that proceeded it showed that things were closing in on the Carlinos. Sam, along with three associates, were charged in the assassination attempt on Baldesareli, with a trial set for that May. Pete was missing, and some presumed him dead. And their money was running out. Sam was being sued by a local car dealer after a test drive the previous year ended in rollover and permanent injuries to the dealer. Midway through that civil trial, Sam Carlino's attorneys withdrew from the case when they realized Sam didn't have the money to pay them.

Afraid of would-be assassins and further arrests, Sam holed up in his Denver house with his wife Josephine and several bodyguards, but even those were running in short supply. Several Carlino associates had been murdered in southern Colorado during the previous couple of months and, with their power and influence greatly comprised, it was getting harder and harder to recruit new men. On May 8, 1931, Sam was holding a summit of sorts with some of his remaining allies, trying to make plans for the coming weeks and his upcoming trial. Among those attending the meeting was Ernie Ligrani, a stocky man in his late 20s with a port-wine birthmark on the left side of his face who had been serving as Sam's bodyguard since the attempt on Baldesareli's life.

The house was full that early evening. Josephine was attending to her and Sam's 3-year-old daughter in an upstairs bathroom. Pete's wife Jennie had stopped by, accompanied by her cousin Fred Gioso, who was taking her downtown to run some errands. Jimmy Gioso, Fred's older brother, was also there, but he was part of the meeting Sam was having in the family room with Ligrani about a possible hijacking of a booze shipment that was supposed to be coming in from Nebraska.

As Fred Gioso and Jennie Carlino went to leave, Fred noticed a red Ford convertible rolling slowly past the house with a couple of men with fedoras pulled low and tight in the front seat, and pointed it out to Sam. Everyone was already on edge, and Sam was seeing assassins hiding in every shadow he came across, so he quickly jumped up and took a look between the drapes.

"Huh," Sam said. "I haven't seen that car on this block before."

Ligrani joined Carlino at the window and took a look for himself. He observed the car and quickly

dismissed their concern, saying "That's nothing. I saw those guys when I came in. They were parked at the house at the end of the street. There's some kind of get together going on."

"That's right," Sam said, remembering hearing about a party a neighbor was having that day. "The Tolvo's are having a birthday party for their little boy."

Satisfied, Jennie yelled up the stairs to Josephine that she was leaving, and she headed out with Fred Gioso. A couple minutes after they left, Ligrani stood and started putting on his overcoat.

"I need to get going, too, if I'm going to make it in time to pick up that package," Ligrani said. He was supposed to travel south to Colorado Springs to pick up some money that was owed to Sam Carlino and return with it the next morning. Jimmy Gioso was taking over the bodyguard duties that night, and was planning on driving Sam, Josephine and their daughter into town for a late dinner.

Sam rose from his couch and shook Ligrani's hand. Ligrani had been with the Carlinos for several years now, and Sam considered him a key asset moving forward. "Thank you, paisan. I appreciate everything you are doing for me."

"You've got it, boss. Anything you need." Sam walked Ligrani to the front door as Jimmy headed to the kitchen. He patted Ligrani one last time on the back and turned to follow Jimmy Gioso into the kitchen as Ligrani opened the door and appeared to head out. But as LIngrani opened the door, Sam saw the red convertible that Fred Gioso had mentioned had returned and was rolling up to the front of the house. At the same time, he saw Ligrani reach into his coat pocket and pull out a blue steel .45.

"Look out, Jimmy!" Sam yelled as he ran toward the kitchen. Ligrani fired, catching Sam between the shoulder blades, sending him stumbling forward to the kitchen floor. Trying to get to the back door, Jimmy jumped over the kitchen table, knocking it on its side. Ligrani stepped into the kitchen and fired a pair of shots at Jimmy behind the table, catching him in the abdomen with the second shot.

Josephine screamed from upstairs and her daughter cried out as Ligrani stood over Carlino and pumped three more shots into his back before dropping the gun at his side. Ligrani then ran out the front door, jumping into the back seat of the waiting Ford which sped away, drowning out Josephine's cries from inside the house.

"That sonuvabitch is dead," Ligrani said, pounding on the passenger side of the front seat while whooping triumphantly.

"Are you sure?" one of the two men in the front seat, the passenger, asked.

"There was no surviving that. And even if he did, he won't last long. I packed and dipped the bullets in garlic. The infection will kill him," Ligrani said.

"Did you leave the gun like you were told?"

"Yeah, I know what I'm doing. Now get me the fuck out of here."

The plan was to take Ligrani to a safehouse in Wheat Ridge, where another car would take him out to Los Angeles where he would lay low until the heat from the Carlino killing died down. But Ligrani would never make it to Los Angeles. Jack Scaglia, riding shotgun in the getaway Ford that was driven by his brother Gaetano, would make sure of that.

CHAPTER 4

Ernie Ligrani woke with a start, a bucket of cold water rousing him out of the brief respite he had enjoyed after passing out the last time. He wasn't sure when that was. It could have been moments ago, or it could have been days. He had lost all track of time.

After doing the job on Sam Carlino, Ligrani figured his life was going to change. He was right, but not in the way he thought. They had sped him away from Carlino's house in the convertible Ford, the same car Ligrani had used in the unsuccessful hit on that federal agent Baldesareli a few weeks back. But instead of heading west and to the safe house in Wheat Ridge, the driver was headed east and north, toward Commerce City or Brighton.

"Hey, this isn't the right way. We're supposed to be headed to the place in Wheat Ridge."

"Plans have changed."

It was the passenger who spoke. Ligrani couldn't make out who it was — the car was dark and whoever it was had a fedora pulled down tight over his forehead. Ligrani didn't recognize either of the men in the car — they were both young and dark, definitely Italians — but it wasn't surprising he didn't know them. Ligrani had mainly worked down south in Pueblo and Trinidad and had only been sent up to Denver for special jobs. But even down south, Ligrani realized things were unravelling for the Carlino family, so a week ago when someone approached him about possibly setting up his boss and aligning with Charlie Salardino's crew, he jumped at the chance. Salardino had told him that after the hit, Ligrani would have to go away for a while but when it cleared up, he would reward Ligrani by making him a capo and setting him up with his own crew. It sounded great — Ligrani had grown frustrated with the Carlinos for not bumping him up while, at the same time, installing a federal agent in the upper echelons of the family.

But now, as they headed somewhere he wasn't sure of, Ligrani wasn't positive he had made the right choice. He was getting an uneasy feeling off the men in the front seat. He wished he hadn't dropped the gun he had used on Sam Carlino, because now he was unarmed. They had pulled off a main road a little way back and, after a few backroads, were driven past a gate that was opened by a man with a lupara slung across his back into a vast farm. They were now travelling on a narrow dirt road that was surrounded by crops of corn on both sides. A large barn-type structure was ahead on the horizon and that seemed to be their destination.

"This isn't what I had agreed on with Charlie." Ligrani was having trouble hiding his nervousness.

The passenger turned around and faced him. "Look, this is how it has to be. The safehouse was blown. Charlie appreciates what you just did for him, so he didn't want to risk anything going wrong getting you out of here. There's a shipment of vegetables heading out of this farm in the morning headed to California. You are going to pose as the backup driver. It's all arranged."

Ligrani looked into the face staring back at him – the dark eyes, dimpled chin and prominent nose. He recognized him now. It was the same kid he had worked over outside the soda shop on Larimer Street years ago. The one they had been instructed to take it easy on.

"Ok. That sounds good," Ligrani said, nodding in agreement. He didn't want him to know he recognized him, but Ligrani immediately began to look for a way out. It was dark out and the rows of corn were immense. If he could make it into there, he might be able to avoid them long enough to get away.

They were now only about 20 yards away from the clearing around the structure and the driver began to slow down. That was Ligrani's chance. He threw open the back door and rolled when he hit the ground. He jumped up and headed toward the safety of the tall rows of corn. Unfortunately, Ligrani didn't account for the small irrigation ditch that ran along the road and badly turned his ankle in it, going down in a heap before reaching the rows of corn. Ligrani tried to get up but he couldn't put any weight on his ankle, which he was sure he had broken.

By this time the two men had exited the car and were standing above Ligrani, laughing. "Where do you think you're going?" the driver asked before hauling him up and over his shoulder. He was extremely strong and handled Ligrani, who wasn't small by any measure himself, easily. Ligrani was struggling but the passenger took a sap out of his jacket pocket and smashed Ligrani across the skull, knocking him out for the first of, what turned out to be, many times.

When Ligrani awoke the first time, his bound wrists had been hung from a meat hook in the middle of the structure, a large drain under his feet. It was apparent this was a multi-use facility; there were tractors and other farm equipment along one far wall, a dock that was used to load delivery trucks along another and hundreds of bales of hay along a third. There was also a processing station near the dock where the vegetables were loaded into boxes and crates before being transferred to the trucks; several large animal pens that looked like they hadn't been used for a while and a small room, most likely an office, tucked in another corner.

Ligrani was hanging about six inches off the ground, a large spotlight illuminated above him. The two men from the car were standing in front of him, the man who had opened the fence to let them into the farm was leaning against a far wall, out of earshot.

"I'm Jack Scaglia," the smaller one, the passenger, said. "This is my brother, Gaetano." The big one nodded at Ligrani. Both brothers had taken off their jackets and had rolled up their sleeves. "Do you remember me?" Jack asked.

Ligrani shook his head. "No. No. Look I don't know who you are. I have a deal with Charlie. Get in touch with him, he'll tell you. You don't have to do this." Ligrani was panicking. "I have money. I can get you money. Lots of it."

Jack shook his head. "This isn't about money."

Jack took a step toward Ligrani and grabbed his port-wine-stained face in his hand, scrunching his cheeks much the same way Ligrani had done to him outside the soda shop. "You're lying. You remember who I am."

"Look, it was just business. It wasn't anything personal. It was business. The Carlinos made me do it."

"At first it was business. But then you made it personal."

"How? How did I make it personal? They told us to beat you guys, to take it easy on you, but to make an example out of the other one. That's what we did."

Jack still had a hold of Ligrani's face. "How'd you make it personal?" Jack then spit right between Ligrani's eyes, his saliva slowly dripping down his face. "That's how."

Ligrani started to struggle, trying to find a way to get free of the hook he was hanging from. But the Scaglia's had secured his hands well; there was no give in the ropes binding his wrists. When Ligrani resigned himself to the fact he wasn't going to get free, he stopped struggling and pissed his pants.

Seeing the urine drip from Ligrani's legs into the drain in the floor, Jack said, "There's that, too."

Jack looked over at Tano, who had slipped a pair of brass knuckles on his right hand, and nodded. Tano stepped up, smiled at Ligrani and said, "Ciao." He then threw a right hook into Ligrani's rib cage, and you could hear the air leave Ligrani's body as several ribs snapped. The pain was tremendous – Tano hit like a truck and Ligrani immediately saw bursts of light erupt in his vision. Ligrani's body was swinging rhythmically on the hook from the force of the punch, and Tano took advantage of that, sending blow after blow to Ligrani's mid-section as he swung back around. It only took six or seven shots before Ligrani passed out again, blood pouring out of his mouth and nose down his body to mix with the piss draining below his feet.

When he woke up the next time, Ligrani was tied to a hard-backed chair and the Scaglia's went to work on him with a ballpein hammer, smashing his toes and every bone in his left foot, the one he hadn't rolled in his escape attempt.

It went like that for a while. Ligrani would wake up and they would work on him until he passed out again. Sometimes they would rouse him with buckets of ice water; other times he'd come to on his own. One time he awoke to find them eating roast beef sandwiches and drinking soda. They let him sit there in agony while they finished their meal before going back to work on him. The pain was a living thing, crawling through Ligrani's existence; there wasn't a blood vessel, a capillary that wasn't screaming out in anguish.

Another time he woke to find a third person had joined them, not the guard that had let them in the gate at the entrance to the farm, but someone else. This person was as young as the Scaglia brothers, but he appeared to be in bad shape. He needed a walking stick to get around, and he had a milky right eye.

"There he is," Jack said to the man, nodding toward Ligrani. "Doesn't look so tough now, does he?"

The man bored a hole into Ligrani with angry eyes, rage roiling like a wildfire beneath the surface. He looked at Ligrani for a very long time, his jaw quivering as he ground his teeth together. Tears started to stream out of his good eye and he started grumbling under his breath "You motherfucker, you motherfucker..." over and over, chanting it like a mantra, getting louder and louder until he let out a scream. He was holding a rubber hose in one hand and, when he was done screaming, he started reigning blows down on Ligrani's head and shoulders. He wasn't powerful like Gaetano, or precise like Jack, but he was fueled by an anger that burned deep and in some ways his blows were the worst that Ligrani had taken.

When the beating finally subsided, Ligrani was laying on the floor, the chair destroyed under the fury of the shattered young man. Ligrani was well past the point where he could move, much less try to escape, so he just laid there with the man shaking above him. The man dropped his rubber hose, and slowly started to unzip his pants. He was unstable on his feet and almost fell over at one point. Jack stepped forward to try to steady him, but the man waved him off.

"No. I need to do this myself."

The man – Ligrani figured it was the other kid they had beat that day – was able to steady himself and get his cock out and unleashed a torrent of piss on Ligrani's head. When he was done, he zipped up his pants, took his walking stick from Gaetano, and hobbled over to lean against a hay bale. And then he began crying, softly at first but then in giant sobs that doubled him over.

That man – the brothers called him Paulie – was there the next couple of times Ernie Ligrani came to, and he watched the Scaglia brothers work Ligrani over a few more times, including another turn with the ball pein hammer. By the end of that session, Paulie looked sick.

"That's enough Jack. He's had enough," Paulie said. Jack looked back at his cousin surprised.

"That's enough? After what he did to you?" Jack walked over to Paulie and cupped a hand around the back of his neck. "After what he took from you? You can't see out of your one eye. You can't walk without a cane. You'll never be the man you were supposed to be.

"No. Whatever we do to him, it won't be enough for this animale."

Paulie shook his head. "I don't know what kind of man I was going to be, but it wasn't this. I'm good. I'm satisfied. You should be, too."

Paulie looked over at Gaetano. "Tell Jack it's enough, Tano. You guys are going to lose your souls if you keep doing this."

Tano scoffed at Paulie, and then looked at Jack and shrugged his shoulders. "You good, Jack?"

Jack looked at Paulie, then down at the lump of bleeding meat that was Ligrani, and then over at his younger brother.

"No. I'm not done yet. Not until this mutt begs me to kill him."

Paulie grabbed his walking stick, turned his back and headed out. He heard Tano and Jack go back to work on Ligrani as he made his way out into the darkness, feeling sick and defeated deep down in his core.

Ligrani had hoped the Scaglias would listen to their cousin, but that wasn't in the cards. The pattern of rousing Ligrani and then torturing him until he passed out again went on for at least another half day, if not longer. Finally, Ligrani had enough. This time when they woke him up by throwing the bucket of ice water on him, Ernie begged for Jack Scaglia to end it.

CHAPTER 5

They found Ernie Ligrani's body in an empty parking lot out by the railyard, next to a burned-out convertible Ford. The coroner determined that Ligrani had been tortured for a very long time, and had more than 100 broken bones, many smashed into a fine powder. His testicles and eyelids had also been removed, along with all of his fingers and toes. The authorities were able to identify him rather quickly, however, because of the port-wine birthmark on the left side of his face, which was left unharmed.

Breaking with the Sicilian code of omerta, Sam Carlino's widow had named Ligrani as the man who had assassinated her husband in their Denver home and there was a statewide manhunt out for him at the time his body was discovered. He was also wanted for the murder of Jimmy Gioso, who had survived the initial gunshot, only to fall victim when the wound turned septic a couple of days later.

The general consensus was that Ligrani had been murdered in retaliation for the assassination of Sam Carlino, and Pete Carlino was an obvious suspect, but no one had seen Pete in Colorado for a long time. Lawrence Baldesareli, the federal agent that had infiltrated the Carlino mob, was the last person who had seen Pete when he had dropped him off in Omaha many weeks prior.

Pete was very much alive and still laying low in Omaha. Already paranoid, when he heard about his brother's murder he panicked even more. Pete knew his life wasn't worth a plug nickel now, and he wanted to see if he could make some sort of deal. Through emissaries, Pete made arrangements to travel to Brooklyn to meet with Salvatore Maranzano, who was the unofficial capo dei capi, head of heads, the most powerful mafia boss in the country. Carlino met with Maranzano at the end of May, where Maranzano agreed to strip Carlino of all authority but vouched for his safety in exchange. They made arrangements for Carlino to return to Colorado under the protection of

Charlie Salardino, where Pete would turn himself in to authorities to face several charges that were awaiting him, including for arson in the firebombing of his brother's house.

Pete Carlino made his way back to Colorado in June of 1931 and was immediately arrested. Maranzano arranged for Salardino, who he had named the boss of Colorado, to post a $5,000 bail for Carlino who was back out on the streets awaiting a trial at the end of September.

On September 10, 1931, Pete left Denver and headed south to visit one of his cousins who was serving time in the Canon City Penitentiary for arson. Pete never made it. His Dodge coupe was forced off the road and into a ditch in Penrose, Colorado. His abductors took Carlino about 12 miles down the way to Siloam Road, where he was shot three times – twice in the back and once in the head, blowing off a big portion of his skull. Pete Carlino's body laid under a small bridge for three days without discovery; it was later moved to a nearby arroyo and was found after an anonymous call came into the police.

Whoever eliminated Pete Carlino didn't have to worry about any blowback from Maranzano, however. For one thing, Carlino hadn't exactly stuck to his end of the agreement, busying himself by trying to recruit soldiers from Wisconsin and Detroit to come to Colorado to help him retake Denver and Pueblo. And for another, Maranzano wasn't around to seek revenge. About the same time that Pete Carlino saw his life snuffed out by a trio of bullets on Siloam Road, Maranzano was murdered in his Park Avenue office in New York by a group of men posing as federal agents on orders from Charles "Lucky" Luciano and Myer Lansky.

It was all part of Luciano's "night of the Sicilian vespers" where he wiped out a number of mafia leaders considered Mustache Petes across the country to overthrow the old guard. In the following months Luciano would create the National Crime Commission and establish himself as its first "Boss of Bosses."

CHAPTER 6

Although things should have gone smoothly following the elimination of the Carlino family, in reality it was a rough period for Charlie Salardino as he attempted to consolidate control throughout the region. The country was in the midst of the Great Depression and money was tight, so profits from bootlegging began to suffer as the average citizen tightened their belts. While there was still a great desire for alcohol, the high-priced product that the Salardino crew peddled fell out of favor as the public was happy with cheap swill and the production of "bathtub gin" was on the rise.

With profits from booze dwindling, Salardino began looking for revenue streams elsewhere, expanding his reach into gambling, bookmaking and loansharking, turning to Raffaele Scaglia and his sons to oversee those operations. Salardino also put a greater focus on prostitution, but the Scaglias were distanced from that; as a devout Catholic, Raffaele Scaglia found it immoral and felt that there was no honor in the peddling of flesh.

The Scaglia's did get caught up in the subsequent crackdown following the shooting of Lawrence Baldesareli and the murders of the Carlino brothers, however, as federal agents found a cache of illegal booze at the family home and looked to charge Raffaele and Trina. Instead, Jack and Tano claimed the stash was theirs and their parents knew nothing about it. The brothers pled guilty to bootlegging and were sentenced to 18 months in Leavenworth Federal Prison in Kansas and fined $1,000 each.

A short time into his sentence, Jack Scaglia was transferred to El Reno, a medium-security facility for young adults recently opened in Oklahoma to ease overcrowding at Leavenworth. For the most part, Jack kept his head down, working out and playing cards with the other inmates. The prison held a little more than 250 inmates at the time, all but three of them white. Even in prison, the blacks were segregated from the whites; they had their own toilet, their own showers and drinking fountain. The blacks were also the last to get fed in the cafeteria, and Jack noticed the portion given to the blacks was much smaller than what the rest of the prisoners received.

One day, Jack was receiving medical attention for a twisted ankle he suffered while playing football in the yard and was late getting to the cafeteria for lunch. When he arrived, he got in line in the back, behind the black inmates. One of the guards, a hulking Irish thug they called Big Mick, told Jack he could move in front of the blacks.

"That's alright. I'm good," Jack replied, staying in place.

Big Mick moved closer, crowding Jack. "I wasn't asking. Get in front of the spades before I crack your dago-wop head in."

Jack didn't move. "I said I'm good. I can wait."

Big Mick stared at Jack Scaglia incredulously, twirling his billy club by the leather strap at the end.

"Is that so?" Mick turned to the trustee who was dishing out the meal, a stew served over potatoes and a hunk of brown bread. "Did you hear that, boyo? The dago wants these fellows to get served ahead of him. Make sure they get his portion; Scaglia must not be hungry today."

The trustee, Donnie, a 21-year-old from Enid, Oklahoma, doing a three-year stint for armed robbery, took the first black prisoner's tray and dished out an extra small portion of potatoes, drizzled about a tablespoon of stew over the top and shoved it back at the man.

"What the hell?" Jack shouted at Donnie. "Big Mick told you to give them my portion."

Donnie, who had a third-grade education and was missing about half of his teeth, looked straight back at Jack and said, "I'll feed who I want and how much I want."

Jack turned back to Big Mick, who shoved the end of his billy club into Jack's stomach, doubling him over. "Donnie must think they're getting fat. He's just looking out for them," Big Mick said, laughing. "If you have an issue with it, take it up with Dr. Donnie."

The blacks got even smaller portions than normal that afternoon, and Jack went completely without. When Donnie's shift was over a little bit later that day, he went out the back door of the cafeteria to have a smoke before returning to general population. As he stepped off the back steps, he was grabbed by the back of his shirt and thrown hard against the building's brick wall.

Before Donnie had time to recover, Jack hit him hard in the stomach, taking the wind out of him. While he would never be the equal of his brother Tano in the physicality department, Jack's time in prison had hardened him. And while Tano could overpower you with shear brutality, Jack was more precise, landing blows in areas that caused the most damage. He took his time with Donnie, delivering a beating that the trustee would not soon forget.

When he was done, Jack stood over Donnie and said, "From now on you give those fellas the same portion as everyone else. If you don't, I'll come back and I'll feed them your liver."

Jack got seven days in the hole for his beatdown of Donnie, but the black prisoners got an equal amount of food from there on out. Word of what happened got back to Charlie Salardino, and when Jack got out of solitary, he was treated differently by the guards, who had been told Scaglia held special standing. The other prisoners also had a newfound respect for Jack after Donnie spent the better part of two weeks in the infirmary.

The day after he returned to general population, Jack was in the cafeteria eating his dinner of chili and beans when one of the black prisoners, a tall lanky man in his mid 20s, sat down across from him.

Jack looked up from his meal, not saying anything.

"I want to thank you for what you did," the man said. "No white person has ever done anything like that for me."

"Don't worry about it," Jack said. "We're all the same in here."

"Maybe so, but most people don't feel that way."

Jack silently nodded, then went back to his food. But the man wouldn't be put off.

"There's been lots of talk about you since that day. The word around the yard is that you're some kind of up and comer over in Denver?" Jack raised his eyes at this but didn't respond.

"I can see that. You have a way about you. You're quiet, but people know not to fuck with you."

"I don't know anything about that," Jack said.

"Look, I don't want to bother you. But I want to tell you, if you ever need something from me, in here on the outside, I'm your man. I've got another six months to go here, but when I get out, I'm headed your way. I have family in Colorado Springs. I can be a useful friend. I have lots of talents, if you know what I mean."

Jack leaned back and assessed the man across from him. Jack had always felt like blacks and Italians shared a similar status in the minds of most Americans as a lower class of people, not much better than dogs. And for the most part they were treated like that, regulated to the dregs of society and forced to do the work that was beneath decent citizens. For that reason, they often walked around like they were less, afraid to look others in the eye. But not this man. He stared directly back at you. He had intelligent eyes, and carried himself with a gravitas that Jack hadn't noticed in most black men he'd been around.

Jack decided then and there this was probably someone worth getting to know.

"Ok," Jack said. "What's your name?"

"Reggie," the man said. "Reggie Jefferson."

"What are you in for, Reggie Jefferson?"

Reggie laughed. "Shit. Mostly for being black."

CHAPTER 7

When Jack Scaglia got out of prison in 1934, the entire landscape of Denver's underworld had changed. Charlie Salardino was firmly entrenched as the boss of the area, having consolidated his power in and around Denver. The deaths of the Carlino brothers had left a leadership vacuum in the southern part of the state and a small war erupted to see who would fill that void. Chicago sent Sam Pelligrino out to help stabilize things and, with his presence and the backing of Salardino, Louis Briola emerged as the new leader of the south. To keep tabs on what was going on, Charlie installed his brother-in-law, Pietro Villecco, as Briola's underboss.

The Irish crew that ran things up in Boulder fell apart when Glenn McGregor literally lost his head and his top lieutenant, Anders Lindgren, went into the flower business, although it was thought he still ran a few brothels and whiskey joints out that way, but they were small potatoes.

Prohibition had been repealed the previous December, and Salardino's focus had shifted to gambling, loansharking, and prostitution. Raffaele Scaglia had been installed as Salardino's underboss, and he was given control of several nightclubs that served as fronts for illegal gambling parlors. Gaetano Scaglia returned from serving his sentence at Leavenworth around the same time as Jack and, along with their younger brother Joe, they helped their father run things.

Jack reconnected with Reggie Jefferson, who was living with some family members just south of Colorado Springs in a town called Fountain. Jefferson, who had been sent to El Reno after being convicted of pandering, and Jack had become fast friends in the joint, spending a lot of time playing cards and talking philosophy. Jack was impressed with Reggie's intelligence and business acumen, so he introduced him to Charlie Salardino. Salardino was reluctant to work with a black man at first, but finally agreed to give Jefferson a shot running a brothel that catered to blacks in Colorado Springs. Jefferson proved so adept at it – it had the highest profit margin and the least number of incidents of all of Salardino's establishments – that Salardino put him in charge of six others that were struggling to bring in a profit. That didn't sit well with Mario Spinuzzi, who was in charge of running all of the brothels for Charlie up until that point.

Spinuzzi, a squat, dark man who was straight off the boat from Naples, didn't like blacks and let Charlie know in no uncertain terms. Spinuzzi threatened to kill Reggie the next time he saw him on the street, and even took a couple of shots at him as he exited a late-night diner on the north end of Colorado Springs.

Fortunately for Reggie, and for Spinuzzi it turned out, he missed. It did earn Mario a visit from Charlie the next day, who brought along Sam Pelligrino as well. With Pelligrino lurking behind Spinuzzi's left shoulder, Charlie slowly explained to Spinuzzi that Reggie Jefferson was not to be touched. Charlie understood Mario's concern, so as a peace offering Charlie agreed to let Spinuzzi have a cut of the six establishments that Jefferson was running, ensuring Mario wouldn't see a drop in his profits. But, Charlie emphasized, if anything happened to Jefferson, Charlie wouldn't be happy and Spinuzzi could expect a visit from Pelligrino, who reached out and squeezed Mario's shoulder, causing him to almost jump out of his chair.

In 1937 Gaetano and Joe Scaglia were arrested after a truck they hijacked carrying popcorn, candy and cigarettes, got stuck in the mud in Adams County, and were each sentenced to two years in Canon City. The arrest of her youngest son, Joe, who was only 17 at the time, hit Pietrina Scaglia hard and sent her into a bout of debilitating depression. Raffaele took a step back in his responsibilities to take care of his beloved wife. Charlie Salardino was fine with this, as he was also devoted to his wife Gina, and besides, as important as Raffaele was to the organization, Charlie recognized that Jack was an even more cunning leader. So, at the tender age of 27, Jack Scaglia stepped into the role of underboss for the Salardino crew, while Raffaele served as a sort of consigliere to both Charlie and Jack.

Jack was very diplomatic in his approach to running things, preferring business solutions to bloodshed. Even though the country was in the midst of the Great Depression, and the cash cow that Prohibition had proven to be over, Jack kept money rolling in. He had a great knowledge about gambling and how to maximize profits and he made almost as much money from small restaurants and bars hosting games of Barbooth as they did from the bigger gambling dens. He also consolidated the "Italian Lottery" in the area, which was very popular amongst the population looking for a little relief from the hardship of surviving everyday life.

While murders and acts of violence declined sharply during this time, Jack wasn't opposed to using it when needed. When he did employ it, it was brutal and devastating. In December of 1937, a man who tried to take more control of a nightclub that he ran with Jack Scaglia in the Denver suburb of Littleton came to a fiery end when he hit the starter on his Ford Sedan and it exploded, sending a fireball, and pieces of the man, 30 feet into the night air. Three months later, four men who had robbed an underground poker game ran by the Scaglias were found stuffed in wood barrels with their hands cut off and a bullet in the back of their head.

Jack Scaglia quickly established a reputation as someone you didn't cross.

But Jack also took steps to endear himself and his family to the people in the neighborhood. The Scaglias paid for the construction of a high school and a gymnasium on the grounds of the biggest Catholic Church in Denver, and regularly donated food, money and clothes to the local orphanage. Every year they made sure they made the winning bid for the right to carry a statue of Saint Rocco through the streets of North Denver during the annual celebration of the patron saint of Potenza.

Jack also fostered a good relationship with the local police, donating money to their fundraisers. No officer or their families, ever paid for a meal at the café that Jack bought for his parents to run off of Pecos Avenue, and they would host weddings and graduations for members of the police free of charge at their assembly hall on Federal Boulevard. During the Great Depression, when police would come to Jack or Raffaele and tell them about a local family in need, the Scaglias would take care of them, donating clothes, groceries and coal to heat their homes. In fact, Jack told all of his family and the people closest to him to never turn down a family in need.

That isn't to say the Scaglia's didn't take their pound of flesh. They were quick to hand out loans to gamblers who ran out of money and wanted to stay in the game, but they charged high interest rates, $5 a day on every $100 owed. If you couldn't pay them back, what was owed compounded daily. If the bill got too high, Jack would take a piece of your business in exchange for avoiding a visit from Tano Scaglia, which was never pleasant.

CHAPTER 8

Times were good for Charlie Salardino in the latter part of the 1930s. There weren't any real rivals to his control of the region; Louis Briola ran the southern part of the state and he was an ally that Salardino had helped put into power. Al Capone, who had sponsored Salardino's move to the Rocky Mountains, was doing time in federal prison for tax evasion, but Capone's successor, Frank Netti, was an old friend of Salardino so he still had the weight of the Chicago Outfit behind him. Jack Scaglia had proven to be a competent and powerful underboss and liked running things, so Salardino was very content with the status quo.

Jack Scaglia's frustration with Charlie Salardino, however, started to come to a head in the fall of 1940. Under the Scaglia's leadership, the Salardino crew brought in more than $1 million a year through sports betting, barbooth games and gambling parlors. They also owned more than 500 nickel plated slot machines spread throughout the state that, for the most part, were legal to operate after purchasing a $100 federal tax stamp.

Some of those slot machines were in the small mountain towns of Central City and Black Hawk, located about 40 miles west of Denver. Both were former mining boomtowns that had fallen on hard times after the gold located in their hills had dried up before the turn of the century. But Central City, in particular, had enjoyed something of a revival in 1932 when the Central City Opera House put on a performance of Camille featuring the movie star Lillian Gish.

The return of the summer opera season brought with it the return of tourists and their money, which led to the return of several gambling houses designed to take that money. The gambling houses operated under a friendly local government, as long as those gambling houses contributed back to the local economy through the "civic improvement fund."

Jack Scaglia was one of the first to recognize the potential those mining towns offered and opened up a casino across the street from the opera house. For three months every summer, Jack's casino offered slots, craps, blackjack and roulette to tourists who were more than happy to be parted from their money.

While there were more than two dozen gambling houses located between the two towns, the largest portion of the operations were run by the Kingman family, and their patriarch Chuck Kingman. The Kingmans were longtime residents of the area, having come to town as part of the gold rush back in the 1850s and remaining there when their gold mines crapped out. When the towns were at their lowest point, the Kingman clan, which numbered in the 30s, took possession of a lot of local property, so when the revival occurred, they were the first to get rich.

Problem was the Kingmans were the exact opposite of the image local leaders were trying to project. They were wild and uncivilized, and their casinos were dirty and dangerous. Fights were a nightly occurrence, and more than a few spilled out of their doors, leaving dead bodies in the street.

The Kingmans knew how the town leaders felt about them, so it didn't take long before they refused to pay into the civic improvement fund. And while money was pouring into the towns at the Opera House and the casinos, the infrastructure was crumbling. The sidewalks were in shambles and the dirt streets were in serious disrepair. Many of the buildings and most of the residences were falling apart. But worst of all there were no sewer or water lines, with all the town's waste emptying into a creek that flowed through the middle of main street.

During the summer of 1941, Tom Drury, the mayor of Central City, approached Jack Scaglia about taking a bigger hand in things there. Drury made it clear that if Jack was willing to help with city improvements, they would have no issues with the Salardino crew removing the Kingmans and taking over their properties. And if that happened, Drury intimated, the Salardinos wouldn't have to worry about any interference from local law enforcement well into the foreseeable future.

It was a sweetheart deal in Jack's mind. A partnership with a friendly local administration to run casinos unfettered? It was a no brainer. Taking out the Kingmans could be problematic because they were so entrenched in the area, but Jack had no doubt he could outthink and outgun those yokels in short order. His plan was to wait until the opera season was over so as to not turn off the tourists, and then wipe them out over the upcoming winter.

Only problem was, Charlie Salardino wanted nothing to do with it. Charlie had spent the better part of the last 25 years in a constant battle, first in Chicago and then in Colorado with the Carlinos, and he was tired. He had been on the winning side of both of those wars, and he was happy enjoying the spoils of his victories. Going into the hills to battle a bunch of uneducated hillbillies wasn't appealing to him, no matter how much money it might bring into his coffers.

Charlie expected to see disappointment on Jack Scaglia's face when he declined the offer; actually, if he was being honest, he would have understood if it was met with anger. But Jack's demeanor remained unchanged, his dark eyes a blank slate, cold and calculating as always. It was one of the reasons Jack was a great poker player – you could never read what was going on behind those eyes.

"I don't understand, Charlie. This could make us millions in the coming years. This has the potential of being our biggest money maker by far." It was Gaetano Scaglia who voiced his opinion, which was not a surprise. You always knew what was going on in Tano's head, Charlie thought.

Jack looked at his brother and shook his head almost unperceptively, then over at his father, who winced at Tano's outburst. The meeting was held in the backroom of one of Salardino's grocery stores. Danny Villeco, a Salardino nephew who had recently become Charlie's driver, and Sam Pelligrino were also there. "Pop, you're the consigliere. What do you think?" Tano asked his father.

Raffaele, whose once jet-black head of hair was now almost completely white, seemed to consider things, then nodded in agreement. "It makes a lot of sense, Charlie. We have a place up there already, and it's doing really well. All we have to do is take care of some montonaros and we'll run those towns."

Charlie stood up and walked over to an icebox in the corner of the room, pulling out a glass bottle of Dr. Pepper. He gestured at the other men in the room, to see if they wanted one as well, and when they declined, he popped the top off with an opener attached to the icebox. He took a long drink before making his way back to the round card table in the center of the room, but he didn't sit back down.

"Those montonaros, those cowboys, may not be so easy to get rid of," Charlie began, looking from Raffaele to Jack, ignoring Tano. "Sure, we have better guns and are better fighters, but they've lived there all their lives. They know every ditch, every rock cropping, every cave. They'll have the advantage in a firefight if we have to try to force them out of the hills. And we'll have to wipe them all out. Every man, woman and child. They won't turn on each other." Charlie glanced over at Pelligrino, who nodded in agreement.

Sam, who hardly ever spoke, said, "It will be difficult. We will be fighting on their turf."

"When have we ever been afraid of a fight?" Tano asked, earning a sharp look from his father.

Charlie finally addressed Tano directly. "No one is afraid of a fight, but we don't have to be reckless." Charlie turned back to Jack. "What do you know of this Drury character?"

Jack considered the question, then answered, "Honestly, not much. Just from our dealings with him there. He seems straightforward."

"Do we have anything on him?"

"No, not on the mayor," Jack admitted. "We have our hooks into the Sheriff, Jim Geary, pretty deep; Reggie has an establishment just outside of town that he likes to frequent, and he's ran up a pretty healthy credit line with us there. He's a lousy blackjack player. But nothing on Drury, yet."

"I don't like that, either," Charlie said, setting his soda down on the table. "Right now, he wants to be our friend, but who's to say that once we get rid of the Kingmans, that Drury decides he doesn't want us in his town, either?"

"Well, that would be a mistake on his part," Jack said coolly. "I understand your hesitation, Charlie. These are all things I've considered. I wouldn't have come to you if I hadn't thought this through. I just feel, long term, this will be the biggest moneymaker for the family by far. Once the government figures out how much money there is to be made up there, they'll get their hooks into it and we'll be forced out. Right now, everyone is concerned with what is going on with Hitler and Europe and whether or not we'll get drawn into the conflict overseas. They're not paying attention to things like this. If we can get established now, we'll have time to position ourselves properly."

Jack got up from his chair and walked behind his brother, putting his hands on Gaetano's shoulders. "Forgive Tano for being so worked up, but he understands this as well. They're never going to allow one of us, a Salardino or a Scaglia, to be the face of things, but if we act now, we can put the right people in place. Then, when the government finally figures out what they're missing out on and they legalize gambling in these towns, not only will we be legitimate, but we'll be printing money. This will set up our families for generations."

Charlie shook his head. "It's too risky. Right now, the pezzonavantes are allowing gambling with a wink and a nod because everyone is making money. What happens when Drury is gone and some do-gooder comes into power and decides to shut the gambling down? All that work. All that bloodshed. And we're just out."

Jack considered what Charlie said and determined he had a point. There was nothing to guarantee that the next mayor would be as friendly, and Jack had no confidence that Drury had the stones to carry through on his promises. Jack thought it was worth the risk, however, and was a little surprised that Salardino was being so short-sighted. Charlie had gotten lazy recently, Jack thought, satisfied to let the Scaglia family do all of the heavy lifting while he sat back and enjoyed the spoils. It was true he asked less than he could, but it was still a little galling the lack of involvement he was taking in day-to-day operations. In more and more instances, the men on the street dealt only with Jack and his family, and often Charlie was completely cut out of the decision making. And Salardino liked it that way. This was too big a decision not to have his input on, however, and Jack was going to live with his answer. Jack felt that if their way of life, the way their "family" was structured, was going to work, certain rules and traditions had to be followed. If Jack said no to the arrangement that they brought him, then no it was.

"Ok. If that's your decision, then the matter is closed," Jack said, and walked around the table to embrace Charlie. Raffaele and Tano also rose and embraced Salardino, although Tano could barely hide his frustration. As they were heading out, Jack glanced back at Pelligrino, who gave him a small, almost imperceptible nod. Jack thought there was something off about the big man, he seemed nervous, almost jittery, which was completely out of character. Jack couldn't place his finger on what it was, but he filed that piece of information away.

The Scaglias climbed into their sedan, which was being driven by young Joe, who hadn't been in the meeting. As soon as they were on the road, Tano slammed his hands on the dash, saying "That old man is stunad."

"That's enough, Tano," Raffaele said, delivering a sharp rebuke to his son. "That was shameful, the way you were acting. Never let people outside of the family know what you are thinking like that."

Tano was still fuming, but he nodded. "Yes, papa."

Raffaele then turned to his eldest son who shared the back seat with him. "So, now that our family is together, I'm interested in knowing what you are feeling, Jack?"

"Charlie's right on some things," Jack started. "Getting the Kingmans cleared out won't be easy, that Chuck Kingman is a real caparbio who thinks he's a .90 caliber. but it is definitely doable. From my interactions up there, I think many of his family members would be glad to see him gone if we took him out. And someone could come into power who would not look the other way on illegal gambling. Drury and that sheriff are weak, and could easily be moved out. A do-gooder, or some crusader who thinks God really cares whether or not people play a card game, could come in and clean house. So, there is a risk. But the potential payoff is worth that risk. If you look at the odds, it's a risk worth taking. Someday gambling will be legal in those towns, and the money will just be flowing in. We're talking millions."

Jack let that hang in the air for a moment before continuing.

"But, because Charlie is the boss of the family, we have to live with his decision. The way this thing of ours is set up, we have to respect what the boss says, otherwise it's just chaos," Jack concluded.

Raffaelle patted his son on his hand. "Yes. That is true," Raffaelle smiled at Jack. "Charlie is a wise man, and we have made a lot of money under his leadership. For the most part, he has good judgement on these issues. That doesn't mean he doesn't make mistakes, however. Take, for example, when he decided you and Paulie needed to take a beating for ripping off the Carlinos so many moons ago. I didn't agree with that – I thought paying a fine would have been sufficient. But Charlie felt the beating was deserved. And it made the Carlinos happy and kept the peace, for the time being."

Jack looked back at his father, the surprise showing on his face. "Charlie okayed the beating?"

"Yes. In fact, looking back, I think it was his idea." Raffaelle could see a brief moment of rage rising on his eldest son's face, and he smiled to himself. Jack was very stoic, rarely showing his emotions. But Raffaelle knew that beating had changed him. He knew what buttons to push to get a reaction from his son.

"So, as long as Charlie is boss of this family, we have to respect his decision," Raffaelle said.

TUESDAY, JUNE 14, 1960, MIDDAY

CHAPTER 1

Reginald Jefferson still cut an impressive figure, even now as a middle-aged man. He remained long and lean with a freshly shaved head and a three-piece velvet suit that was more violet than purple, complete with a matching fedora. He had an ornate walking stick with a black Beachwood staff and a crystal fox head handle. His soft leather loafers and tassels were a matching violet color to his suit. His cologne was a crisp citrus scent that floated around him without being overwhelming.

Jack rose from behind his desk at his office at Danilo's and embraced his old friend, genuinely happy to see him.

"Two-Guns," Jack said, calling his friend by his nickname while taking a half-step back to assess the man in front of him. "You look great. You don't age."

"You don't look half bad yourself, Mr. Scaglia," Reggie replied with a warm smile. "It's great to see you again." Reggie gestured to the man who had accompanied him to the meeting, a young Irishman with a bright red shock of hair and a Van Dyke beard. "This is Seamus Killkelly, my driver."

Jack shook the man's hand, Killkelly's grip dry and limp. Killkelly wore a peasant shirt over olive green trousers held up by suspenders. He had a gold tooth on one of his upper incisors. "Good to meet ya, Mr. Scaglia," he said with a heavy Irish accent.

Jack moved back around his desk and took a seat, Reggie doing the same on his side while Killkelly remained standing. Reggie reached into an inner pocket of his suit jacket and pulled out an envelope thick with cash and put it on the desk.

"Business has been good," Reggie said, smiling. Jack picked up the envelope and gauged its weight in his hand. He didn't look in the envelope or attempt to count it; placing it in a top desk drawer instead. "It appears so," he laughed.

The prostitution business had changed in the years since Jack and Reggie had met back in El Reno. There was still a desire for forbidden flesh, but the brothels and music and dance halls that offered patrons more than a turn on the dance floor had fallen out of favor. Now hot sheet motels and street walkers were more prevalent. Reggie had adjusted with the times. While he still ran a few high-end places that were well known and well protected, he had recently bought a half dozen motels along the Front Range that charged by the hour.

Raffaele's feeling on prostitution hadn't changed, so Jack still kept the business at an arm's length, although he never turned away Reggie's envelopes and was quick to send Tano to clean up any messes that may arise.

The two friends caught up on pleasantries for another couple of minutes before Reggie turned to Killkelly. "Seamus, why don't you go down to the bar and get yourself a Roy Rodgers. I have some private business I need to discuss with Mr. Scaglia here."

Killkelly, nodded and headed out the door. "Sure, Reggie. Let me know when to get the car."

They watched Killkelly exit the office and head down the door before continuing.

"Where'd you find him?" Jack asked, gesturing toward the area Killkelly had just left.

"His sister worked for me down in the Springs a few years back. He was always hanging around and asked me for a job." Reggie took out a silver cigarette case from a different pocket in his jacket, offering one to Jack who declined. The case didn't hold cigarettes, however. Instead, Reggie lit a thin cigarillo as Jack pushed a glass ash tray his way. "Don't let his appearance fool you, he's very capable."

"I never understood why you use the Irish so much," Jack said. "Wouldn't you feel more comfortable with one of your own?"

Reggie laughed. "I didn't say I trusted him. But, and this may surprise you my dear friend, even in the year of our Lord 1960, there's plenty of places that a beautiful black man like myself finds closed off. So, I need a white man to get me access. And as far as I can remember you dagos still find what I do beneath you."

Reggie took a deep drag on his cigarillo, letting the smoke fill his lungs before exhaling a giant ring that traveled to the top of the ceiling before dissipating. He stubbed it out in the ash tray and then looked across the desk at his old friend. Reggie had recently approached Jack about another business venture. He had an in with a marijuana grower who was looking for distribution help and Jack was considering it. There was a lot of money to be made with illegal drugs and many of the rank and file in the Scaglia crew was tempted to dip into the narcotics trade. Jack was still opposed to having anything to do with cocaine and heroin – the risk was too great and the legal penalties too severe. But marijuana was something different. Jack thought it might be a way to placate his crew without having to get involved in the harder drugs, which carried heavy prison sentences for those that dealt them.

Reggie was also looking to open up a pair of "burlesque" clubs – one in Denver a mile west of the capital and one in Colorado Springs near the Air Force Academy – and was hoping Jack would help secure financing for the ventures. Reggie was confident Jack would get him what he needed – Jack owed a debt to Reggie, and he knew it. There was no reason for Reggie to remind him.

The two men stood up and embraced by the side of the desk. Jack watched his old friend descend the stairs before walking over to the bar cart behind his desk and pouring himself a scotch, downing it in one gulp. He poured another; this time adding a couple of ice cubes to the tumbler. He was going to invest in the burlesque clubs Reggie was proposing; there was little risk to a venture like that. Jack was more intrigued by the marijuana proposal. The Donatos would be there shortly and they wanted Jack to go into business with them growing one kind of flower, how different could the flower Reggie was talking about be? Sure, one was illegal, but that had never deterred Jack before.

SATURDAY, FEBRUARY 7, 1942

CHAPTER 1

Danny Villecco was wrapping up his visit with his dad, Pietro, at the prison in Canyon City when a guard came in and told them about the assassination of Charlie Salardino in Denver. Pietro, who was doing an 18-month stint for extorting Western Slope gas station owners, was the older brother of Charlie's wife, Gina, and his immediate concern was for her safety.

Pietro, or Peter as he was known, was also Pueblo mob boss Louis Briola's underboss, so he started to go over the angles of what Charlie's death meant for him, Briola and the Pueblo faction and, most importantly, for his 22-year-old son Danny, who had spent the past two years as Charlie's driver and bodyguard. Peter's immediate assumption was that the Scaglias were behind the hit and it wouldn't be long before they would try to consolidate power. Would they consider Danny a threat, and move to eliminate him? Were they also going to make a move on Briola and the Pueblo crew? Peter knew that Briola was loyal to Salardino because he helped him come into power and had the backing of the Outfit in Chicago, but he simply tolerated the Scaglias. Briola had made it known that, with the Scaglias taking a bigger hand in things, he didn't appreciate having to kick up to a crew in Denver that hadn't been south of Colorado Springs in two years. With Charlie eliminated, maybe Briola would see this as an opportunity to expand his reach.

There were close to three dozen actual members of the Salardino family spread throughout Colorado, and maybe another 50 or so associates. Most would side with whoever was winning, if there was a war, and with Charlie out of the picture, it sure looked like that was the Scaglias. Hell, most probably had no idea a war was coming. Charlie certainly didn't or he wouldn't have been caught unaware in his own living room.

The Scaglias were popular amongst the rank and file, but they were also pretty insular. They made decisions amongst themselves, only trusting blood relatives with the really important matters. So that meant their numbers weren't overwhelming. If Briola and the Villeccos could convince others to take up arms with them, Peter thought they may have a chance.

One troubling report he had received, however, was that the Scaglias had recruited Sam Pelligrino to their side. Pelligrino was a force unto himself and could win a conflict on his own. Pelligrino and Tano Scaglia together on the same side? It was a frightening thought.

Peter couldn't concern himself with that right now, however. He felt he had a real chance to wrest power away from Denver, but only if he could act quickly. He was pretty sure he could convince Louis Briola and the Southern Colorado faction they could outgun and outmaneuver the Scaglias, so making sure the Pueblo crew was on his side was his first priority. He instructed Danny to get up to Denver as quickly as he could to make sure that Gina was safe and taken care of, and then sent word out to Briola that they should meet as soon as possible.

Peter used the prison chaplain to relay messages back and forth to Briola, who was sitting across from Villecco less than two hours later. Built like a fireplug, Briola was a dark, humorless man of Neapolitan background born in New York around the turn of the century. His father was a distant cousin through marriage to the Carlinos, and the family made its way to Southern Colorado when Louis was still a toddler. His father, Tomasso Briola, wasn't particularly bright but was a hard worker and was strong, so he was useful to the Carlinos. Unfortunately, Tomasso Briola was one of the first casualties of the Carlino-Danna war, forcing Louis to grow up faster than he should have. Louis proved to be level-headed and serious, and he was the go-between between the Carlinos and Charlie Salardino when Charlie was first sent out to Colorado by Al Capone and the Chicago Outfit.

Charlie was impressed with Briola, so after the Carlinos were eliminated, Salardino put him in power, and Louis ruled the South efficiently and with an iron fist.

As expected, Briola told Peter that the Scaglias hadn't approached him about taking out Salardino, and he wasn't on board with the move. He agreed that it was an opportunity for them to gain more power, and he was ready to go to war.

"It's been a while since there was a real war," Briola said. "It needs to happen every once in a while. Thin out the herd a little. It's been almost a decade since the last one. Everyone's gotten soft. And, seriously, fuck the Scaglias."

CHAPTER 2

Louis Briola left his meeting with Pietro Villecco at the prison in Canyon City with a plan in place that, if executed successfully, would put him in control of organized crime in Colorado and put the Scaglias in the ground six feet under. They agreed that they needed to end this as quickly as possible, so Briola sent one of his top lieutenants, Gus "Whispers" De Marco, along with the Picolli brothers, down to Denver to join up with Danny Villecco. He also sent word to Salardino's top pimp, Mario Spinuzzi, that he could keep his spot running Charlie's brothels if he would join up, and he had their permission to take out Reggie Jefferson. Briola had done a stretch with Spinuzzi's driver, Carl Riggio, and he had agreed to deliver the offer. Briola thought Spinuzzi was a disgusting human being, but he was good at his job and he hated that ditsoon Jefferson. The fact that Jack and the Scaglias were so comfortable working with the blacks never sat right with Briola, and it was another reason to get rid of them.

Briola put out the word that any member of the Salardino/Scaglia crew from Denver found south of Colorado Springs was to be killed on sight. Early the next morning, Briola jumped into his 1935 Ford Sedan with three of his lieutenants and headed to his ranch in Vineland, just east of Pueblo proper, to grab a cache of Tommy Guns and BAR rifles before making their way to Denver to try to end this conflict before it heated up. There was a big storm scheduled to hit Denver that afternoon, so he was hoping he could beat the snow and be in town before the first flakes fell.

Briola and his men never made it to Vineland, however. As they used the Baxter Street Bridge to cross the Arkansas River near the Old Sante Fe Trail, they found the south side of the bridge blocked off by a pair of vehicles pulled across the roadway. Briola tried to reverse his way back north as gunfire erupted, causing him to crash into the guard rail, disabling his vehicle. Briola and his men emptied out of the car, returning fire at the group of men on the south end, as another trio of gunmen emerged from nearby cornfields on the north end of the bridge.

Briola and his men were easily cut down in the ambush, with Briola tumbling over the bridge face first into the Arkansas River, where his lifeless body floated half a mile downstream before getting hung up on a sandbar in the middle of the river.

CHAPTER 3

Mario Spinuzzi was midway through a giant plate of spaghetti aglio e olio when there came three sharp raps on the kitchen door at the back of his house on South Broadway in Littleton. Spinuzzi's wife, a short, ugly woman with a dark mustache in a shapeless grey housedress, looked up from the dishes she was doing in the sink to ask her husband "Cos'è quello?"

"How am I supposed to know who it is?" Spinuzzi spat back at her. He hated his wife, and he knew the feeling was mutual. "Go see who it is. And speak English, you scrofa."

She hissed "Va a fanculo" under her breath, wiped her hands on her apron and then went to see who was at the back door. Spinuzzi twirled a big fork-full of the pasta, splashing olive oil all over the front of his shirt and the checkerboard tablecloth before bringing it up to his mouth. As he was slurping the last noodle into his wide mouth, his wife led Carl Riggio, his driver, into the kitchen.

"Carl. What are you doing here? I didn't expect you for another hour." Spinuzzi wasn't ready to go out yet, but the less time he spent around his wife, the better. He wasn't dressed for the night, remnants of his meal showing all up and down the undershirt he was wearing. He would have to freshen up before he could go.

Riggio tried to hide his disgust as he looked at Spinuzzi. Carl thought Mario was a pig – a real gavone – but he was his boss.

"There's news out of Denver I thought you'd want to hear right away," Riggio said. "Charlie Salardino has been taken out."

"Taken out?" Spinuzzi said, surprise covering his greasy face. "Like, taken out for good?"

"Yeah. Someone pumped more than a dozen bullets into him in his living room this afternoon."

"Shit," Spinuzzi said, sinking back into his chair as he dropped the fork onto his plate. "I didn't see that coming."

Someone took out the boss. The wheels started turning for Spinuzzi as he tried to figure out what that meant for him. He wasn't interested in moving up in the hierarchy; he was satisfied running his brothels and making a little book out of his establishments. It kept him in the two things he loved – pussy and money – and kept him out of his house and away from his wife most of the time. So, he honestly didn't care who took over, as long as he kept his position.

"Was this Black Jack's doing?" Spinuzzi asked, pouring himself a big glass of dago red.

"I don't know," Riggio answered. "It was either him, or Pueblo. I'm not sure, everyone seemed to love Charlie.

"But, I do have some news from down South, from the prisoner and his boss," Riggio continued as he grabbed a crust of bread from the basket on the table, slathering a big pad of butter on it. "They said if things go their way, they'd like you to stay on."

That's good, Spinuzzi thought. It seems like the killing of Charlie was only going to be the first domino, that the South was prepared to go to war with whatever was left of the Denver crew. And no matter who won, Spinuzzi was going to be able to keep his spot. "They did have one request however."

Here it is, Mario thought. He knew it couldn't be so simple. "What is it?"

"They said they would like you to take care of a little problem they perceive in the family," Riggio said. "They don't see why there should be two people in charge of the brothels in the area, especially when you can't see one of them in the dark. And they said sooner rather than later."

A smile broke out on Spinuzzi's face as he realized Briola and Villecco had just given him permission to take out Reggie Jefferson. That decision had never sat right with Spinuzzi, why should he share in the spoils, especially with a moolie. He never understood why Charlie ruled that way, or why Jack Scaglia protected Jefferson the way he did. But now that Charlie was gone, and Jack maybe soon to follow him, Spinuzzi could take care of the biggest thorn in his side.

Mario got up from the table, using a big cloth napkin to wipe his face. "Give me a second to get ready," he told Carl. "I want to go coon hunting tonight."

Carl smiled. "I thought you might."

Mario headed to the bedroom to finish getting ready, smacking the backside of his wife's rear as he passed her in the hallway, probably harder than he should have. Who cares, he thought. All she did was complain about how she missed Sicily and wanted to go back and how Mario was a terrible man with his whores and his criminal friends. The truth was he wished he could send her back – he would send her back in a box if he could - but he liked having someone to cook his meals and clean his clothes. And, she was a distant cousin of Charlie Salardino's wife, even though with Saint Charlie playing his mandolin with the angels, he didn't know if that mattered anymore.

Mario peeled off his undershirt, which was surprisingly drenched in olive oil and flop sweat. He was always messy, but tonight more so than most. Mario assessed himself in the full-length mirror on the backside of the bedroom door. Spinuzzi had gained considerable weight since being put in charge of prostitution by Charlie Salardino many years ago, and now checked in at more than 300 pounds. He was covered in dark, dense body hair and had saggy tits like an old woman. The thought of trying to get in better shape briefly crossed his mind, but then he laughed it off. Why put the effort in?

Spinuzzi went into the adjoining bathroom and slapped on a generous amount aftershave and used tonic to slick back his hair. He then put on his nicest dress shirt and tie, topping it off with a dark suit jacket. Tonight was going to be a special night, so he wanted to look good.

Mario was surprised when he didn't pass his wife on his way back to the kitchen, and was even more surprised when he found Reggie Jefferson sitting at his kitchen table, a small pistol pointed at Spinuzzi's massive midsection.

"Sit down, Mario," Reggie said, gesturing to the chair across from him. "We have a few things to talk about."

Spinuzzi looked over at Carl Riggio, who was stationed in the doorway leading out of the kitchen to the back door. He also had a pistol out, one much larger than the single-shot model Jefferson was brandishing.

"You're in on this?" Spinuzzi asked Riggio, who gave a little nod. "And Marie? That cow knows about this?"

"Your wife had nothing to do with this, Mario," Jefferson said. "She's on her way to the airport and she'll eventually board a boat back to the homeland. She's happy."

"I don't give two shits if she's happy," Spinuzzi spat, raising the fingers of his right hand to under his chin before flicking them forward. "Ehi, fottila."

"Classy, as always," Jefferson sighed before gesturing to the chair again. "Sit your fat, greasy ass down before I shoot you where you stand."

Spinuzzi looked at Jefferson and knew he wasn't kidding. Spinuzzi had begun to sweat, which wasn't unusual, but it was nervous flop sweat that dripped from his hairline into his eyes, which he wiped at with a meaty hand. The aftershave he had used wasn't making a dent on the body odor he was exuding now; he was even disgusting himself. But, he had a glimmer of hope, since the skinny spook hadn't already shot him. Mario pulled out the chair from the kitchen table and sat down, leaning forward with his hands clasped in front of him.

"Look, Reggie, I always liked you. We can work something out," Spinuzzi pleaded.

"Always liked me?" Reggie looked at him incredulously. "Didn't you take a shot at me outside that café a while back? And I couldn't help hear about you constantly running me down to the girls and the customers. 'That spook doesn't know shit from shinola," Jefferson did a pretty fair impression of Spinuzzi nasally voice. "He shouldn't be running one of your houses; he should be shining my car. I don't know why we have to keep him around. If it wasn't for Charlie, I'd take him out myself.' Who are you trying to bullshit?"

"No, no, no. That wasn't me," Mario said while shaking his head furiously. "That was Charlie. It was all Charlie." Spinuzzi gestured wildly at his driver. "He didn't want to work with blacks. He told me all the time that it was only because of Jack Scaglia that he kept you around. He said you were lower than the dog shit on his heel.

"It was him. I promise," Spinuzzi smiled at Reggie, trying to look sincere. "I always liked you. I'll come work for you, I promise. Let's work something out."

Reggie laughed at this, looking over at Riggio. "Do you believe this guy?" Reggie asked. "Carl just told me how you wanted to go 'coon hunting tonight.' Was he lying about that?"

Spinuzzi's eyes flicked over at Carl and then back to Reggie and he shook his head again. "No, no, no. I only said that because I thought that's what Carl wanted to do. I promise. I'm your man, Reggie. I'm your man," he continued, almost crying.

"My man," Reggie repeated, nodding his head slowly. "My man."

Reggie raised his pistol and fired a single shot, hitting Mario in the forehead, bits of hair and skull and blood blowing out the back of his head. Spinuzzi's big head flung back violently and then abruptly stopped by the rolls of fat on his neck. Mario slumped forward, his rotund body hitting the edge of the table and toppling it over, bringing it down on top of himself.

Reggie Jefferson slowly rose from his chair and walked over to the sink, using a mopine to wipe the pistol clean before dropping the gun on top of Spinuzzi's corpse. Jefferson returned to the sink, using his elbow to turn the water on again before washing his hands, using the same mopine to dry them.

Reggie turned to Carl and said, "Well, that's that.".

CHAPTER 4

Chuck Kingman took a look down Eureka Street toward the front of the Central City Opera House, guessing there was still another half hour remaining in the current performance before the doors would open and the patrons will spill out into the streets and the surrounding businesses, including his Riviera Casino, which he was standing on the sidewalk outside the front entrance of. It was a brisk night with the temperatures already dipping down into the single digits. Kingman could see his breath when he exhaled, and he knew another round of snow was probably not too far off. That meant the non-locals would get stuck up in the hills, and his run-down hotel off the main highway would fill up, as would the Riviera and his other gaming halls around the town.

Things were already starting to heat up behind the saloon doors of the Riviera, as it was a favorite of the local crowd. His brother Stan was banging out a Cole Porter song on the upright piano. Seven of the Riviera's twenty poker tables were already filled, and there were another three patrons camped out at the long bar along the west wall. One of the four upstairs rooms, where patrons could buy some time with a saloon girl, was currently occupied. Almost all of the current patrons were locals, and that was fine, as long as they moved on to one of Chuck's other establishments when the out of towners started to come in when the Opera was concluded. Of all of Kingman's establishments in the town, the Riviera was the nicest and the one that out-of-towners would flock to and spend their money at before heading back down the hill.

Chuck went through the swinging doors and walked up to the bar, getting a shot of whiskey from Frank, another one of his brothers that was tending the bar tonight. Chuck slammed it back, telling Frank to bring him another.

"It's going to be a busy one, isn't it?" Frank asked as he filled Chuck's shot glass, wiping down the bar top with a dish towel.

"It should be," Chuck answered as he gulped down the whiskey, the liquid warming him after being out in the cold night air. He looked down the length of the bar, seeing Red Link, a local drunk, slumped over in his stool near the end of the bar. "As long as the people don't have to look at pieces of shit like that," Chuck said, gesturing to Red.

"Red, what in the hell are you doing here?"

"Hi Charlie," Red mumbled, limply raising his left arm in greeting while cupping a beer with his right hand. "Just having a drink or two before I go home."

Chuck turned to Frank and cuffed him on his ear. "I thought I told you not to let his drunk ass in here."

Frank pressed the dish towel to his ear. "Damn, Chuck. I was going to move him out before it started to fill up."

Chuck walked down to where Red was sitting and grabbed him by the scruff of the neck. "I thought I told you I didn't want to see you in here?" Chuck shook Red violently, Red's beer sloshing over the side of his mug.

"Frank told me it was okay," Red said, putting his hands over his head in defense.

"Frank's an idiot," Chuck said, shaking Red again. "And so are you."

Karen Kingman, Chuck's younger sister who oversaw the saloon girls and the upstairs operations, came running down the long staircase and put her hands on her brothers' shoulders, trying to calm him. She knew Chuck had a violent temper, and she also knew that Sheriff Geary and Mayor Drury were looking for any excuse they could find to put Chuck behind bars. Plus, three of the four saloon girls she had working tonight were her teenage daughters, including the one currently working in Room One.

"Chuck, Red was just getting ready to leave," Karen said softly. "Just let him leave." She felt that Red was harmless, a local who worked as a handyman around town for the past 30 years. But Red's wife, who had been his life-long love, was buried in an avalanche and died three winters ago, and Red had been a drunk ever since. Most had a lot of sympathy for him, but Red had always blamed Chuck for his wife's death because he had been using a tractor to push snow off of the driveway of his house at the top of the hill when the avalanche occurred. And he made the mistake of telling Chuck that he blamed him for it a couple of months after his wife's death when Red was in his cups, and Chuck hadn't appreciated that.

Red quickly discovered that blaming Chuck for anything in Central City was a losing proposition, so he just resigned himself to being a drunk. But Chuck had never forgotten the accusation, which was made in front of a bar full of people, so he took every opportunity he could to humiliate Red.

Tonight was one such opportunity. Chuck looked at the beer that had splashed out of Red's mug, and became furious. "Get your hands off of me, bitch," Chuck hissed at his sister through clenched teeth, then turned back to Red. "Look at the mess you made, you fucking drunk."

Red actually looked at the spill, and turned his head up to Chuck. "I'm sorry Chuck, I'll clean it up. I promise," Red said, starting to rise from his bar stool.

Chuck slammed Red back down on the stool, saying "You keep your ass right here. You have to finish your beer." Chuck then picked up the mug and poured what remained over Red's head, drawing laughs from some of the people in the room.

"Now you're done." Chuck grabbed Red by the back of his shirt and his pants and ripped him off the stool, dragging him toward the front door. Chuck reared back and threw Red through the saloon doors out onto the sidewalk, directly in front of Mayor Drury and Sheriff Geary, who were getting ready to enter the establishment.

Drury looked down at Red on the sidewalk, and then over at Chuck. "Evening, Mr. Kingman."

"Evening, Mr. Mayor," Chuck said, giving the mayor a big smile. "Fancy seeing you tonight."

Sheriff Geary was bent over, helping Red up. "I'll make sure he gets home," Geary said to Drury.

"Thanks Ed," Drury said, then turned back to Chuck again. "Do you have a minute?"

Chuck looked at him and said, "For you Mr. Mayor? Of course I do." Chuck went back in through the saloon doors, grabbing a bottle of whiskey and a couple of shot glasses from the bar. "Follow me, Mr. Mayor."

Kingman led Drury to a small office at the back of the building that had a desk and a couple of chairs in it. Chuck grabbed a stack of papers off of one of the chairs and gestured for Drury to sit down as he closed the door behind them. Chuck moved behind the desk and put down the two glasses, filling them both before slamming a shot back. He refilled his glass before sitting down behind the desk.

"What can I do for you?" Chuck asked, downing another glass full of whiskey. Drury picked up his glass, taking a small sip before setting it back down on the desktop.

"Have you given any more thought to our latest proposal?" Drury asked, watching Kingman down another shot of the whiskey. "We could really use your help with this, Chuck."

Kingman looked at Drury, rubbing his hand on the whiskers on his face and laughed. "You mean your proposal for me to give some of my hard-earned money to your 'Civic Improvement Fund?' You mean that proposal?"

Drury shook his head slightly because he knew the conversation was pointless. "Yeah, Chuck. That proposal." Drury grabbed his shot glass, took a look at it and then slammed it back. Screw it. He might as well plead his case one more time. "Look, it will only benefit you if we can improve the infrastructure around here. The buildings are falling apart, the roads are practically unpassable and there's a stream full of sewage running down the middle of the town."

Chuck stood up and moved from out back to sit on the edge of the desk, inches from Drury in the cramped room.

"I agree that our little town needs lots of work, and I think you should do all of that to pretty it up," Chuck leaned forward, getting right in Drury's face. "But you're not going to get one dime from me or my family to do it."

Kingman was so close that Drury could feel spittle hitting his face and smell the alcohol on Chuck's breath. Chuck's face was beat red and his eyes were wide and bloodshot. "For years everyone in this little pissant town wanted nothing to do with the Kingmans. We were always the trash from the hills who couldn't strike it rich in the gold mines. Well, that's true. We crapped out as gold miners. But I struck it rich with the casinos. This city may be falling apart, and when it does, there will be a Kingman here to build it back. We don't care if it's fancy, it's our home."

Chuck finally leaned back, allowing Drury to gulp in some fresh air. "All of you look down your noses at us. Even though we have money coming in hand over fist, we're still the inbred goat-fuckers that you would rather have run out of town than be your partner. I know you talked to that dago, spaghetti-eater about getting rid of us. But I'm here to tell you we will still be here long after some other greaseball puts him in the ground."

Chuck picked up the bottle and started drinking straight out of it, foregoing the shot glass. When he was done with a huge drink, he smacked his lips and turned back to Drury. "And that stream that runs through the middle of town? Us Kingmans have been shitting in it for more than 60 years, and we'll still be shitting in it long after you're gone as well. Now get the fuck out of here."

It was a good night for Chuck Kingman. Not only did he kick Red Link's ass, but he also told off that no-good Mayor. His businesses were filled to capacity as snow began to fall shortly after the Opera let out. The Riviera was particularly busy with out-of-town folks who were stuck by the storm and who would eventually need a room at his hotel so they didn't get stuck in a snowbank on the way down the hill.

Things finally started to slow down around 3 a.m., and Chuck closed out the night by spending some time with a saloon girl in one of the upstairs rooms. She was young with pale red hair and a smattering of freckles across her face; Chuck was pretty sure it wasn't one of his nieces, but he didn't really care. He had so many damn relatives in this town now, or at least locals who claimed to be relatives, that he didn't even try to keep track anymore. This one was tangled up in the sheets, fast asleep before he even finished putting his boots on.

Chuck made his way down the stairs to find his brother Frank wiping down the bar top, a shot of whiskey waiting for Chuck as he pulled on his overcoat.

"It was a good night, Chuck. One of the best ones of the season."

Chuck slammed back the shot, maybe his twentieth of the night. He could definitely feel it. If he was smart he'd just go back upstairs and sleep it off in one of the rooms up there. But he didn't want to share a bed with no whore, especially if it was one of his nieces – his bitch sister Karen wouldn't like that.

No, he would take the short trek down Eureka Street to the Liberty Bell, another one of his establishments, where he had a bigger office with a cot in the corner.

"How much snow did we get?" he asked Frank as he put a hat on his head.

"Only about half a foot. It wasn't too bad," Frank said.

"Hrmmph," Chuck said, heading toward the door. "Alright, kick all these assholes out. And I'll see you in the morning."

Chuck stepped out of the relative warmth of the Riviera into the dark, frigid night. The sky was starless because of the storm clouds, and the temperature had dropped below zero. The awning had kept most of the snow off the sidewalk around the Riviera, but there was about six inches in the street. Chuck stepped off the sidewalk into a path that previous travelers had trudged in the snow, heading toward the Liberty Bell, which was three blocks to the east. The streets were deserted now, with no sane person out and about at this time of night in this cold.

Chuck was uneasy on his feet, as much from the liquor he had consumed as the snow on the ground. He took his first tumble into a snowbank about 50 feet from the front door of the Riviera, but was able to scramble back to his feet, losing a glove in the process. He went another 10 feet before falling again. He rose to his knees and took a look down toward the Liberty Bell, still a good 500 yards away.

The cold and the wet snow had sobered him a bit, and he realized he'd never make it. He climbed back to his feet and looked back toward the Riviera, deciding to sleep it off there. As he started back that way, he noticed the flame of a cigarette on the porch of a long-closed restaurant to his left.

Chuck cocked his head and squinted, trying to make out who was smoking in the dark. "Who's that?" he asked, moving towards the steps as Sheriff Geary stepped out from the shadows.

"Geary? What the fuck you doing there in the dark?" Chuck mumbled; his tongue heavy with drink. "You're going to freeze to death out here."

"I'm not," Geary said. "But you might."

"Ha," Kingman laughed out loud. "I was born in these hills. This cold runs in my veins. You and your buddy Drury don't understand that. You may have your fancy titles and might get your picture in the paper with whatever fat cow is singing at the opera this month, but you'll never run this town."

Chuck climbed a couple of steps up to porch, poking Geary in the chest. "I run this town, and I always will."

Despite Kingman's aggression Geary stood his ground, taking a deep drag off his cigarette before flicking it into a nearby snowbank. "You're wrong, Chuck. Your time is up here."

This caused Kingman to laugh again. "You think so? Why, because that little wop Scaglia's on your side? If that fucking guinea wants to come up and battle it out in my hills, I'll send him back to the boot in a box." Kingman spit on the ground and then turned his back on Geary. "If Scaglia wants me, tell him I'll be at the Liberty Bell, sleeping it off."

Kingman went down the steps toward the snow-covered street, slipping on the last step and going down to one knee. That caused Kingman to laugh again, saying "I must be drunker than I thought" as he reached out for the handrail to get back on his feet. As he did, Geary slipped a burlap sack he had hidden in his coat over Chuck's head, cinching its drawstrings tight at his neck while wrenching back with all his might.

Kingman was a powerful man, and kicked and fought like a marlin on a line, but he was drunk, and Geary was equally as strong. After a half-minute of struggling, Kingman finally started to fade and dropped again to his knees. But, just as Geary thought it was over, Kingman had a final burst of panic and reared back, getting back to his feet and actually lifting Geary off the ground. The sheriff held tight to the drawstrings of the burlap sack and, in a final desperation move, Kingman fell backward into the stairs, bringing his full weight down on Geary, causing the air to rush out of him.

That was the opening that Kingman needed as he broke free from Geary's grasp, ripping the sack from his head as he sucked in huge mouthfuls of air. Geary, meanwhile, was having trouble breathing himself as he was pretty sure he had broken a couple of ribs on the concrete stairs when Kingman had fallen back on him. Geary's vision was filled with stars, but he could see well enough when Kingman stood over him for a second before bending down, putting his big meaty hands around the sheriff's throat. Geary's breathing was already troubled; Kingman could hear him wheezing as Kingman started to squeeze. Geary's eyes started to bulge, and he was spitting blood bubbles from his rapidly purpling lips.

Geary resigned himself to the fact that he was going to die right here in the snow and the mud at the hands of Chuck Kingman, that inbred dirty hick that had been a thorn in his mangled side from the day he became sheriff of this backassward mountain town. His life wasn't exactly flashing before his eyes, but he did have a moment of clarity about how worthless his time on this earth had been when, out of the blue, Chuck's grip around his throat slackened.

Geary saw the side of Chucks head explode and pieces of his skull and thinning hair go flying into the cold night air before Geary actually heard the shot. Kingman remained frozen in place for a beat before he slid to his right and down the steps into the street, crimson blood from the wound in his head spreading in a large pool on the formerly pristine white blanket of snow. Geary could just make out the form of Red Link, who stepped over Geary and fired three more shots into Kingman's lifeless body.

"That's for killing my wife, you mean motherfucker," Red said as big flakes of snow started to fall again out of the winter sky.

SUNDAY, FEBRUARY 8, 1942

CHAPTER 1

Raffaele Scaglia arrived at the home of Charlie and Gina Salardino just before noon on the day following Charlie's death, his youngest son Joe in tow, to pay his respects to his longtime friend and business partner. A large group of people had gathered at the home, and they all watched in stunned silence as the Scaglia's came through the front door and presented themselves to Gina, who was perched on the edge of the plastic covered couch in the sitting room, her sister-in-law Marie Villecco with a protective arm around her shoulders next to her. Raffaele took off his hat and handed it to Joe before going to his knees in front of Gina, taking her small hands into his own.

For the next five minutes Raffaele held his head close to Gina's, whispering comforting words to her that only Gina could hear. She quietly sobbed the entire time, gripping Raffaele's hands with a strength that belied her small stature. Finally, Raffaele hugged Gina tightly, kissing her softly on the top of her head before rising and turning to his sons.

"I'm going to go fix her a plate," Raffaele said to Joe. "After paying your respects, why don't you go wait for me out front."

Standing in a far corner of the room, Danny Villecco watched with disgust as Raffaele Scaglia made his way into the kitchen while Joe offered his condolences to his aunt Gina before heading out the front door. Most troubling to him was the two that were missing, Jack and Tano Scaglia. Where were those two cocksuckers? Word around town was that Tano was seen late last night sporting two black eyes and a fresh bandage across his already fucked up nose. Although you couldn't tell it now, but the room they were in was a complete mess less than a day earlier, Charlie's body slumped on the floor and brains and blood splattered all over the walls. They had found Charlie's beloved mandolin reduced to a pile of splinters next to the piano; it had obviously been smashed on something. Something like Tano's ugly face, Danny thought.

Danny watched as Raffaele Scaglia made his way back into the sitting room with a small plate with cheese cubes and grapes on it, Marie Villecco moving over to make room so Raffaele could sit next to Gina. His aunt was convinced the nice man Raffaele, who was Charlie's good friend, and his sons had nothing to do with the murder, despite Danny telling her the opposite. Gina would not hear of it. Charlie and Raffaele had been friends, Gina said through her tears. The two had spent so much time together – Raffaele and his wife Trina had just been over for Christmas. No, Raffaele and his sons had nothing to do with Charlie's murder. It had to be someone else.

When Danny started to argue, his mother, who was on her knees scrubbing the blood off Gina's floor, gave him a sharp look and shook her head once. Danny understood it was not to be brought up again, at least not to his aunt. At least not until they got through the weekend.

That was last night, but no matter how hard Danny tried, he could not let it die. Then word came this morning that Louis Briola had been gunned down outside of Pueblo, and Danny wondered if the war had already been lost. Whispers De Marco and the Picolli brothers were currently out scouring the streets for the Scaglias, and two of them had the balls to show up at Charlie's house. Danny thought about taking them out right then, but there were too many witnesses, and besides, Rafaelle and the half-wit Joe weren't the two crucial Scaglias to put down.

Watching Raffaele comfort Gina, Danny could barely contain his anger, however. He sat the coffee cup he was holding on the top of the upright piano and made his way out the front door, where he found Joe Scaglia on the porch, picking at a non-existent thread on his overcoat while nervously sucking on a cigarette.

"Danny," Joe nodded toward him. "Sorry for your loss. Charlie was a great man."

"Yeah, if he was so great why aren't your bothers here?"

"What?" Joe seemed surprised by the question. "They had some things they had to take care of. I'm sure they'll be by later. They both respected Charlie."

Danny spit on the ground at Joe's feet. "I heard Tano's face is even more fucked up than usual. What happened to him?"

"He was sparring over at the 20th Street Gym and some big coon caught him with a right hook," Joe said, stubbing out his cigarette.

Danny laughed. "Some big coon?" Danny shook his head and then spat on the ground again.

"You okay, Danny? Why you keep spitting like that," Joe took a half-step away from Villecco. "Be careful, you almost hit my shoe with that last one."

Danny shook his head at this and started to walk away, intending to get in touch with Whispers and his crew to let them know that two of their targets had been located. But before he could get away, Joe grabbed his shoulder from behind.

"Hey Danny, why weren't you with Charlie yesterday? Aren't you supposed to be his bodyguard?"

Anger flashed over Danny's eyes. Was he trying to push his buttons? Joe Scaglia wasn't highly thought of in the life. He was thought of as weak, and considerably less intelligent than his brothers, particularly Jack. But that question cut to the quick for Danny, especially because it wasn't the first time he had heard grumblings about his whereabouts when Charlie was gunned down.

"I went to see my dad down in Canon City. Uncle Charlie okayed it before I went. What are you trying to say?" The volume of Danny's voice had risen, and the dozen or so people also out front of the Salardino home were starting to take notice of the conversation between him and Joe Scaglia.

"I was just wondering," Joe said while lighting another cigarette. "Kind of lucky you weren't here, or you might have been killed, too.

"So, what have you heard? Do you have any idea who did this?"

Danny laughed incredulously. "Any idea who did this? You guys did this. Who the fuck you trying to fool?" He couldn't contain his anger any longer. He grabbed Joe by his lapels, shoving him against the front porch railing outside his dead uncle's house.

"Danny!" His mother, Marie Villecco had stepped out the front door in time to see Danny grab Joe. "Cos'hai che non va? Let go of Joe."

Danny looked up at his mother, failing to register what she was saying because he was so angry. She had to shout his name again before he snapped out of it. He finally loosened his grip, making a show out of smoothing out Joe's lapels. He leaned in close so only Joe could hear and told him "This isn't over."

By this time Raffaele had joined them, and he put a reassuring hand on Danny's shoulder. "Danny, why would we want to hurt Charlie? Think about it. It makes no sense. We were partners, making lots of money together."

"Bullshit. You wanted the big chair for your family. Now that Charlie's gone, Jack's in line to be the boss."

Raffaele looked at Danny and squinted his eyes and shook his head. "Why would Jack want that headache? He doesn't want to be boss. No, we didn't kill Charlie, believe me."

"It was probably Briola, out of Pueblo," Joe offered. "That's what I'm thinking."

"It wasn't Briola, and you guys know it," Danny said. "He wasn't even in town. And he was killed this morning, him and a couple of his guys."

"Briola was killed?" Raffaele said, a look of surprise coming over his face. "I hadn't heard that."

Danny didn't know who Raffaele was trying to convince, maybe the small nearby crowd, but it was a good performance. If he didn't know better, he'd almost believe it. Again, Danny scoffed in response. "Unbelievable."

"With Briola gone, doesn't that mean your dad is in charge in Pueblo?" Joe asked.

"That makes sense," Raffaele nodded. "With Charlie out of the way, your dad could be in line to run it all..."

Raffaele let that thought float into the air, and it took a second for Danny to understand what Raffaele was implying, but when he finally did, all he could do was shake his head and walk away. He had to give it to the Scaglias, to an outsider it would make sense that Pietro Villecco had made moves to become the boss of Colorado from behind bars. The cops would probably even buy that scenario. But Danny knew that wasn't true. The Scaglias were the ones pulling all the strings and had done it brilliantly.

CHAPTER 2

Shortly after Raffaele and Joe Scaglia left the mourners at Charlie Salardino's home, the February sky opened up, dumping large heavy flakes of snow that crippled the metro area for the next several days. After being contacted by Danny Villecco, Whispers and the Picolli brothers rushed over to Charlie's house, hoping to get on the trail of the Scaglias, but after picking up Danny they were caught in the fast-moving blizzard and had to take refuge in a safe house on the southwest outskirts of Aurora. When they got up the next morning, more than 18 inches of snow had fallen on the metro area, making their search for the Scaglias even more difficult.

They weren't the only ones looking for Jack and his family, as the police had put out a statewide alert that the Scaglias were wanted for questioning in the murder of Charlie Salardino. They weren't officially suspects, but the police figured if anyone knew who rubbed out Salardino, it would be Raffaele and his boys.

For their part, the Scaglia's plan was to lay low in the aftermath, and if things got too hot, they would head to Central City while things played out, but the snowstorm took that off the table. Central City was hit even harder, with reports saying it was buried under two feet of snow.

Instead, the Scaglias were holed up in the basement of one of their grocery stores in Wheat Ridge for the time being.

The storm had left Sam Pelligrino stranded as well. He had split from Tano after leaving Charlie's and his plan was to spend the night at his girlfriend Rita's place before heading up to a small piece of land he had recently bought in Laramie. Instead, he was stuck in Rita's third story apartment off of Market Street, waiting for the roads to clear enough for him to make his way out of the city.

Sam wasn't worried about anyone finding him at Rita's; no one knew about her. She wasn't involved in the life, and he had never mentioned her to anyone. And no one asked about his personal life. Sam knew what his reputation was, and he enjoyed the fact everyone was afraid of him. Well, everyone except Jack, but Jack respected him.

Sam's reputation was well earned. He killed his first man at the age of twelve, a low-level associate of Big Jim Colisimo's crew who was dating his mother and enjoyed using her as a punching bag when he was in his cups. After one such beating, Pelligrino went up to his bedroom, took his little league baseball bat out of his closet, and sneaked out his window to hide in the alley next to his apartment. When the man came out a bit later to go continue drinking at a local beer joint, Pelligrino emerged from the shadows and beat the man to death, leaving him in a broken heap in the gutter.

No one missed that creep, but it did bring Sam to the attention of Colisimo, who let Pelligrino hang around and do menial tasks for him from time to time.

Sam befriended a young Al Capone and, after Capone and Salardino helped Johnny Torrio eliminate Colisimo and form the feared Chicago Outfit, Pelligrino became one of their top enforcers.

Killing never bothered Pelligrino. He did not believe in God, so the thought of hell never scared him. He figured people were just sacks of meat taking up space on this planet. Pelligrino had a talent for killing and he liked to do it in as many ways as possible. While still in Chicago he became proficient with the garrote and used an ice pick on more than one occasion.

After one particularly brutal incident, where he had slowly lowered a rival gang member in a barrel of acid, forcing the victim's associates to watch as the skin was eaten off the body as it was submerged, a $25,000 bounty was placed on Sam's head by Capone rival Dean O'Banion. That led Capone to send Pelligrino out to Colorado, taking care of two problems; one, helping Salardino shore up his position in the Rocky Mountains and two, getting Sam out of town until the heat died down.

Sam immediately took to the area, loving the mountains and the weather. While most people thought Colorado was always cold and snow covered, Sam quickly found out that for much of the year, it was sunny with mild temperatures. And after the Carlinos were eliminated and Salardino had established himself as the boss of the territory, things settled into a nice rhythm and Pelligrino brought in good money. He asked Capone if he could stay permanently, and Al agreed.

Everything was going great until last winter when, on one of Colorado's infamous snow days, Pelligrino slipped and tumbled down a flight of concrete steps, injuring his back. The pain was intense, and there were many days when he could barely move, and he had trouble sleeping most nights. He did not tell Charlie, or anyone else in the family about the injury, however, because he knew it would be seen as a weakness, and he could not afford to be seen as weak. He went to three different doctors without getting any relief, and even saw a chiropractor, who he did not trust as legitimate physician but was willing to try because he was so miserable.

And that was when the real trouble started.

When the chiropractor saw that his treatments were not working and that Sam was still in a tremendous amount of pain, he gave Sam an injection that immediately took the pain away. At first Pelligrino was extremely grateful, going pain free for more than 24 hours.

When the pain returned the next day Sam returned to the chiropractor and found out he had been given morphine.

When Sam understood what the chiropractor had done, he almost killed the man, pinning him up against a wall with his massive arm while cutting off the man's ability to breath. But that movement wracked Sam with pain, and he fell to his knees.

Defeated, Sam took the morphine, and the results were immediate. A warmth blanketed his body, and the pain left his back. Sam felt joy, something that had been sorely lacking in his life. He was not sure what euphoria meant, but he now understood what it felt like.

The next thing he knew, Sam was taking morphine daily. The chiropractor kept him supplied and knew if he told anyone, he would end up in a hole that no one would ever find.

And that was how he met Rita, a bank teller who had injured her back after falling off a horse. She was also a patient of the chiropractor, and on occasion would run into Sam picking up his "prescription." They both knew what was going on, although they usually avoided eye contact when they came across each other. But Rita liked the way Sam carried himself, so one night she asked him to dinner.

Sam's world was usually dominated by lies and deceit, so he was immediately smitten with the refreshingly honest Rita, who made no qualms about her need, and love, of morphine.

Pelligrino, who until that point never had a relationship that lasted longer than an hour with a girl usually using a fake name, started to spend all his free time with Rita. He was not sure if it was the morphine or if it was true feelings, but he was in love for the first time in his life. As their relationship grew, so did their drug use, eventually growing beyond morphine to cocaine and heroin. Rita lost her job at the bank, but Sam agreed to support her. Part of that support came through a bank heist that Sam oversaw, and which Rita may have helped with knowledge of the bank's layout and operations.

Sam never let his addiction affect his work, or at least he did not think it did. But he was getting worried. Charlie was starting to get increasingly guarded around him, and even asked at one point if he was on something. Sam of course denied it; he understood that being an addict meant a death sentence in Charlie's eyes.

That is why he approached Sam about taking Charlie out following the meeting concerning expansion into Central City. He was not around the Scaglias as much, so his recent erratic behavior was not noticed. And when Charlie turned down their proposal, Sam figured Raffaele and his sons would agree to take Charlie out.

When Sam went to Jack and proposed that very thing, it sealed Charlie's destiny. In addition to taking out Salardino, they put plans into place to take out Louis Briola and put Sam in his place in Pueblo. Sam's plan was as soon as he was in charge in Pueblo, he would move Rita down there with him and the two of them would get clean and put this all behind them.

Now, after teaming with Tano Scaglia to kill Charlie, he ended up at Rita's because of the snowstorm. He told her of his plan to move south and get clean, and he wanted her to do it with him. After a tearful hours-long conversation, she agreed to kick the drugs as well. There was still a good amount of drugs in the apartment, so the plan was to finish it off while the city was crippled by the snow and then to start their new lives together.

After back-to-back days of above freezing temperatures the snow had melted enough that the city was starting to move again. Sam, who had spent the better part of the last two days watching the road out of his girlfriend's window, decided it was time to get moving. He did the last of the cocaine that was spread out on the nightstand, kissed Rita goodbye, telling her he would be in touch when he could, and then put on his winter coat and hat. Before leaving the apartment, he checked his pistol, making sure it was loaded, and then headed down the stairs and out into the street.

Pelligrino was greeted with a blast of frigid air as he walked out the front door of the apartment, so he pulled his scarf a little tighter around his neck. He looked up and down the street, but there was no traffic to be seen. It had been quiet that morning, with the milk delivery truck and a few random cars the only activity he had seen for the past few early morning hours. He had decided against heading north to Laramie; instead, he was going to meet up with the Scaglias at their grocery store and discuss next steps. The snowfall had changed everyone's plans.

Sam had parked his car three blocks north and two blocks east of Rita's place and he started walking that way, all the while alert for anything out of the ordinary. Halfway to his vehicle, a car turned onto the street a few blocks behind him. Sam unbuttoned his coat, putting his hand on his pistol as he eyed the car suspiciously, but it turned a block before it pulled up even with him. He reached his car without any other incidents and then made the slow trek across town to the Scaglia grocery store in Wheat Ridge.

Sam again parked several blocks away, trying to avoid the puddles of melted snow and the few banks of packed ice that remained. By the time he reached the edge of the grocery store's parking lot, his feet were soaked, his leather wing tips ruined. And the cocaine was wearing off. His back started hurting and he was jittery. Still, he stopped under the relative obscurity of the low hanging branches of a group of trees cattycorner to the main entrance of the grocery to scope out the situation. A delivery truck was pulling around back, and there were about a half dozen cars in the small parking lot, but they all appeared empty. He watched for several minutes before deciding it was safe and stepped off the sidewalk toward the front of the store.

Just as he did a four-door sedan pulled out of a nearby side street and roared up behind him, the vehicle's suicide doors thrown open. Danny Villecco and a tall, thin man Sam did not recognize jumped out the doors; Danny aiming a Browning shotgun at him while the other man had a Thompson submachine gun. Sam went for his own gun, but the heavy winter coat he was wearing slowed him down. Still, he was quick enough to get a shot off that clipped the man with the Tommy gun in the leg as Villecco fired the shotgun, the force of the blast blowing Pelligrino out of his shoes and five feet through the air.

Laying on his back in a puddle on the edge of the parking lot, bleeding from multiple wounds from the shotgun blast, Sam saw another man jump out of the back seat and go help the man who had been shot in the leg into the car. Sam thought he recognized the driver as Whispers De Marco out of Pueblo. Villecco walked over and picked up the Tommy gun the man had dropped after being shot and walked over to Sam.

"Hello Pilgram," Danny smiled down at him. "I guess you weren't as tough as they said."

"Fuck you, Danny." Sam found enough strength to spit at Danny, a combination of phlegm and blood landing on his shoe.

"Nice," Danny said before looking down at the Tommy gun. "I actually have never fired one of these. Well, there's a first time for everything." Danny pointed the gun at Sam.

"Goodbye, Pilgram."

Danny pulled the trigger, putting a burst of bullets into Sam Pelligrino, whose dead body bucked with each shot. Danny then used Sam's face to wipe the phlegm off his shoe as Whispers shouted from the car, "C'mon. Let's get out of here." Danny laughed at that. Whispers, who you could barely hear most of the time, was able to be loud when he needed to be.

Danny put another short burst of bullets into Sam Pelligrino's body before heading back to the car.

"I love this gun," Danny said.

CHAPTER 3

It had been a frustrating couple of days for Danny Villecco in his quest to avenge the murder of his uncle, Charlie Salardino. First there was the confrontation with Raffaelle and Joe Scaglia at Charlie's house, which they had manipulated to make it seem that if Danny wasn't complicit in Charlie's murder, than at the very least he was incompetent as a bodyguard. Then the snow came, bringing the city to a stand-still for 48 hours, and then when they were finally able to hit the road there was no sign of Jack Scaglia or Sam Pelligrino anywhere. It didn't help that they slid off the road twice while traversing the city, and Gus "Whispers" De Marco and the two guys he had brought with him – some stunad named Turk and his brother Sante, who was even dumber, if that was possible – were ready to pack it in head back south to Pueblo. Their boss, Louis Briola, had been taken off the table, so they were ready to get back to their city and help stabalize things.

But Danny caught a huge break when he convinced them to take one last look at the grocery store out in Wheat Ridge. As they slowly rolled to a stop on a side street just north of the building, Villecco saw a large man staking out the place, trying to look inconspicuous amongst some trees on the southeast corner of the parking lot.

Although Danny couldn't see the man's face, he seemed similar.

"Gus, do you see that?" Danny said, gesturing to the man who was stamping his feet to try to stay warm. "I think that big fucking gorilla is Pelligrino."

"What? Where?" Whispers looked from side to side. "I don't see any...wait, I see him now."

They watched the man, who took another look around before appearing to come to some decision and finally step out from the cover the trees were providing. When he did Danny was able to see for certain that it was Sam Pelligrino.

"That's him. That's Sam," Danny shouted. "Go, go. Let's get him."

When it was done, Danny couldn't believe his luck. They had taken out Pelligrino, the most dangerous killer out there. Sante, who was built like a scarecrow, had taken a bullet to his leg and wouldn't stop wailing about it, but it was worth it. Danny was now beginning to believe they could win this war. With Pelligrino gone, he may be able to convince others to join his cause.

They took Sante to a veterinarian with a rather substantial gambling debt to sew up his wound, which was mostly superficial, and then headed back to their safehouse. When they got there Danny was in the mood to celebrate, grabbing a couple of Mile Hi beers from the Tivoli Brewery out of the icebox. He offered one to Whispers, who had a concerned look on his face.

"I don't think we should be celebrating," Whispers said.

"Why not? We just took their most dangerous piece off the board. What's not to celebrate?"

"Sure, we took care of Pilgram, but Jack and Tano and the rest of that fucking family are still out there," Whispers said. "I guarantee they were holed up in that grocery store. Why else would Sam be headed there? Why were we even going by there? Because we thought they might be in there."

"So, what should we have done? Just let Pilgrim go and hook up with them?" Villecco looked at him incredulously.

Whispers sighed. "Yeah, honestly. That's what we could have done. We could have called in some more men, and then we could have gone in after them. Now, it's going to be even tougher to get to Jack. I'd be surprised if we see a hair on his ass in the next six months."

"Well then, we're just going to have to wait him out, aren't we?" Danny answered sharply. He was getting tired of the Pueblo crew. But he understood he needed them, however, so he softened his tone. "What do you suggest we do?"

"We can't wait him out. We will lose the war of attrition. They have twice as many guys in their crew than we do, and we just lost our boss in Briola. With your dad in prison, there's a leadership vacuum in the South." Whispers did finally accept a beer from Danny and took a long drink. "And sorry, I don't think most of the guys down here will side with you. No offense, but Jack has really been running things for the last couple of years while your uncle has been napping. Jack has made the family a lot of money, and in turn, the guys in the crew a lot of money. No, they're not going to pick Charlie's wet-nosed nephew bodyguard over Jack Scaglia."

Danny was offended by the slight, even though he knew it was true. Before Sam Pelligrino earlier that morning, Danny had never killed anyone. In fact, he had never even fired a gun at a living person before. And although he had been by his uncle's side for a while now, he wasn't a decision maker. Most of the time he didn't even listen closely when important matters were being discussed.

"Ok, you're right. But like I asked, what do you suggest we do?"

"We need to find them and hit them now. We should be back out on the street looking for them."

"You just said that it's going to be harder than ever to find Jack now? How are we going to do that? Should we go back to the grocery?"

"No, that's too hot now. It will be crawling with cops. Plus, they'll be on the move as soon as they can." Whispers thought for a second, then finished off the rest of his beer in one long gulp. "Reach out to anyone you think might be loyal to your uncle and see if you can find out anything at all. I'm going to send for a few more of my guys that I know are loyal, and when they get here, we'll hit the streets again. And we won't rest until the Scaglias are wiped out."

CHAPTER 4

Jack Scaglia watched as they put Sam Pelligrino's corpse in a body bag and loaded him up into the back of the morgue wagon. He was standing next to Denver police detective Harry Tate, who had spent the better part of the last half hour questioning Jack and his brothers about the murder of Pelligrino, as well as the assassination of Charlie Salardino a few nights earlier.

Tate, a 17-year veteran on the force, closed the door of the wagon and then slammed his hand on the top, signaling to the driver that he was good to go. As the vehicle pulled away, Tate looked over at Jack.

"What are you going to do now? You can't stay here."

Jack shook his head. "No, we can't stay here." He was still a little stunned at what had transpired in the parking lot of the grocery earlier today. Sam Pelligrino had seemed indestructible, and with him at his side Jack had no doubts that they would have dealt swiftly and easily with Danny Villecco and whatever crew he could have put together looking for revenge. But for Villecco to get to Pelligrino was shocking.

In truth, Pelligrino had been sloppy. To get gunned down in the parking lot? Jack was having trouble wrapping his head around it. The fact that Sam had even showed up here, exposing where Jack and his family were hiding out, was unconscionable. They had no idea he was coming and would have discouraged him if they had.

Jack took a look around, scanning the neighborhood outside of the parking lot. Onlookers that had gathered were being kept at bay by the police, and he did not see anything that set him on edge. But he would not be surprised if Villecco had someone with eyes on the place, looking for another opportunity to take out the Scaglias.

"Is there anything we can do for you?" Tate asked while stamping his feet, trying to ward off the cold. "I could leave a patrol car with a couple of officers. They could escort you where you need to go."

Jack considered the offer. He knew he could trust Tate; his relationship with Raffaele Scaglia went back to when he was a rookie patrol officer, and Jack had recently loaned him money so Harry's daughter could get braces. But Jack also had no interest in letting anyone know where they were headed next, especially a policeman, no matter how much they were compromised.

"No, just make sure that this clears up any suspicion anyone might have about us being involved in Charlie's murder. We're being hunted, too."

Tate knew it was ridiculous, but he could sell it to his superiors. They weren't looking very hard for Salardino's killers, and if the Italians wanted to kill each other off, so be it. "Sure Jack. I can do that."

"One other thing," Jack said, stopping Tate as he was walking away. "If you hear anything about where Danny Villecco is, let me know, okay?"

"Through the normal channels?" Harry asked, getting a nod from Jack. "Will do. Be safe."

Jack went back into the grocery, waving off the inquiries of the store manager and a couple of workers and headed to the back office where his father and brothers were waiting. "Well?" Raffaele asked as soon as Jack closed the door.

"The one positive is this should clear us, at least in the eyes of the authorities, in Charlie's murder. Tate believes he can convince who he needs to that we were being targeted along with Charlie in a takeover bid," Jack said as he loosened his tie and sat down at a card table in the middle of the room, lighting a cigarette. "It looks like Danny has a couple of guys with him out of Pueblo. I'm sure he figures if he can take us out, then when Peter gets out of prison they can rule the whole region."

"Is all of the South with them?" Joe, the youngest of the Scaglia brothers, asked. He stood off in the far corner of the room, nervously chewing on his fingernails. He had been anxious ever since they had made the decision to take out Salardino, and had been a complete mess since last Saturday's hit. The murder of Pelligrino in the parking lot had sent his anxiety to an entirely different level, and Jack was contemplating sending for a valium for his younger brother. Until now, Joe had never been part of any real conflict, and he hadn't handled his prison stint well. Jack had serious reservations about whether or not Joe was cut out for this line of work. Although Raffaele had said Joe had handled himself admirably when confronted by Danny at Charlie's house the day after the murder.

"I don't know Joe," Jack said, setting his cigarette down in an ashtray on the table before rubbing his temples, trying to ward off a tension headache. "The blizzard really threw a wrench in things. We have that crew that Pilgrim put together that took out Briola for us, but they all scattered after the hit. And with Sam dead, who knows where their loyalties lie? For now, we have to assume the rest are against us, but that's not what I'm concerned about."

Raffaele, who was chewing on an unlit cigar, stood from behind the desk in the room and went over to the card table where Jack was sitting. "So, what is it that concerns you, mio figlio?"

Jack took a deep drag on his cigarette and blew the smoke out while leaning back in his chair. "Pete Villecco is smart. He has to realize that his best shot at winning this thing is taking us out as quickly as he can. The longer this goes on the less chance he has. We have more men, more guns and more money. And I'm sure I could get half of his crew, if not more, to join us If I could get word to them. He knows that Danny is di peso leggero, so I'm sure he's pulling all the strings, even while in prison. If he's going to make a move on us, he's going to do it soon. So, we need a new place to hole up."

Jack turned to his other brother, Gaetano, who was seated on a couch, bent over at the waist looking at his hands in his lap. "What's going on with you, Tano? Usually, I can't get you to shut up, and you haven't said one thing."

Tano remained silent for a moment, before nodding to himself and looking into his brother's face. "I've just been thinking of Pelligrino, trying to figure out how that dumb-fuck Villecco was able to get the drop on him. And then I remembered, when we went to go take Charlie out, he mentioned something to Sam about what he was up to, and how we wouldn't be happy when we found out. I didn't think nothing of it then, but maybe Charlie knew something. Sam had been acting strange lately, even for him. And he seemed jittery that day. The fuckin' angel of death seemed nervous as we drove to Charlie's.

"I don't know. Maybe he was on drugs?"

"Drugs? You think Sam was on drugs?" Joe asked, almost angrily. "Why wouldn't you say something?"

"Hey, calm down Joe. I don't know what it was, and my mind was on other things at that moment. But it certainly could have been drugs Charlie was talking about. Sam never showed any ambition to be anything other than what he was. And the guy was a stone-cold killer. And he was jittery before going to see Charlie?

"I will say one thing though. Once we got there he had nerves of steel. Even if he was on something, it didn't change how he was on the hit."

The four men remained silent for a moment before Raffaele asked, "Okay, so what do we do now?"

Jack stood up and walked to the windows on the far wall and looked out at the back of the grocery. There was a delivery truck from Leprino Farms unloading pallets of lettuce and corn at the dock at the rear of the store.

"I've got an idea," Jack said, turning back to his family. "Let's get going."

CHAPTER 5

Carlos Perez didn't want to get involved. He really didn't. He had read the papers about the big mob boss in the area getting gunned down over the weekend, and he knew that his boss, Phil Leprino, was cousins to the Scaglias, who more likely than not had been the ones to gun that mob boss down. And he knew that those same Scaglias were hiding out at the grocery store in Wheat Ridge where he had just taken a load of lettuce and corn and tomatoes to, because he saw them talking to local police about a body that was apparently found in the parking lot of that grocery store.

So what? What did that matter to Carlos? Let all of the Italians kill each other, as long as they didn't bother him, and as long as they left Mr. Leprino, who he really liked and who took care of him and his other employees, alone. So what if the Scaglias wanted to catch a ride in the back of the delivery truck back to the farm? What did it matter to Carlos? It didn't.

But then the big one, the one with the smashed-up nose, laughed, and it all came crashing down. That big gorilla with the ugly nose and the stupid laugh. That was the same laugh he had used a couple of weeks earlier when he had broken two of the fingers on Carlos' left hand over a late payment on a loan to pay off his barbooth tab.

And fuck that stupid game. Barbooth. What kind of game was that, really? Barbooth. Roll a couple of dice and hope you get the winning combination. If he hadn't drank so much tequila that night, he wouldn't have even started playing that game. And if he hadn't drunk so much he wouldn't have lost, and he wouldn't have had to borrow money to keep playing to try to get his original money back. And then who knew that since he couldn't pay it all back the next week, that he would owe more and more. And that eventually he owed twice as much as he originally borrowed.

Sure, the big one said he only broke those fingers so that Carlos could keep working, and out of respect for Mr. Leprino, who was ugly nose's cousin. And he made sure Carlos knew it was only because of Mr. Leprino, otherwise ugly nose would have broken every bone in his body. But still. It hurt like hell and the bastard laughed at him when Carlos starting crying after he did it. Sure, it was only his pinky, and the other finger next to it whatever that was called, and Mr. Leprino covered Carlos' debt and was only taking $5 a paycheck out until he paid it all back, but it still pissed Carlos off. Fuck that game and that ugly-nosed motherfucker.

So when that bastard laughed as the Scaglias made their way into the back of the produce truck to be driven to the Leprino farm, Carlos decided he was going to get involved. He had heard that people were looking for the Scaglias, and they were willing to pay to know where they were. As soon as he got back to the farm and got off for the afternoon, he went over to the bar in Brighton, the same one where he had lost the money playing barbooth, and told the bartender what he knew. The bartender took ten twenty dollar bills out of the register, gave them to Carlos and went into the back to make some calls.

Carlos looked at the two hundred dollars in his hand, and took a big drink of the cold cerveza the bartender had poured him and smiled. It sounded like there was a game of barbooth going on in the back corner. Carlos figured it had already been a good day – he might as well go over and see if his luck held.

CHAPTER 6

Reggie Jefferson took a flavored cigarillo out of the cedar box on his desk, settled back in his high-backed velvet chair and lit it with a round crystal lighter, admiring the flame for a second before snapping it shut. Reggie took a deep drag, letting the sweet-smelling smoke enter his lungs before blowing a giant ring toward the ceiling, which was covered in copper-colored tin panels. He looked around the room, his ornate third-floor office at his south Colorado Springs brothel. He loved this space – it was all purple and gold and gaudy, just like Reggie. Outside of the carved writing desk with the white granite top and brass fittings Reggie was currently sitting at, the rest of the room was designed for pleasure. There were a couple of soft oversized couches adorned with numerous decorative pillows, and a huge four-poster bed with lace curtains next to windows that looked west towards Pike's Peak.

This was also his favorite of all his establishments because it had a mix of girls – white, black, Irish, German, Chinese. There was even a couple of Hispanics and an Italian. Reggie liked to call it an international buffet of pussy. The first floor had a long bar and a small dance floor. There was a raised stage and a grand piano in one section, and a decent sized kitchen and dining area in another. The second floor was all working rooms, while the upstairs had Reggie's office and a couple other living quarters for some of the girls. It wasn't the nicest place that Reggie ran, but it was his favorite.

Reggie was having trouble enjoying it this evening, however. The news out of Denver, that Sam Pelligrino had been gunned down outside a Scaglia grocery store earlier that morning, was unsettling. After taking out Mario Spinuzzi, Reggie was even more tied to Jack Scaglia now, so it was in his best interest that Jack emerged from this skirmish in control. It was almost assured with Pelligrino around. Now, anything could happen.

Although Reggie had never seen the Pilgrim in action personally, he had heard all of the stories. It was believed that Pelligrino could win most conflicts on his own, and to think that Danny Villecco had taken him out was shocking. Villecco was a lightweight, honestly someone of no concern. At least he was, until he took out the Pilgram.

The word was there was a loyal faction of Louis Briola's crew that was backing the Villeccos in their battle against the Scaglias. There was currently a member of that crew, Fat Chucky Blanda, enjoying the company of one of Reggie's ladies in a room one floor below. This also dismayed Reggie; he wasn't considered a "soldier," so he was under no obligation to do anything himself about Blanda, but he was loyal to Jack, so he considered making a call up to Denver. But Reggie also understood that once he did that, he couldn't claim to be neutral in the conflict and he would fall under the crosshairs of the Villeccos if they happened to win. Reggie wasn't afraid to get his hands dirty if he had to; shoot, he had enjoyed taking out a Spinuzzi just days ago. But first and foremost, he was a pragmatist and a businessman, something his friend Jack would understand.

So, Reggie Jefferson sat in his comfortable chair, smoking his flavored cigarillos, contemplating what his course of action should be. He heard Jacklyn, one of his girls that he was currently seeing, start to stir on the bed in the corner. She stretched her arms high above her head, wearing only a sheer black nightgown and matching panties, and that settled things for Reggie. She was a vision, with long dark hair that spilled halfway down her back and perfect breasts with nipples that always pointed up. Reggie could feel his interest rising. He decided he wasn't doing anything but joining her in bed right now. Reggie stubbed out his cigarillo in a glass ashtray and stood up, telling Jacklyn to "stay right there, baby. Daddy's on his way."

Just then there were the sounds of an argument followed by a door slamming shut coming from the floor below. Reggie reached into his desk and pulled out a pearl handled pistol and headed out the door and to the stairs while yelling "What the fuck is going on?" When he got to the landing and started to head down, he stopped dead in his tracks. Fat Chucky Blanda was in the hall pulling up his trousers, while another man pointed a Tommy Gun up the stairs at Reggie.

"You stay the fuck up there, you dumb smoke, or I'll pump you full of lead." Blanda had managed to get his pants fastened and was now pulling on his shoes. Selina, a mocha-colored teenager that Blanda had been with, poked her head out her door and said, "He hasn't paid me yet, Reggie."

Reggie spread his arms out wide, his gun pointed harmlessly away from everyone. "Hey man, I don't want any trouble. But you got to pay the girl."

Blanda looked first at Reggie, and then Selina. "That black pussy wasn't any good anyway."

"That's just because you got a little dick, fat boy," Selina screamed, stepping toward Blanda, who turned on her and slapped her hard across the face, knocking her down. "Fuck you, you black cunt."

Reggie took a couple steps down the stairs, saying forcefully, "That's enough."

The man with Blanda raised the submachine gun at Reggie again while taking a step up the stairs, saying "I'm not kidding, motherfucker. I will cut you down right there where you stand."

Reggie nodded, saying, "I don't doubt that. But you know who owns this establishment, right? There won't be a place safe in the Rocky Mountains for you if you do that."

"Yeah, we'll he might not be owning it for much longer," the man said.

"I don't know anything about that," Reggie said, keeping his voice calm. "Look, I'm going to put my gun down, alright?" The man nodded and Reggie set his pistol on the top step behind him. "Now, I don't know what is going on here, and why you guys are in such a hurry to get out of here, but you have to pay the girl."

Blanda looked up at Reggie and scoffed. "What if I don't?"

"Well then, my good friend Mr. Riggio behind you there is going to put your brains all over the wall."

While the confrontation was going on, Carl Riggio, who was now acting as Reggie's bodyguard and driver, had come up the back stairs and had a shotgun levelled at the two men. He was close enough and the hallway was narrow enough that there was no doubt what the outcome would be if he pulled the trigger.

"Now, you go ahead and pay the girl and we'll all call it even. You don't even have to apologize for hitting her or the hurtful words you said. You can get your stuff and go," Reggie said. "Do we have deal?"

Blanda looked at the man with the Tommy Gun and shrugged. "We have to get going anyway." Blanda took a cash roll out of his pants pocket, peeled off five ten-dollar bills and threw them at Selina, who had curled into a ball on the floor.

"There you go, you fucking whore." Blanda then nodded at the other man and they started to head down the stairs and out the front door.

"One other thing," Reggie called out to them, and they turned around to hear what he had to say. "You two are never allowed back here. Understand?"

"Whatever," Blanda said. "After tonight, I may end up running this place."

When the two men had left, Reggie came down to the second-floor landing and gathered Selina up in his arms. She was crying softly and the welt on the side of her face where she had been hit had started to swell. "I'm sorry, Reggie."

"Shhh. Don't worry about it, baby," Reggie said. He turned to Jacklyn, who had come down the stairs, and told her, "Go get her some ice for her face." He then started gently rocking Selina back and forth, drying her tears. "Tell me what happened."

Selina looked up at Reggie, her left eye completely swelled shut. "We were doing it, we had done it before, and everything was going fine. He was really liking it. Then that other guy came bursting through the door, telling Chucky to get up and get dressed. They had to get going."

Selina started to cry again. "I'm so sorry, Reggie."

"It's okay, baby. You did nothing wrong," he said, kissing her on top of her head. "Go on, what happened next?"

"So, Chucky says, 'What are you talking about?' And the other guy goes, 'They found Jack. They found Jack. We're going to go help kill him.' That's when he jumped up and started to get dressed. I asked him for my money, and he told me to shut the fuck up. That's when you showed up."

Reggie kissed her on the top of her head again. "You did good. Everything is good, Selina. Why don't you go up to my office and go to sleep in my big bed. You can stay there tonight with Jacklyn."

"Are you sure?"

"Yeah, baby, go on up."

They found Jack. Shit. That wasn't good.

Carl Riggio had just come back up the stairs after making sure the two men left without causing any more trouble.

"What do you need me to do, boss?"

Reggie thought for a moment, then made up his mind. "Did you see what car they got into?"

"Sure did."

"Would you recognize it if we caught up to it on the highway?"

"I sure would," Riggio said, a big smile going across his face.

"Go get the Caddy and another couple of guns. We're going to Denver."

CHAPTER 7

Jack Scaglia hadn't been to the Leprino farm in more than a decade, since the Ernie Ligrani business back during the war with the Carlino brothers. The building hadn't changed much in the ensuing years and it served the purpose Jack needed it to; you had to be let in through a gate on the south side of the property to access the only road that led up to it, and then you had to travel more than a quarter of a mile on a washboard rough dirt track to get to it. A surprise vehicular assault was out of the question.

But the vast farmland surrounding the structure was an issue. It would be impossible for the four of them to monitor it all, so a ground assault was a probability. Jack sent for reinforcements, and they were joined by Nicky Pauldino and his cousin Roxie Gioso, and Phil Leprino and his sons Joe, Tony and Phillip. Leprino's wife and daughters had brought sandwiches and drinks for the men, and they had set up cots outside of the office near the loading dock in case anyone wanted to catch some shut eye.

Jack looked around the massive structure, which was pretty empty considering it was the farm's offseason. The Leprinos had agreements with several farmers in California to provide some vegetables and lettuce throughout the winter months, which was what had been delivered to the grocery earlier that day. But for the most part, the barn was currently being used for vehicle repair and upkeep. There was a half-empty hayloft accessible by a couple of ladders where Pauldino and Gioso were stationed, watching the horizon for any sign of approaching vehicles. It was getting close to dusk, with the sun setting behind the mountains to the west, and the temperature had dropped precipitously in the last half hour or so.

Raffaele and Gaetano Scaglia were currently playing a game of pinochle with Phil Leprino and one of his sons on a card table just outside the office, where Jack was currently sitting behind its simple desk making calls. His first call had been to his mother, assuring her that they were all safe and they would be coming home soon, and then he called his own wife Frances to check in. Then he made a call to Harry Tate, who informed him that the Scaglias were no longer considered the prime suspect in the murder of Charlie Salardino.

Afterward he called a few of his trusted associates to see if they had any updates. To a man they were all shook by Pelligrino being taken out, but no one had any real information on Danny Villecco or Whispers De Marco. Jack understood that most were hedging their bets after the removal of Salardino to see who would come out on top between him and Villecco, but he was still hoping he might pick up a crumb or two of information.

Brad Carnahan, a young bartender who sometimes provided muscle and made book for the family at Nettie's Place in Denver, did mention that Reggie Jefferson had called looking to get in touch with Jack several hours earlier.

"What did he say?" Jack asked.

"Nothing really. He seemed rushed, and just asked if you were around or if I knew how to get in touch with you," Brad said. "We were only on the phone for about twenty seconds before he got off."

"OK, thanks Brad. I'll be in touch." Jack hung up, making a mental note to himself to get something extra to Carnahan when he could. Even though he wasn't an Italian, Jack trusted him.

Jack walked out of the office and watched the card game for a moment. His youngest brother, Joe, was pacing nervously nearby, glancing out the window in the entry door every couple of minutes or so. He was not doing well, and Jack was worried he wouldn't be able to handle another day or two of this.

"We're leaving in the morning," Jack announced, getting surprised looks from his father and Tano. "It's time. The police aren't looking for us anymore, and I'm not going to continue to hide from Danny Villecco. We go back to business as usual."

Raffaele nodded his agreement, saying "I think that's right."

"But we have to get through tonight. If I was Whispers I would figure this was my last, best shot. After tonight, I think he cuts his losses and heads back down south."

"Well, then, we should be good, right?" Joe asked. "No one knows we're here, right?"

Jack looked at his younger brother and nodded, "I don't think so, but you never know. We shouldn't have let that driver leave after he brought us here."

"Carlos?" Phil Leprino asked. "No, he's good people. He's been with me a long time."

"Maybe. But it wouldn't have hurt to make him stay with us, just to be safe," Jack said, sitting down on the edge of one of the cots. "I've been sloppy and careless. I should know better than that."

Jack gestured to Tano. "And I think you're right about Pelligrino. About the drugs. There was something off about him. When he came and approached me about taking out Charlie, he seemed fidgety. And that wasn't like him. I shrugged it off as nerves, taking out a boss is a big decision. I was just happy he was on our side, so we wouldn't have to go to war against him. I overlooked it then. I shouldn't have."

Jack sat silently for a moment, looking at his father. "I'm sorry, Pop. I should have planned this better." He then got up and went to Joe, affectionately cupping his hand around his brother's neck. "And I'm sorry I put you in this situation, Joey. When this is all over, we're going to sit down and figure out your future. I don't want you involved in things like this."

Joe looked back at his brother, hurt in his eyes. "You don't have to do that, Jack. I'm with you and pops and Tano, no matter what."

"I know that. I've never questioned that," Jack said, bringing his forehead to his brother's. "I love you, fratello."

The moment was broken up by Nicky Pauldino, who called out from his perch on the second floor, "Hey boss, I think you should come see this."

CHAPTER 8

Nicky Pauldino was using a pair of binoculars to survey the perimeter of the farm from his second-story perch, and although the light was quickly fading, he was able to make out a trio of vehicles that had stopped under a small cluster of large oak trees about 100 yards south of the main entrance. Seven men had gotten out of the vehicles and were gathered around the rear of one of the cars, although it was hard to make them out in the diminishing light.

But Jack had no doubt about who the men where, or what their purpose was.

"They're here," Jack said, handing the binoculars back to Pauldino. He leaned over the railing, addressing the men below. "Everybody get ready."

A palpable sense of calm seemed to come over the group, even Joe Scaglia, as they prepared for the inevitable showdown. Roxie Gioso and Nicky Pauldino took up positions on the second level with Springfield sniper rifles that Phil Leprino had brought back from the Great War, while the rest of the men each had a shotgun and a couple of pistols. They checked their loads, and then placed additional ammo where it would be easy to get to.

Currently, they had Villecco outmanned, but Jack wasn't sure that would remain the case. Backups could be on their way right now. Jack was sure that they would wait until it was darker to start the assault, so it would be hard to see them until they were almost right on the barn. Although there were electric lights on all four sides of the structure, they only put out a small circle of illumination. There was a hundred yards of empty field on each side of the structure, so it would be impossible to monitor it all. Instead, he made sure all entrances were firmly secured and the only way in or out was the single door next to the barn doors on the south side.

Jack was pissed at himself. He had been sloppy, which was not like him, and he had put his family at risk. If he had taken out Villecco at the same time as Charlie, then none of this would have happened. And he felt like there wasn't something right with Pelligrino, but he was just so happy to have him on his side he overlooked it. Then letting that driver leave after he brought them to the farm was just stupid. Jack was sure it was the driver who had sold them out.

Jack vowed he would never make mistakes like that again. If they survived tonight's assault, he would never put his family in danger.

Close to an hour had passed since Pauldino had first spotted the group on the outskirts of the farm, and darkness had fully enveloped the area when they spotted two pairs of headlights coming northbound before stopping near where the first group was and cutting the lights. Jack was right, they were waiting for reinforcements. Two more vehicles, which could mean anywhere from two to eight more men.

"Dammit," Jack muttered under his breath. It wouldn't be long now.

"Ok, they're coming," Tano said, checking his pistols for the third time in the last half hour.

"Pop, I want you in the office. You stay out of the way as much as you can."

Raffaele started to protest, but Jack cut him off. "No, this is the way it has to be." He then turned to his youngest brother. "Joe, I want you right outside the office door. You don't let anyone get to pop. Understood?" Joe nodded.

Jack had Phillip and Joe Leprino sneak out the east door and go hide in the field, one on the southeast corner and the other looping around to the north side of the building. The thought was to let Villecco's team go past them and then to come up on them once the assault started. After securing the east door, Jack joined the rest of the men near the entrance. There were doors on the north and west side of the barn which they locked, and then secured with several hay bales. If they were able to get through the door, it would take considerable effort to get past the hay bale barrier, which would allow Jack and his crew to pick them off. There wasn't a door on the east side; the south side had the big barn doors which were secured with big two by fours and would be almost impossible to get through. The only real way to get in to the structure was through the single door on the south side, which is where Jack's men were waiting. They had arranged several hay bales in a semi-circle aimed at the south door, hoping to provide cover and to use that entrance as a bottleneck.

Nicky Pauldino and Roxie Gioso would patrol on the level above, using the sniper rifles to take out anything that they could see.

"Two vehicles are on the move," Pauldino called down. "They're going around from the west to the north side."

That makes sense, Jack thought. They'll let men out there to encroach from the north and east. "Can you hit them from this distance?" Jack asked.

"Doesn't hurt to try, does it?" Pauldino said. Both he and Roxie Gioso took up firing stances at one of the windows on the second level, aiming out to the distance, using the headlights to target the vehicles. "I'll take the trail car, you get the one in the lead," Pauldino said. "On three..."

Pauldino counted down and they both fired, both missing. They ejected the spent shell before reloading, taking aim again. Understanding what was happening, the lead car switched off its headlights right as Roxie Gioso fired another shot, this one striking the front door on the passenger side. Pauldino's shot also found its mark, blowing off the driver's side headlight on the trail car, which slid into the ditch on the side of the road. The remaining headlight illuminated the car ahead of it enough for Pauldino to see three men jump out its doors and head toward the field. Leprino was able to fire off two more shots, catching one man in the chest as he emerged from the passenger door, before the other two escaped into the darkness.

Pauldino, meanwhile, fired three more shots into the trail car and it looked like he may have caught one man in the shoulder as he attempted to get out of the passenger door. The driver rolled out of the vehicle on his side, and Tony Leprino lost sight of him as he ran into the field and the darkness.

"There was five of them coming from this side," Pauldino shouted down. "Roxie took out one of them, but there's still four left. I think I winged one, but I'm not sure."

"Ok, can you see anything on the west side?" Jack asked. Pauldino went over to the window on that side of the structure but couldn't see anything. "It's too dark, Jack. But I'm sure they're coming."

"Yeah, I am too," Jack responded. "Keep on the lookout there, and Roxie, keep your eyes peeled up north. Shoot anything you see."

"You got it."

"Alright, let's be sharp," Jack told the other men. "This door here should be their only access point, so as long as we don't let anyone breach this, we should be fine."

It seemed interminability long as Jack and his men waited for the assault to begin. Villecco and his crew were taking their time traversing the land between the road and the barn. Jack figured it couldn't be an easy trek; there were remnants of last season's crops, and the rows were undulating at the best of times. The recent storm further made them a mess, although the temperature was low enough that the ground was hard and frozen.

Still, it came as a shock to the men when the first shots rang out as Villecco and his men targeted the lights on the west side of the barn. The muzzle flair of the shots exposed them a bit, however, and Pauldino was able to hit one man in his center mass before the light was finally shattered. Moments later the unmistakable sound of a Thompson submachine gun filled the air, with bullets smashing through the west wall. Jack and the men hunkered behind the hay bales until the barrage of gunfire ended.

"Everyone good? Anyone hit?" Jack called out, learning that everyone survived the initial onslaught unscathed. Intermittent shots rang out now, as they targeted the rest of the lights on barn, taking out the one on the north and east side. The assault team also had reached the north wall and were trying to breach the door there, but there was a barrier of about fifty hay bales barricaded against it, so Jack wasn't worried about them getting through.

"Can you see them trying to get in that door on the north?" Jack asked. Roxie Gioso was trying to target the men from the loft but couldn't get a shot off. "The angle is all wrong," Gioso said, just before a shotgun blast splintered the wood next to his head, knocking him off his feet and sending shards into his right side. The wounds were superficial, but it still shook everyone.

"Be careful," Phil Leprino called down from below.

Another round of Tommy Gun fire erupted along the west wall; this time much closer to the southwest corner of the structure. Most of the bullets didn't penetrate all the way through the wall, but a handful did and shattered most of the glass of the office where Raffaele was stationed.

"Pop," Jack called out. "Are you alright?"

"No!" Joe yelled, coming into the office as another burst from the Tommy Gun penetrated the wall, sending Raffaelle diving underneath a metal desk.

"Get him out of there. These walls aren't going to hold," Tano shouted. "This isn't' going to work, Jack."

"Old wood," Phil Leprino said.

Jack had hoped that the walls of the structure were solid enough to withstand most of the gunfire, but the higher caliber munition was penetrating it like it was made out of cheesecloth. To make matters worse, one of the men trying to breach the north side had brought an axe with him and made short work of the door. As soon as he finished with that door, the man with the axe headed around to the west side to work on that entrance, while the other three men tried to make their way past the hay bales that had been stacked behind the door. Each bale weighed in excess of fifty pounds, and there were several dozen stacked up there. It was going to take them a while to get in. After tossing five or six aside, one of the men said, "Fuck this." He reached into his pocket and fished out a lighter, putting the flame to the nearest bale of hay. "We'll burn those motherfuckers out."

As he was doing that, Joe Leprino, who had been hiding in the northeast corner of the property, snuck up behind the men and opened up with his shotgun, cutting them down with a couple of well-placed blasts. Unfortunately, he wasn't in time to stop the hay from catching fire, and it was quickly spreading, flames rising to lick the wall of the barn.

CHAPTER 9

Carl Riggio and Reggie Jefferson pulled up to the south of the Leprino Farms property a half hour after the sun had set and about two minutes behind the cars carrying Fat Chucky Blanda and his friends. They had been able to tail the entourage pretty easily; Carl was an excellent driver and Blanda didn't have any reason to believe anyone was following him. Carl had caught up with them on the freeway just outside of Castle Rock, staying about 100 yards back. He was even able to refuel the same time the others did without detection, using a gas station on the other side of the street from the one that Blanda's crew was using.

Reggie had tried to get word to Jack Scaglia, both before leaving Colorado Springs and again when they were refueling, to no avail. Carl and Reggie were flying blind, not knowing where they were going or what they were going to. Reggie was a little surprised when the procession made its way through Denver and continued north into more rural territory. When they finally stopped it seemed like they were in the middle of nowhere to Reggie. He instructed Carl to kill the lights and pull under a copse of trees a way back from where Blanda had stopped. In the distance to the north there appeared to be a rather large barn surrounded by empty fields.

"What do you want to do, boss," Carl asked as he reached behind him to grab a shotgun from the back seat.

"We're just going to watch for now. I have no idea what they're doing, or if the Scaglias are even here," Reggie said while lighting one of his cigarillos. "We're going to wait and see."

They didn't have to wait long. A couple of minutes after Blanda arrived, two of the five vehicles gathered outside of the gate turned on their headlights and started moving, heading to the west side of the property.

"They're on the move," Carl said, but the headlights were quickly lost in the distance. "I can't see where they went."

"It's too fucking dark," Reggie agreed. "See if you can roll up closer to where they were originally without attracting attention."

Carl started the Cadillac up but didn't turn on the headlights, and carefully rolled up the road until they were about 100 yards away from the original group of vehicles.

"Okay, stop here," Reggie said as Carl pulled to the side of the road again. "Let's go see if we can figure out what's going on."

Carl and Reggie quietly got out of the car, making their way along a large irrigation ditch that ran along the east side of the road. When they were about fifty yards away from the vehicles the unmistakable sound of a Tommy Gun erupted from the area west of the barn. Flashes of gunfire illuminated the night sky, both from an upper area of the barn and the land surrounding it to the west.

"Let's move," Reggie said as he and Carl picked up the pace. When they got a little closer, they were able to see that the group of men had cut the barbwire fence on the side of the main gate to gain access to the field. There was one person, a tall man who was leaning on a crutch, that had been left behind with the vehicles, but he was distracted, watching the firefight going on in front of him, and didn't notice Reggie and Carl coming up behind him.

"That's Sante Picolli," Carl whispered to Reggie. "He's one of Louis Briola's guys."

Reggie nodded before leaving the side of the road, quickly moving behind Picolli and kicking the crutch out from under his right shoulder, Picolli went down in a heap, the shotgun he was holding skittering under a nearby car. The fall brought a tremendous amount of pain to the leg that he had injured in the firefight with Pelligrino, and Picolli yelled out like a wounded animal.

"Quit that crying," Carl said while putting the barrel of his shotgun to Picolli's forehead. "Hello, Sante."

Sante looked up. "Carl," Sante said, tears coming to his eyes from the pain. "What're you doing here? Are you here to help?" Sante looked over and saw Reggie Jefferson and confusion came to his face. "Why are you here with that ditsoon?"

"Nice," Reggie shook his head. "It never stops with these crackers."

"Who's all with you, Sante?" Carl asked.

"Turk's here, and so is Danny Villecco. Did you hear we hit the Pilgram?" Sante tried to sit up and grunted in pain again. "He shot me in the leg, but we killed him."

"That's great, Sante. Who else is here?"

"Whispers is with us, and then Fat Chucky and a couple more guys just came down," Sante said. "The Scaglias are in that barn and we're going to take them out. That's why you're here, right?"

"This guy and Danny Villecco took out Sam Pelligrino?" Reggie asked, incredulously. "Really?"

Sante looked from Carl, to Reggie, then back to Carl. "Seriously, Carl. What are you doing with this ni..."

Reggie put a pistol to Sante's temple and shot him before he could complete his thought.

CHAPTER 10

This wasn't working out how Jack Scaglia had planned. The Leprino farmhouse wasn't the fortress that he had hoped. The walls were being shredded by the gunfire; the hay bales they had stacked up to solidify the north entrance were now on fire and the bottle neck they had designed to ensnare their enemies was now working against them. They were trapped, with no way to get out.

The good news was they hadn't lost anybody yet; at least not anyone in the barn. Nicky Pauldino appeared to have broken his leg when he jumped from the loft to avoid the spreading fire on the north wall, and Raffaele Scaglia had superficial cuts from when the glass was shot out of the office he had been in.

Tano Scaglia was champing at the bit to actually be able to confront someone, and Jack could tell he was on the verge of doing something rash. Jack needed to get the situation under control and do it quickly, or things could turn out poorly for them.

Danny Villecco and what remained of his men had now all gathered outside the south wall where the barn doors and the main entrance was. There was Danny, Whispers De Marco, Fat Chucky Blanda, Turk Picolli and two others from Pueblo that Jack didn't recognize. Danny and Turk had Tommy Guns; the rest had at least a shotgun.

"I got you, Jack," Danny shouted. "You're trapped in there. You guys are either going to burn, or we're going to shoot you down as you come out the door."

"He's right, you know?" Raffaele said to Jack inside the barn that was heating up and filling with smoke. "If we stay in here," he gestured to the back wall that was now completely engulfed in flame, "we'll burn to death. But if we go out the door they'll cut us apart."

"I'd rather go out fighting," Tano said, heading toward the door.

"Wait, Tano," Jack said while reaching out to grab him. "Give me a chance. I got us in this mess, let me see if I can get us out."

For a moment all Danny and his men heard in reply to his pronouncement was the crackle of the growing fire. But then Jack shouted back, "You're right, Danny. You got us. You win."

Danny wasn't sure how he expected Jack to respond, but that wasn't it. Admitting that Danny had won? This day kept getting better and better.

"We're going to put our weapons down and come out, okay?" Jack said. "Don't shoot, alright?"

Danny raised his Tommy Gun, aiming at the door. "I'm going to blow him away as soon as I see a hair on his ass." But Whispers put his hand on Danny's gun, pushing it down.

"Let them come out," Whispers said. "You won. Enjoy this."

Danny thought for a second, then nodded. "Okay," he shouted at Jack. "Put your weapons down and come out and we won't shoot. You have my word."

"What are you doing?" Tano hissed at Jack. "We're just going out there to be executed. Fuck that."

"Tano," Raffaele barked at his son. "Knock it off. Just follow Jack's lead."

"If it will make you feel better, Tano, you can keep your pistol in your back waistband. But everyone put down the rifles and shotguns. Don't give them any reason to open fire."

The men reluctantly agreed, setting down their long guns. Tano did slip his pistol under his shirt in the back of his pants, but everyone else was unarmed as they headed out the door. Everyone but Phil Leprino, who had been a sniper in the Great War and was set up behind a hay bale about 15 yards back with a Springfield rifle, aiming out the door. Jack figured Danny Villecco had no idea how many men were actually in the barn, just like he probably had no idea that both Joe and Phillip Leprino were out in the fields somewhere, hopefully close.

Tony Leprino emerged from the door first, empty hands out in front of him, followed by Joe and Raffaele Scaglia. Roxie Gioso helped Nicky Pauldino and his broken leg out next, then Tano came out, his face a mask of anger. Finally Jack emerged, his hands high above his head. He looked around at Villecco's men who had them surrounded in a half-circle, nodded at the ones he knew, before setting his gaze on Danny.

"Hi Danny."

"Go fuck yourself, Jack."

"Nice," Jack said.

"I don't know what you think this is going to accomplish here, Jack," Danny said, gesturing to Jack's unarmed crew. "You're not going to be able to talk your way out of this. And you can't save them, either."

Jack nodded. "You're right. You won. You have the right to take us all out," Jack said. "That's what I would do. But it just proves that the sun shines on a dog's ass every once in a while."

That brought a few chuckles from the men, and a look of confusion from Danny. "What are you talking about?"

"It's hard to imagine, that when they talk about this moment in time, that they're going to say someone like you was able to take out Sam Pelligrino and Jack Scaglia all in one day. You're a lightweight, not even in our league. No one will believe it."

Danny stepped forward and hit Jack in the gut with the butt of the Tommy Gun, bringing him to his knees in front of the opening of the door. The blow hurt, but Jack was okay with it. Danny was getting flustered, which was what he wanted.

"Well, they're going to have to believe it, because that's what is happening," Danny said, handing the Tommy Gun to Whispers while taking a pistol out of his pocket and putting it to the back of Jack's head. "Anything else to say, smart guy? You better make them good, because they're going to be the last fucking words you ever say."

"Yeah, I do. I just want you to know I underestimated you," Jack said. "I thought you were weak-brained, not someone to take seriously at all. That's why I didn't even consider you when I made the plans to take out your uncle. I thought about Briola, of course, and your father, even though he's in prison. But you, you never crossed my mind."

"What do you mean, you considered my father?" Danny said, pushing the barrel of the gun hard into the back of Jack's head.

"I knew with Charlie gone, Briola would be upset, and so would your father, especially since Gina is his sister. So I made plans for him as well. I couldn't have him run the south with an obvious grudge against me. I was going to put Pilgram in the big chair. If not him, I actually thought about Whispers."

Danny looked over at Whispers, his gun hand faltering a bit. "Did you know about this?"

"First I heard of it," Whispers said quietly. "That's interesting, though."

"Yeah, Danny. Sorry. I really underestimated you. I guess it's a lesson learned. Too bad about your dad, though."

"What?" Danny was panicking now; his face had turned bright red and he appeared to have tears in his eyes. "What are you doing to my dad? You need to stop this, now."

"It's too late. With me dead, no one can call it off."

"Goddammit Jack. Tell me what you're planning to do to my dad."

Jack just stayed there silently on his knees as Danny continued to get more frantic. Finally, Danny took a look around, his eyes stopping on Raffaele Scaglia.

"Fine, if you won't tell me, I'll kill your dad."

Danny moved the gun from the back of Jack's head to point it at Raffaele. But, as he was raising the pistol to take aim, Phil Leprino fired from inside the barn, Danny's head exploding like a pumpkin, bone fragments and pink mist filling the air.

Everything erupted at that point, with Joe Leprino coming around the west corner of the barn firing his shotgun at the man closest to him, cutting him almost in half, and Phillip Leprino popping up from the field just to the east of the barn, firing wildly and missing everyone.

Turk Picolli opened up with his Tommy Gun as he dove to his right to avoid Phillip Leprino's errant shot, the bullets cascading in an upward arc. He winged Raffaele Scaglia in the hip with his first shot, and then his spray caught Nicky Pauldino in the chest and Roxie Gioso full in the head, blowing his face out the back of his skull. Whispers leveled Danny's Tommy Gun at Joe Scaglia, but Tano was faster, pulling out his pistol and putting three in Whisper's gut before he could pull the trigger.

Fat Chucky Blanda had his shotgun trained on Tano and Joe Scaglia, while Turk Picolli had recovered from his dive to get on one knee, preparing to spray everyone in front of him with the Tommy Gun. But neither Fat Chucky or the Turk got a shot off, as Reggie Jefferson emerged from the dead fields with a silver pistol in each hand, his left-handed shot going in Fat Chucky's ear while the blast from the gun in his right hand hit Turk in his eye.

Reggie, who was still donning the purple velvet suit he had been wearing at his brothel earlier in the evening, looked around at the chaos in front of him; the gun smoke rising in the air to mix with the smoke from the fire at the back of the barn, the smell of cordite and copper stinging the nostrils, to all of the dead bodies lying on the ground, to his friend Jack Scaglia on his knees with Danny Villeco's brains and blood all over him.

"Shit, Jack. You Eye-talians sure do know how to throw a party."

Jack laughed at Reggie. "You looked like the Grim Fucking Reaper emerging from the corn fields, with two guns blazing, except for that purple clown suit you have on."

"Ha. You wouldn't know style if it hit you in the head."

Tano went up to Reggie and clapped him on the shoulder. "Man, I'm glad to see you. But who the fuck fires two guns at once?"

CHAPTER 11

The Leprino barn was completely engulfed in flames by the time firefighters reached it early the next morning, and there was no trace of the battle that had occurred a few hours earlier. All of the bodies had been loaded in cars and taken elsewhere to be disposed of. A knocked over lantern was blamed for starting the fire, and the Leprinos would have a new, state-of-the-art building up and running in time for the next planting season.

The Scaglias were caught up in the suspicion surrounding the murder of Charlie Salardino by the local authorities and were questioned but were able to provide solid alibis. Raffaele and his wife Trina had spent the day at a retirement party for a Denver police sergeant. Jack and his wife, along with Joe and his girlfriend, had attended a double feature at a movie theater on Curtis Street before going out for a chili dinner, and hadn't heard about the murder until running into Tano later that night. Tano Scaglia, it was said, had spent the day working out and sparring at the 20th Street Gymnasium, and several well-paid witnesses vouched for him being there.

Other theories were floated, but the one that gained the most traction was that Salardino, and Louis Briola as well, was taken out by Pietro Villecco in an attempt to take control of the Colorado mob ahead of his impending release from prison. That theory gained even more credence when Pietro's son, Danny, went missing following the big storm that blanketed the Front Range shortly after Charlie's murder.

Salardino's funeral was one of the grandest ever seen in Denver, with more than 2,500 citizens lining the streets around the home on Vallejo Street. Before the actual internment, a short ceremony took place in the sitting room where Charlie had been killed. Salardino was placed in a polished copper casket covered by a glass dome, and an elaborate, colorful floral display sat atop the casket, a bright white sash with the word Husband in gold lettering adorning it.

For several hours Gina Salardino allowed visitors to pass by the coffin and view Charlie's remains through the glass dome. Although Charlie had been shot in the forehead, the undertaker had done a masterful job hiding the wound. Of the 12 bullets that Charlie had taken the day of the murder, 11 were to his body so Gina was able to have an open casket. It became a thing of honor for locals to say they were able to see Salardino's body, and the line of mourners stretched out the front door and down the block for much of the morning of the funeral.

Following the ceremony in the sitting room, Salardino's casket was placed in a hearse and the floral arrangements were put on a flatbed truck and the procession crawled slowly through streets lined with mourners in the North Denver neighborhood before arriving at Crown Hill Cemetery, where Salardino, who was just 48, was entombed in the Tower of Memories, his crypt surrounded by dozens of beautiful arrangements and two large candles standing more than six feet tall. The two biggest floral arrangements at that entombment featured several hundred carnations purchased from Colorado Wholesale Florists and designed by Asunta Donato and were paid for by the Scaglia family. The entire Scaglia family attended the ceremony, including Raffaele who had injured his hip, apparently in a bad fall, a few days earlier. He walked with a cane and held tightly to the arm of his son Gaetano Scaglia, whose face still showed the remnants of a busted nose and black eyes he had suffered while sparring on the same day Charlie was murdered.

CHAPTER 12

About the same time as Charlie Salardino's body was being placed in his crypt in Denver, Pietro Villecco entered the small prison chapel in Canyon City to light a candle for his dead brother-in-law and say a prayer for the safety of his sister and his son. Peter felt like Gina would be alright – although it wasn't unheard of during the days when the Black Hand ran the underworld to go after someone's spouse or family, it was generally frowned upon by the people that currently made up the association and ran the mob across the nation.

Danny, on the other hand, was a totally different story. He hadn't been seen for several days, and Peter feared the worst. Word on the street was that Danny had actually taken out the feared Sam Pelligrino, which Peter found hard to believe. He loved his son, but he had doubts he was cut out for the life. Now he was missing. Peter hoped that Danny was just in hiding, even if he knew better.

When Peter was done in the chapel, he was going to attempt to get word out to Jack that he wanted to negotiate a truce with the Scaglias, to save not only his son's life, but his as well. Peter was willing to give up power in the south in exchange for their lives. The Villecco's had relatives in southern California, and life next to the ocean sounded mighty appealing right now.

The morning services in the prison had wrapped up more than an hour earlier, so Peter was the only one in the chapel. A guard that was on his payroll was posted outside, and he should have a half hour or so to himself before he needed to return to general population. Peter lit a candle in front of the altar to the Holy Mother, before making his way to the front of the chapel, where he knelt down and started silently reciting The Lord's Prayer. He had just gotten to the part where he was asking for forgiveness for those that trespassed against him when Anthony Carpineto came up behind him and slipped a garrot over Peter's head.

Carpineto, a powerfully built former Denver policeman, was doing time for manslaughter after beating a rape suspect to death with his department issued flashlight. Cops who ended up in prison usually had a hard time, but not Caprineto. On his first day in the joint he was approached by a giant black inmate who demanded his lunch tray. Carpineto grabbed the man and drug him to the far side of the cafeteria, slamming his head three times into the concrete wall before letting him crumble to the ground. He then went back to his table and resumed eating his bowl of chili, never uttering a single word. After that, no one messed with Carpineto, who earned his nickname The Ram that day.

Now, Carpineto reared back, lifting Peter off the ground. The smooth rope cut into Peter's neck as he kicked out with his feet, but Carpineto held firm until the body went limp and his bowels released. Carpineto held the garrot tight for another two minutes just to be sure, then let the body slide to the floor. Pietro Villecco was dead, laying in a puddle of his own shit and piss.

Carpineto glanced at the altar and crossed himself, and then lit a candle of his own before walking out of the chapel, handing the rope to a bull who had been standing guard outside its doors. "There's a mess in there," Carpineto said, gesturing back toward the chapel before heading back to general population.

CHAPTER 13

Carlos Perez woke to the smell of frying eggs and potatoes and burning bacon, his mouth watering before he rolled out of bed. His abuela was in the kitchen cooking up breakfast for him even though it was just past noon. Man, he had really tied it on last night and he was paying for it this morning, actually afternoon. He couldn't remember how many shots of tequila he had drank, but what the hell? He had earned it. Carlos had been on a hot streak ever since collecting $200 for dropping the dime on the Scaglias a week ago.

His good fortune started that night as he was able to turn that two hundred into three-fifty playing barbooth, the same game that had gotten his two fingers broken by the ape Tano Scaglia. The next morning he found out that the big barn had burned down at the Leprino farms, the same barn that Tano and the rest of the Scaglias had been hiding in when Carlos left work that previous afternoon. That was good Carlos thought, especially if Tano and the rest of those spaghetti benders had been in it when it went up in flames. His boss, Phillip Leprino, had sent word not to worry about coming in for work for a few days while they sorted things out, but that Carlos would get paid anyway.

That was good. Phillip Leprino was a good guy, unlike his cousin with the smushed nose. He felt a little guilty about giving up the information, but not very guilty and not for very long, when he remembered how Tano had laughed after breaking Carlos' fingers. So Carlos had spent the last few days celebrating his newfound fortune, playing barbooth and drinking his weight in tequila. He even bought himself a whore after a particularly successful night of barbooth, and he was up at least an additional three hundred and fifty dollars, even after paying for all the alcohol and ass.

But he learned during last night's barbooth session that Tano and the rest of the Scaglias had survived the fire. One of the other players said they were seen at the funeral for the other Italian, the one whose death had started this whole thing. That was surprising for Carlos. Now he was worried that they would find out he was the one that ratted them out. So Carlos cashed out early and ran to the bar, to the bartender who he had delivered the information to. He told the bartender, he thinks his name was Jerry Healy or something white like that, that he was worried. But the bartender, Jerry, assured him he had nothing to worry about. If the Scaglias knew he was the one that sold them out, he would be dead already. Hell, Jerry said, he'd probably be dead right alongside Carlos.

That made sense to Carlos, so he had another beer and then went back to the game, winning another fifty dollars before calling it a night.

Carlos went into the bathroom and splashed some cold water on his face to wake himself up, then went into the kitchen and kissed his abuela on the forehead. She was spooning the fried potatoes out of the skillet onto a plate, telling Carlos to sit down and eat, that there were tortillas and eggs and bacon already on the table. She told him she had to leave; she was going down to the church to play bingo with her friends but asked him to feed the chickens when he was done eating. He said fine, and that he loved her and would see her when she got back.

When he was done eating Carlos got up and went out the back door, urinating on the sunflowers that grew on the side of the stoop. His abuela had about a dozen chickens, and they were all out doing chicken things, looking for feed in the dirt and sparse grass in the fenced back yard.

"Hello chickens," Carlos called to them. "Are you hungry? I bet you are."

Carlos went over to the plastic bin attached to the small coop he had made for his abuela a couple of summers ago. He had attached the bin to the wall of the coop off the ground so the chickens couldn't get to it, and it appeared to have something dripping out of it. That was strange. Maybe it had gotten wet? But it hadn't snowed for a few days, so that didn't seem likely. And, whatever was dripping from it was dark. Carlos felt it and it was slick, but it also seemed to be crusting over in spots. He smelled his fingers and they smelled coppery, almost like blood.

Carlos opened the top of the bin with some reluctance, thinking maybe an animal had gotten in there and died. Maybe a chicken even. When he took the lid off a smell came out, but at first he couldn't see anything out of place because feed covered whatever was in there. Carlos thrust his hand in the feed, reaching down until he touched something hard and covered in hair.

Was it a cat? A fox? Whatever it was, it smelled. Carlos grabbed the hair and pulled it out of the feed.

Jerry Healy's severed head popped out of the grain, his eyes frozen open, staring straight at Carlos, who was screaming at the top of his lungs. He was screaming so loud he didn't even hear Tano Scaglia come up behind him, and didn't know he was dead until Tano cut his throat.

CHAPTER 14

With the death of Pietro Villecco, the victory of the Scaglia family was complete. In less than a two-week span, Jack Scaglia had orchestrated the elimination of his rivals and the takeover of organized crime in the Rocky Mountain region. His guile and savageness in the execution of the operation solidified his reputation as someone to be taken seriously, both regionally and nationally. He was now seen as a "Man of Respect," partly because of the reverence he had shown others before making the move on Salardino.

Jack had sent word to The Outfit in Chicago, to both Frank Nitti, who was recognized publicly as the boss, and Paul "The Waiter" Ricca, who actually ran things, that he was going to take Charlie out. Jack made arrangements to install Sam Pelligrino, who got his start in Chicago and was still a legend for his savagery in The Outfit, to run things down south in Pueblo and Trinidad, replacing Louis Briola and Pete Villecco. Sam's murder derailed those plans, but The Outfit still appreciated the gesture. And although they had no issue with Salardino personally, Jack's promise that the tributes sent East would be larger and more frequent, helped grease the wheels.

Jack also reached out to Charles Binaggio who ran the rackets in Kansas City, an up-and-coming territory that was gaining traction in the Midwest, and Jack Dragna in Los Angeles. He also let it be known that the Scaglia's would be willing to work with both families on criminal enterprises moving forward. While Jack Scaglia didn't ask for permission to take out Charlie Salardino, the fact that he let these other organizations know he was making a move earned him a lot of respect and raised his profile nationwide.

News of the takeover made its way back to The Commission, the national governing body of the Italian-American Mafia based in New York. Charles "Lucky" Luciano, who formed The Commission following the Castellammarese War in 1931 and currently served as its chairman despite being imprisoned for pandering, was impressed with Jack's planning and execution, and agreed that he was someone to keep an eye on.

For the most part the transition from the rule of Charlie Salardino to the Scaglias went smoothly, as Colorado's general public was more concerned with the United States' growing involvement in World War II than a conflict between a group of Italians. The police were convinced that Danny and his father Pete Villecco were the ones behind the sudden outburst of violence in a failed takeover attempt. With the Villecco's eliminated, police officials — more than a few who had outstanding gambling debts forgiven -- were willing to put the investigation to rest.

BOOK III

TUESDAY, JUNE 14, 1960

CHAPTER 1

John Donato pulled his Packard station wagon in the lot across the street from the entrance to Danilo's Restaurante and turned off the ignition, the engine knocking a couple of times as it cooled down. He would have to have Johnny take a look at it. The vehicle was 20 years old now and, even though John had kept it meticulously maintained, its best days were behind it. It may be time to get something newer.

John turned to his older brother Anthony in the passenger seat and smiled. "You ready for this?"

Anthony put his hand on his forehead before running it back through his hair, which just recently had started to recede. He let out a big breath he hadn't realized he was holding and said, "As ready as I'll ever be." He started to open the door when John reached across and grabbed his arm.

"We're doing the right thing, Anthony. I know you have your reservations, but this is the right thing. Mom is right. If we are going to survive, we have to look out for ourselves," John said, squeezing his brother's forearm reassuringly.

"I know," Anthony said, getting out of the car. "But that doesn't make it any easier."

The decision to approach the Scaglias for help had been made that previous Sunday during the meeting of the Italian carnation growers at the Donato farm. It hadn't come easily, or unanimously. When Joe Carabetta told his story about his friend wanting to help, and John Donato explained that the friend Joe was talking about was Raffaele Scaglia, the gathering erupted in discussion. John Donato was surprised to hear that most of the group was okay with being associated with the Scaglias, while there was less than a third of them that were opposed to any such partnership. Several of those opposed were adamant that they wanted nothing to do with the Scaglia family, who they considered criminals and, even worse, sinners.

The debate raged on for close to half an hour, with both sides presenting their arguments, sometimes loudly but always passionately. Many, who were fine with working with the proposal, brought up the old country, where partnerships with men who were outside the law were very common. While the other side pointed out that many of them had to come to America to get away from that very practice.

It seemed like they would be hopelessly deadlocked, and John Donato was convinced that the gathering would end with the group splintering, with parts of it fine with approaching the Scaglias while another, smaller portion would stay with the devil they already knew, Anders Lindgren and CWF.

In the end it was the words of Asunta Donato that sealed the decision to approach the Scaglias.

At one point the conversations ebbed, and the volume of the meeting reduced as the two factions were speaking amongst themselves. Suzy Donato took this opportunity to take one of the hard lemon drop candies she always carried out of her pocket, unwrapping it before popping it in her mouth. Although she was under five foot tall and in her mid 60s, Suzie's voice was still strong and clear, and cut through the other chatter.

"My father, Natale, was born In San Cipirello, a little village in Western Sicily," she began, while sitting down at the head of the first table. "He was a quiet man, but strong, big for a Sicilian, maybe five-and-a-half feet." That brought laughter from the assembled group, who were already entranced by Suzy's story.

"Papa worked as a," Suzy stumbled for the right words here, English being her second language, "como se dici,... a cowboy," the appropriate English word coming to her finally. "Yes, a cowboy, for the local gabelloti of a wealthy lemon grower who lived in Palermo. Whatever the gabelloti asked of him, my father did. It was an honest living, but it wasn't a good one. He would come home late at night, tired and sore and covered in the day's dust, only to go out again the next morning before the sunrise.

"Papa Natale struggled to keep food on the table for him and his new wife, my mother, Catarina. Papa would see the nice things the wives of the rich people had and would want that for his beloved Catarina. My mother had beautiful, raven black hair that hung down to her waist. My papa wanted nothing more than to buy her a fancy brush because there was nothing he loved more than watching her brush her hair every night. But, he couldn't even afford that. So, he would go out under the moonlight," Susie paused here, searching for the right word before continuing, deciding on "'freeing' baioccos from alms boxes in the little chapels that were set up for travelers in the mountainsides around Palermo. It wasn't much, baioccos were the pope's coins, worth about a penny, but he was good at it, and was able to put together a pretty substantial stash. He wasn't proud that he was doing that, becoming a thief, but it was the only way he knew to be able to buy fine things for Mama."

Suzy stopped here for breath, taking a drink of wine from a small tumbler Big John had placed at her side. She looked out at the men gathered before her, seeing that she had all their attention before continuing. "Papa was so good at … freeing these coins and his stash grew substantial enough that it eventually came to the attention of his gabelloti, who was a local mafioso. Now, we're not talking about the Mafia like what they have here in America, the one they talked about in those senate hearings a while back with that big shot Frank Costello. The mafia in Sicily back then was more of a way of life, a moral code that they all lived by. But that isn't to say there wasn't still people who ruled things, capos that had to be taken care of. I'm not sure if it was the gabelloti that Papa worked for who was this man in San Cipirello, or if it was the man the gabelloti worked for, but either way, someone came to Papa and demanded a portion of the baioccos he had freed."

Suzy took another sip of wine, and then slipped another lemon candy into her mouth before continuing. "Well, Papa wasn't about to give up what he had risked so much to, como se dici?" Again, she struggled to find the right word. "Ehh…put together. So Papa was threatened. If he didn't turn over part of his stash, then he may get hurt. Or even worse, his beloved Catarina might see harm." Suzy looked down at her hands, collecting herself before continuing. "Papa was a proud man, and he refused, telling the man he was mistaken, that he didn't have any secret money anywhere. When he returned from work the next evening, he found my Mama crying at their kitchen table, her head in her hands. When Papa went to her, he saw that someone had come and cut off most of her beautiful hair." This brought a gasp from the gathered men. Suzy took a moment to gather herself, a single tear streaming down her face before she continued.

"My Papa was ready to kill someone and grabbed his lupara and headed out the door. But Mama grabbed his arm as he was trying to leave and begged him not to go. She said her hair wasn't worth his life. And neither was his pride." Suzy sighed. "She was able to convince him to stay. They stayed up all night talking, and Papa agreed to pay the man the next day. The sun rose a short time later, and my dad went out to work and to pay his gabelloti what they felt they were owed. They were herding goats that day on the side of a rocky hill. The man laughed when Papa walked up to him with his small bag of baioccos, telling him not to be so glum because hair grew back. Papa said he clenched his fists but had promised my Mama he wouldn't do anything, so he just turned his back and went to go check on a goat that appeared hobbled. The gabelloti, meanwhile, went to put the bag of coins in a pack on his nearby donkey and must have slipped on a rock or something, because he went tumbling down the mountain side, breaking his neck when he hit the bottom." Suzy looked every man there in the eye, knowing exactly what she was saying. "Papa took this as a sign. He went and got his bag of coins out of the pack on the donkey, and there happened to be a couple of other bags that also had coins in them, and he quickly headed to the gabelloti's home to tell them about the tragedy and deliver the bags of coins. When he got to the home, he could not find anyone there, the wife and children must have went into town to have lunch. He did find more bags of coins and, worried that someone might come along and steal them, gathered them up for safe keeping."

Suzy glanced around at the men, seeing smiles on most of their faces as she told her story. She smiled back before continuing on with the tale.

"So Papa got back home, where he found that Mama had packed their things. She told him that she wanted to leave, and leave now. Papa always did what Mama wanted, so he gathered up their belongings and headed to Naples to find passage to America," Suzy said, taking another drink of wine. "In all the excitement, he must have forgotten that he had gathered up all of the gabelloti's coins for safe keeping. This bothered him, but he didn't have time to return them, so he used some of the stash of baioccos to buy passage on the sailing ship Moshulu, vowing to return the money once he arrived in the new country. So, Papa and Mama, Natale and Catarina, along with about five hundred other Italians, headed across the ocean to America and a new life.

"During that journey to America, that journey that took more than three months to cross the Atlantic, they were blessed with a beautiful baby girl, me!" Suzy laughed and clapped her hands. The rest of the group laughed and clapped along, raising their glasses in celebration.

Suzy smiled to herself, waiting until the men quieted down again.

"Well, so that's how I came into this world, amid a mass of dirty, starving piasians trying to escape our homeland to find a better life in America. And, for the most part, we were able to do that, to find a better life here. But that isn't to say it's been easy. The Italians were looked down upon, treated no better than animale by the pezzonovante and the whites. We've had to work hard for everything we have, but that's the way it should be. But we should be able to keep what we've worked hard for, not have someone else take it away.

"I'm not complaining, mind you. I've been lucky. I was able to find a good man who loved me and we had the most wonderful children in the whole wide world," Susie looked over at Big John and Anthony, taking another sip of her wine before continuing. "And then God decided he needed to call my beloved James home."

She paused again here, another single tear dropping from the corner of her left eye that she briskly wiped away before going on.

"I don't have too much to say about that. I don't know why God felt like he needed James more than our family did, but that's something I'll ask him when I get to heaven. And believe me, he better have a good answer," That brought out a couple of quiet laughs.

"So, with James gone, things were hard. But I had to do what I had to do for my children, for my familia. We did okay. I worked hard, the boys worked hard. But times were tough and, no matter how hard we worked, we couldn't make all the bills. So, I had to sell off some of our land, and as part of that deal, I took ownership of the greenhouse on Federal. A greenhouse. What do I know about running a greenhouse? Lo niente. But, luckily, my family, my boys, and many of you gathered here today, helped this poor little widow find her way."

Suzy, reached across the table and grabbed Joe Carabetta's hand and gave it a squeeze. "Joe, my cugino, you were especially helpful. Grazie." Joe nodded and squeezed her hand back.

"So, with a lot of help, and a lot of hard work, I was able to keep some plants alive." This brought more laughter. "Like all of you, I joined up with Anders Lindgren and CWF. And it was good, he took our flowers and distributed them and we made a little money."

"Very little money," Pete Villano said.

"Yes, it seemed like we should be making more. So I called up Mr. Lindgren and asked him if he could give me some advice. Was there anything I could be doing better? Any way my little greenhouse could generate more profit? Mr. Lindgren agreed to come by and look at my little operation. I walked him through the growing houses, and our grading room and even our little retail shop. He looked at everything really closely and nodded his head a lot when I talked about our operation. When we was done with the tour, we went into my office and I asked him, 'So, what do you think?'

"So, Mr. Lindgren says he's really impressed with my greenhouse. That I have it running great. That my flowers are strong and healthy, some of the best that come through his doors. But there's only so much money to be made. CWF has to make a profit, and he has a lot of overhead. And he goes on and on about all of the hard work he does, maintaining the trucks that deliver the flowers to the different shops across the region, blah, blah, blah. He says he hears it from all of the 'Eye-talian' growers, that they're all complaining they aren't making enough. But where are they going to go? He asks."

Suzy took a big drink of wine here, finishing her cup. She gestured over to Anthony, who refilled it from a nearby jug. Suzy took another sip before continuing.

"Then Mr. Lindgren, that big pasty Swede who looks like a giant lo spettro, got up from his chair and walked over to the door of my office and closed it, locking it behind him. He walked over and sat on the edge of my desk and took my hand into his. He was so close I can remember what he smelled like, like tobacco and schnapps, And he looks down at me all sincere and says, 'You know, there is one way I can think of where I might be able to get you a bigger percentage of the profits.' I pulled my hand back and tried to back away, but I was in my chair so I couldn't move. I told him, no, I don't think so. But he leaned closer, and he said, 'Look, I know your husband has been gone for a while now. I'm sure you're lonely. We could help each other out. If you be my friend, then I'll give you a bigger piece of the pie.' Then he leaned down and tried to kiss me."

A hush had fallen over the assembled group, and Anthony's face had turned beet red. Big John's face remained impassive, blank as a stone. Suzy saw there were several of the men looking at her sons, wondering how they could let this pass and quickly responded.

"Look, I never told my boys because I knew what they would do to that man. We didn't need that trouble. No, they didn't find out about this until a couple of weeks ago. I handled it myself. I grabbed a letter opener off my desk and aimed it at Lindgren's crotch and told him if he came another inch closer, I would hang his testicolos on my wall."

This brought out cheers and laughter from most of the men. Joe Carabetta reached over and squeezed Suzy's hand again, and others raised their glasses in salute to the fiery woman they all loved and respected. Her sons didn't join the quick celebration, however. Anthony grabbed a glass of wine, stopping the grinding of his teeth only long enough to down his drink, while John remained stone faced.

After Suzy's story, there was a little more back and forth about whether or not the assembled group should accept help from the Scaglia's so they could leave CWF, but it was only cursory. The decision had been made. The group took a vote and only one grower – Abe Notary – was opposed to making the move. But he agreed to go along with what the rest of the group decided was the best course of action.

CHAPTER 2

Big John and Anthony Donato stepped out of the bright sun into the dark, cool entryway of Danilo's where they were greeted warmly by Raffaele Scaglia. He had them sit on a couple of round stools as he made his way behind the long bar before pouring each man a shot of anisette. Raffaele raised his shot glass, saluting them by saying "cent'anni." John and Anthony raised their glasses and responded in kind before the three men shot down the sweet tasting liqueur.

"Jack will be ready for you in a bit," Raffaele said, gesturing to see if the men wanted another shot, which they both declined. "I'm so glad to finally meet the two of you. It should have happened a long time ago. My father Danilo, who this place is named after, was very good friends with your grandfather Rocco back in Potenza."

"Yes, we've always heard that," Anthony said. "And I know you and my father-in-law have become good friends."

"Ah, yes, Joe. We spend a lot of time together at The Sons of Potenza." Raffaele leaned forward with a big smile, patting Anthony's forearm with his hand. "I love Joe, but I think he cheats at bocce."

That brought a laugh from all the men. "He probably does. He definitely cheats at pinochle," Anthony said. "He was going to come with us today, but his wife was feeling under the weather this morning and he stayed home with her. He said to tell you he'll catch up with you at the lodge."

"Bueno. Tell Joe I hope she feels better."

"I will."

The three men sat in silence for a moment, before Raffaele looked at each man in their eyes.

"Look, I'm not sure why our families grew apart, but I hope you and my son can come to some agreement today and we can come together again," Raffaele said while wiping down the bar top with a dish cloth. "I know you are probably aware of all of the things that are said about my family, and the fiction told in the newspapers and on the radio and television. I'm not going to lie to you. Some of it is true, some not so much. I did what I had to do for my family to survive. And then I let Jack take over. It's not easy running a family while a lot of people count on you. I'm sure you two know this better than most."

John looked over at his older brother, he nodded his head in agreement. "Hard choices have to be made sometimes," John said.

"Exactly. So, we have a reputation. We're lumped in with those mobsters back east and in Chicago," Raffaele said. "That's simply not the case. You don't have to worry about any of that. We're businesspeople. And we always make money for ourselves and our partners. We can all make good money here, and you can set up your family heading well into the future. Does that sound good?"

"Of course," Anthony said.

"It does," John agreed.

Raffaele looked at the two men, smiling before embracing a forearm of both with his hands. "Buono."

Just then Anthony Carpineto made his way from the back and over to the bar.

"Hey Mr. Scaglia, Jack is ready for them." Carpineto turned to the Donatos, shaking each man's hand. "I'm Anthony. Follow me."

Carpineto took them by the swinging double doors of the kitchen to a hallway that led past the restrooms to a narrow staircase. There was a folding security gate that went across the entrance to the stairs that was open. Carpineto let the Donatos pass him, telling them to go on up as he turned and locked the gate behind them.

The stairs led to a sparsely furnished landing area that had another, larger staircase on the opposite end. There were several doors off the landing area, including an open one by the northwest corner of the floor that Carpineto gestured for the men to go into.

Jack Scaglia was sitting behind an ornate desk in the northwest corner of the room, the day's edition of the Denver Post broadsheet splayed out in front of him. Jack raised his head as the Donatos entered the room, a smile coming to his face.

"Ahh, it's so good to see you," Jack said as he rose from behind the desk, shaking each man's hand before offering them a seat in hardback chairs situated in front of the desk. "Please sit down."

John Donato was getting his first real look at Jack Scaglia, and he was impressed. Like most Sicilians, Scaglia was small in stature, but he projected a much bigger presence. He appeared fit and had freshly groomed salt and pepper hair and wore a sharp white dress shirt with a burgundy tie and dark trousers held up by a pair of suspenders. As he made his way back around the desk he looked at the Donatos and asked "Do you want Anthony to get you a drink?"

Both men waved the offer off, with Anthony Donato saying "We've already had a few with your father."

"Ah, yes," Jack laughed. "Papa likes his drink more and more these days. We'll save it until after we're done when we hopefully have something to toast." Jack gestured to Carpineto. "Do you mind if he joins us? I trust Anthony with my life."

"That's fine," John said.

Anthony Carpineto closed the door before taking a seat next to it and Jack settled behind his desk. "So, gentlemen, I have a pretty good idea about what you came here to discuss, but I'd like to hear it from you. What can I do for you?"

Anthony Donato deferred to John, who ran down the Italian grower's history with Colorado Wholesale Florists and Anders Lindgren, and how they felt they were being shortchanged by the Big Swede. John told them about deciding to go out on their own, but how they didn't have the infrastructure and capital to do it properly. John then told Jack about Joe Carbetta's conversation with Raffaele and his suggestion that Jack might be able to help them out.

"So," John continued, "we're here to see if we can come to some kind of partnership."

Jack, who had been leaning forward with his elbows on his desk, listening intently, nodded his head before leaning back into his chair.

"I appreciate that you came to me with this offer. It means a lot to me personally, especially coming from you two, who are from the same hometown that I come from." Jack stood and walked over to a wet bar along the north wall, pouring himself a scotch.

"I know it can't be easy, legitimate businessmen like yourselves to come to someone with the reputation I have." Jack took a sip from his tumbler before returning behind the desk, but not sitting. "I know what is said about me and my family, what is written in the papers. And, to be perfectly honest, much of it is true. We were bootleggers and made a lot of money providing alcohol to the public when the government wouldn't allow it. And I'm not going to apologize for that."

Jack finished off his drink, setting it on a coaster before continuing on.

"It was our involvement in that venture that allows me to be in position to help you guys out today. I have a building that we used to store the booze in that would be perfect for your warehouse and distribution hub, and we have a fleet of trucks we used for bootlegging that can be used to transport your products."

At this point Jack stopped and bent over, putting his hands flat on his desk while looking directly at both Donatos.

"I understand why that could be problematic, why individuals such as yourselves wouldn't want to be associated with that. Because believe me, if we go into business together, there will be people out there that will call you criminals, that will call you gangsters, whether it is true or not," Jack stood up straight. "For the next few years, at the very least, that's what they will say about you because of my family. But I'm telling you right now, we are diversifying. We own restaurants, nightclubs, grocery stores. We own property and office buildings. I'm negotiating right now to have a piece of the greyhound racing track over in Commerce City. We just opened a deli in Wheat Ridge and a bakery in Arvada. Hopefully, ten years from now when the Scaglia family name is mentioned, people won't immediately think of Al Capone. They'll think of titans of industry. But I understand that it may take some time.

"So, I guess what we need to decide right now, is if that acceptable to you? Because if not, there's no reason to continue."

The two brothers looked at one another, John giving an almost imperceptible nod to his older brother.

"We are well aware of your reputation, in the newspapers and in city hall," Anthony said. "We're not naïve. We are coming into this with our eyes wide open. We know being associated with the Scaglias carries a certain 'shine' along with it. But we also know how hard it has been to be an immigrant in this country, especially an Italian immigrant that is looked down upon by much of the respectable crowd. We know your family did what it felt it needed to do to survive. Hell, we may have done the same things if the opportunities had presented itself."

Anthony looked over at his brother, who nodded in agreement.

"But we also know what the community, our neighbors, say about you. About how you guys are the first ones to lend a helping hand when it's needed. How if you need money to keep your heat on, or if your daughter needs braces and you don't have the funds to get them, the Scaglias are always willing to help, often not expecting to get paid back. When the church needs new windows, or when the school needs new uniforms for the basketball team, who do they turn to?

"Like I said, we're not naïve. We can't get to where we want to be without some help, and who better to turn to then a paisan? No, we will be proud to be in business with you."

John looked at his older brother with admiration. Anthony didn't enjoy the spotlight on him, so that is why John did most of the talking even though he was the younger brother. But John knew it was important for Anthony to say what he had said. And he was especially proud that Anthony hadn't mentioned that their partnership had to be completely legitimate. Several of the other growers, although agreeing to go into business with Jack Scaglia, had wanted the Donatos to insist that it was all above the board. But John and Anthony had discussed this in private, and they both felt it would be an insult to even bring that up.

When Anthony was done, Jack seemed pleased. "Buono. Buono. I think this will be a great partnership." He moved around the desk and shook each brother's hand again. "Ok, let's figure this out."

Over the next two hours, Jack Scaglia and the Donatos hammered out the details of their partnership. Jack laid out how he would use his connections to get their products into grocery stores, retail shops, catering halls and restaurants throughout the Front Range. And he would do it for a fraction of what Lindgren and CWF was taking. The Donato brothers were surprised – Jack's offer was so good they didn't even feel like they had to negotiate it down.

This actually worried John, and he said so.

"I'm not sure why you are being so generous to us. I feel like this deal is almost too good to be true," John Donato said.

"I understand that," Jack said, loosening his tie. "I could ask, and rightfully so, for a bigger portion of the pie. But that would place you and your fellow growers in a more precarious position. And I see this as a long-term investment for my family. This agreement we are making today will be good for five years. After that we will negotiate. We have the money to survive the next five years without pulling a big profit out of this venture. I want you guys to have the best chance you can to succeed, so when we sit down again in five years, it will be a much bigger, and stable, pie that I will take a piece of. Capisce?"

John and Anthony nodded. They both could see the logic in that.

"There is one other little detail we need to discuss," Jack continued. "Anders Lindgren. He is not going to be happy with this little partnership we are forming here."

The Donatos knew that Lindgren would be upset with a good portion of his growers leaving, but it was perfectly legal. The Italian growers didn't have contracts or any signed agreements that locked them in with CWF for any length of time, and that was the way that Lindgren had wanted it. It was to his advantage. He probably never thought that the Italians would leave in a mass exodus.

Losing the Italians wouldn't cripple Lindgren's business, but it would take a big chunk of change out of his wallet.

"Sure, Lindgren will be upset. But what we're doing is perfectly legal," Anthony Donato said. "What can he do?"

"Well, that's the thing," Jack said. "We don't know what he will do. Anders Lindgren isn't exactly what he appears to be. He didn't get a mansion down the street from the Governor just by pedaling flowers."

"What do you mean?" John asked.

"Back in the day, Anders was a bootlegger, much like my family. He ran with a crew that was headed by an Irishman, Glenn McGregor," Jack said. "We actually worked with McGregor for a short time – he had a connection that could get Canadian bonded whiskey, which was extremely popular. So, we went into business together.

"Lindgren was one of McGregor's muscle. They were a brutal crew, leaving bodies all over Boulder and Longmont. Lindgren was considered particularly vicious, not someone you mess with. Rumor has it that he had a falling out with McGregor shortly before the end of prohibition, something about how profits were shared. McGregor went missing, and Lindgren took over the crew. A couple of weeks later McGregor's wife heard some kind of ruckus outside her front door. When she went out to check, she found McGregor's head in the milk box on the porch."

The color drained out of the Donato's faces hearing this, but they remained silent, John staring out the window while Anthony looked down at his hands in his lap. After a moment, John returned his attention to Jack.

"We know there are risks with doing this. We knew Anders wouldn't be happy, and we've heard rumors about his temper," John said. "We've actually had this discussion amongst ourselves, and we're determined to make this move. We may not be soldiers, or what anyone would consider hard men. But we've had to endure, all of us. We've fought for our families, for our place in America. We are hard men and will do what we have to. We won't be scared off by Anders Lindgren, or anything he might try to do to us."

"Good," Jack said, rising again from behind his desk. "I wasn't trying to scare you. I was just letting you know who you are dealing with. And I highly doubt that Lindgren would do anything drastic. He's older now, and that was a long time ago. No one knows for sure who killed McGregor, but even if it was Anders, he's been out of that life for a long time. Still, it wouldn't hurt to be careful. We," Jack pointed at Anthony Carpineto as he said this, "will make sure nothing happens to you and the rest of your group. That's part of the agreement we have here – we will look out for you. I just want you to know who we are dealing with."

Jack poured each of the men, including Carpineto as well this time, another tumbler of whiskey. "Here's to a long and prosperous partnership," Jack said, raising his drink high in the air. "And hopefully to a renewal of a long-standing friendship."

CHAPTER 3

With few exceptions, the partnership between the Scaglias and the group of Italian growers went relatively smoothly in the beginning. As expected, Anders Lindgren was furious when the Donatos told him about the group's intention to leave and strike out on their own, and the Big Swede vowed to destroy them and grind their operation into the ground. But when he learned that the Scaglias were backing the move, Lidgren relented a bit, telling the Donatos they were making a big mistake going into business with "a bunch of red-sauced criminals" and they would come back, begging to rejoin CWF.

Although Lindgren immediately froze the Italians out, Jack Scaglia was able to use his connections to keep income coming in for the new company, which they christened Bel Fiore Florists, as they built up their network. And when a grower did find themselves in financial straits during that early period, Jack would provide an advance that they could pay back in very small increments over a long period of time.

As summer turned to fall somewhat of a normal routine returned for all involved. Jimmy helped his dad and uncle run their greenhouses and got engaged after asking Connie to marry him during a trip to the hot springs in Glenwood at the beginning of August. Joey Carabetta became a delivery driver for the Scaglias and began spending most of his free time between Nettie's bar and Danilo's. Tano Scaglia took a real shine to Joey Cars and started using him to run little errands and to be his driver at night and on the weekends.

Little John returned to high school and earned a spot on the varsity football team, earning all-conference honors as a nose tackle. He also turned 16 and got his driver's license and took a weekend job as a delivery driver for the Scaglias alongside Joey Cars.

It was on one of those weekend deliveries where the first real trouble started. Little John and Joey Cars were working as a tandem duo on a two-day delivery run from Denver south to Grand Junction and back. The initial part of the trip went fine; they made six stops along interstate 70 – Avon, Edwards, Eagle, Gypsum and Glenwood Springs before the final delivery in Grand Junction, where they stayed overnight. The following morning, they were having breakfast at a local café before heading back to Denver when someone burst through the restaurant doors yelling about a vehicle that was on fire in the parking lot. Sure enough, it was the Bel Fiore truck that was ablaze, exploding in a huge fireball seconds after Joey and Little John had exited the café.

Over the next several weeks a handful of Bel Fiore trucks had their tires slashed, a small retail shop that switched from CWF to BFF had its front window shattered and its inventory destroyed and Ted Losasso's youngest son, Enzo, was mugged and beaten to the point he had to be hospitalized after leaving a bar in Brighton.

Still, things were going pretty well for the growers and the Bel Fiore group. The Donatos were contracted to provide the flowers for the wedding between the lieutenant governor's beloved daughter and a popular local news anchor in the final week of September 1960. It was the biggest wedding the state had seen for several years, with close to 750 guests invited to the reception, and would be covered by both the Denver Post and the Rocky Mountain News social pages, as well as local television. It would be a great opportunity for the Donatos, and all of Bel Fiore's growers, to showcase their products.

The arrangements for the ceremony were completed and stored at the Bel Fiore warehouse on the Friday before the wedding, to be delivered to the Cathedral Basilica of the Immaculate Conception in downtown Denver Saturday morning. Suzy, however, insisted that the bride and groom's bouquets, along with the place settings for the reception be as fresh as possible. At 4 a.m. the day of the wedding, Suzy and her son's Anthony and John, along with their wives and kids, went to the 32nd Avenue greenhouse to finish the work, only to find that someone had broken in overnight and smashed all of the vases and shredded the flowers that were going to be used for the table place settings.

CHAPTER 4

Little Johnny Donato poured the last of the oil from the can into the funnel, watched the dark viscous fluid slowly drain down before replacing the fill cap on his Granny's 1958 Lincoln Continental. He checked the dipstick to make sure the level was correct before using a shop rag to close the hood, not wanting to leave dirty fingerprints on the paint. It was a nice car, Shasta Blue with white interior, and his Granny Suzy loved it. Johnny preferred the body style of the '50 Continental, but he wasn't going to complain. Granny Suzy was in her mid 60s now and didn't drive much, letting Johnny have it whenever she didn't need it.

It was early evening the day after the big wedding and things were tense around the Donato compound. That day's Sunday pasta had been a subdued affair, with none of the usual loud conversations and laughter served up with the plates of spaghetti and sugo. Johnny's dad, in particular, was really quiet, barely saying two words during the meal. And when it was over, there were no card games or sing-alongs; the relatives and guests just helped clean up and then headed out to their own homes.

Johnny was worried about his dad. For the past several weeks, ever since Johnny had taken the trip to Grand Junction with Joey Cars when the Bel Fiore truck was blown up, his dad seemed to be carrying extra weight around. Johnny had to admit the truck blowing up was frightening; he wasn't able to sleep for a solid week after that and played his worst game of the football season that Friday night. He still was able to get a crucial quarterback sack late in the game to help his team win, and then later that night while they were celebrating with burgers and shakes at the Scotchman, Lannette Bryer, a sophomore cheerleader, leaned over and kissed him. By the next morning he had forgotten all about the giant fireball and the heat the burning truck put off, so hot it melted the tar on the pavement of the parking lot of the café in Grand Junction.

But he knew his father didn't forget, and he made Johnny give up his weekend job driving trucks for Bel Fiore. He didn't think his dad was sleeping at all, guzzling pot after pot of black coffee. He looked terrible, even forgetting to shave a couple of mornings, which was not like him. Big John Donato even shaved when they went on vacation.

As bad as Big John looked to Johnny, his Uncle Anthony looked even worse. Uncle Anthony had a grey pallor on him and had taken up smoking cigarettes, something that disgusted his wife, Aunt Mary Anne. Uncle Anthony and Jimmy had even gotten into a heated argument one evening that ended with loudly slammed doors and with Jimmy peeling out of the driveway, barely missing the mailboxes as he fishtailed onto the road.

Then things seemed to have reached a boiling point the previous morning when they got to the 32nd Avenue greenhouse and found the front door kicked in, and all of the glassware smashed, and flowers shredded. After looking at the destruction in stunned silence for several moments, Granny Suzy grabbed a big push broom and started sweeping things into large piles.

Anthony looked at his mother and shook his head in disgust. "Ma, what are you doing?"

"I'm cleaning up, what does it look like I'm doing," Suzy snapped back. Granny Suzy never seemed to lose her temper, so the sharpness of her response shocked Johnny.

Big John, meanwhile, was walking around looking at the destruction, his jaw clenched tightly and the vein at his temple visibly throbbing.

"I can't believe that piece of shit did this," Anthony said, waving his arms at the mess in front of him. "That motherfucker is going to pay." Again, the vulgarity was out of character for his family, so it felt like a slap to Johnny.

"John, we can't let him get away with this," Anthony said to his younger brother. "We need to go down to wherever he is at and kick his fucking Swedish ass!"

"You'll do no such thing," Granny hissed at her son.

"Ma, stay out of it," Anthony snapped back. "He's insulted our family, threatened our livelihood. There needs to be consequences.

"At the very least we need to call 'Black Jack' Scaglia and have him take care of it. What good is it going to bed with a mobster if you're going to have to deal with shit like this?"

Big John looked hard at his older brother and finally spoke. "No. We're not calling Jack. We'll handle this." He took another look around at the mess, and then seemed to make up his mind and started handing out assignments.

"Milly, love, go put on coffee and keep it coming. Strong and black. Mary Anne, see if anything can be salvaged out of this mess. Johnny, take your cousins Mike and Peter and go out into the greenhouse and bring us anything that we might be able to use. If it's even close to being ready, go ahead and cut it."

"What are we going to do?" Anthony asked. "I hope we're headed downtown to kick that Swede's ass."

"No, Anthony. I want you to help Ma clean up. I'm going to make some phone calls, and we're going to do what we can to make sure the reception has the best arrangements possible," Big John said. "We'll deal with the Swede and all of this later. For now, we're going to do what we were hired to do."

Little John was glad to see his dad take charge. He liked seeing him like this. People looked to his dad as a leader, and it filled him with pride to see it.

Johnny went and got a cutting knife and a tape thumb from the tool tray by the door to the actual greenhouse, and then headed out with his two young cousins in tow. It was just recently that his dad trusted him enough to actually cut the flowers and Johnny loved doing it. He would go up the different aisles, looking for blooms that were open enough to be cut. Once you located one, you had to reach in and find the stem, usually about 18 to 24 inches from the bloom and use the knife, squeezing from one side until the blade went through and hit the tape thumb, which was just duct tape you worked around your thumb so you wouldn't cut it with the blade.

Usually, the blooms had to be pretty open to get cut, not fully bloomed but close enough that they would be in the next day or two. Saturdays were a bit different because you cut the blooms tighter than the rest of the week due to not doing a cut on Sundays. And today, with the emergency situation going on, Johnny was cutting them even tighter than normal. When he had cut enough to fill up his younger cousins' arms, they would run the cut back to the office while Johnny moved on to the next aisle.

While Johnny was cutting flowers out in the greenhouse, his father worked the phones, calling all of the growers that had left CWF to form Bel Fiore to explain the situation and ask for their help. Not a single one turned Big John Donato down. When Johnny had finally made his way back to the office after cutting the entire greenhouse a couple of hours after starting, he was shocked at what he saw. There was no trace of the destruction that had greeted them earlier in the morning, instead the grading room was filled with people working together to create floral arrangements for the wedding later in the day. The parking lot was full of delivery trucks from Italian greenhouses throughout the area. Some had brought vases, some had brought flowers, some had brought both. Music was playing on the radio and the women were singing along to Connie Francis' "My Heart Has a Mind of Its Own" while the men were smiling at them, nodding their heads to the beat. There was no talk of what had happened earlier in the morning and of Anders Lindgren and what was going to happen next, there was just a group of people working together for a common cause. Even though it was the Donatos who had been hired for the wedding, the rest of the group understood this was a big moment for Bel Fiore if it was going to survive.

Even Uncle Anthony seemed to be in a good mood. While Johnny was out cutting, someone had went and picked up a couple of grills and Uncle Anthony and Jimmy were manning them, cooking up sausage and peppers to feed everyone.

The reception was slated to start at 4 p.m. that afternoon, and by a little after noon that day the Donatos had been able to put together a little over 300 arrangements and centerpieces, a hodgepodge of different vases and plants. It wasn't exactly what Granny Suzy had in mind when she had awoken that morning, but she admitted they turned out better than she could have hoped.

They loaded up the trucks and headed over to the reception hall and had the arrangements on the table and ready to go by 2:30 p.m., well before the first guests arrived. And the flowers were a smash hit with people raving about them, even more so than the food which was prepared by an award-winning chef. The Denver Post society page praised the result, writing that "the floral arrangements at the reception were worthy of royalty, all unique and all beautiful. No two tables were the same, from the vases down to the flora contained within them. Carnations, baby's breath, tulips, calla Lilies, hydrangeas, alstroemeria, roses and Peonies from as far as the eye could see. If there is a heaven, it would be hard pressed to match the splendor that greeted Denver's high society Saturday afternoon."

The glow of what they were able to accomplish working together and from turning a sure disaster into a rousing success had worn off by the following morning, however, as concern about the outright assault being perpetrated by Anders Lindgren and CWF returned to the forefront of everyone's thoughts.

A short time after the conclusion of Sunday pasta, Granny Suzy summoned her two sons to her kitchen table. As Little John finished cleaning up following changing the oil on the Continental, he saw his dad and his uncle Anthony go into Granny Suzy's house, both with stern looks on their faces. He could hear his younger cousins playing hide and seek in Uncle Anthony's yard to the east, and the thump of the ball as Dominic played basketball on the driveway to his west. His mom was in the house giving Bella a bath.

Little John walked over to the trash barrel to dispose of the empty oil cans. The barrel was almost full, they would have to burn it in the next day or two. He looked over to Granny Suzy's house and he could see the three of them through the kitchen window, sitting at the table having what appeared to be an animated conversation. His Uncle Anthony was smoking a cigarette, a habit he had just recently picked up, and was continually running his hands over his head as he listened to Granny Suzy talk.

From where he was at, Little John couldn't hear what was being said, but he knew if he walked to the west side of Granny Suzy's house, because the kitchen window was open to let in the evening breeze, he would probably be able to overhear their conversations. He was conflicted about this, because he knew it wasn't right to spy on people like that, especially his parents. But, his dad had been unusually stressed recently, and he was concerned about him. Little John knew his dad hadn't been sleeping much and had been eating even less.

Little John slowly made his way over to the side of Granny Suzy's house, putting his back against the bricks which were cool in the early evening air. He bent down to tie his shoes, and if anyone caught him there he would just tell them he was resting for a second after working on the car. From where he was at, he was able to catch most of the conversation going on in the nearby kitchen.

"...just found out Enzo Losasso didn't make it," Anthony was saying.

"What? He didn't make it?" Suzy gasped, her mouth falling wide open.

"No. I just got a call from his brother, Pete. He said Enzo never woke up from the beating they gave him."

Anthony let that sit with his mother and brother for a moment before continuing.

"And then what they did to us, breaking into the greenhouse and destroying everything? We're fortunate we were able to pull off the wedding the way we did. But how much are we supposed to take."

There was a break in the conversation here, and Little John imagined his dad looking down the way he often did when he was deep in thought. His dad was a measured man, always weighing his words carefully, even with those closest to him. It could be infuriating for some waiting for him to speak, when the rest of the family tended to be hot tempered and apt to fly off the handle at any moment. It was a trait Little John had inherited from his dad, however, and he appreciated the thought his dad put into every word.

"It ends now," Big John finally spoke, and Little John could picture his dad looking directly into his uncle's eyes the way he did when he came to a decision. "We knew Anders wasn't going to take us leaving lightly, but I didn't think this would be his response. I had heard rumors that his past wasn't squeaky clean, but I didn't realize he was as big of a thug as he turned out to be. And, I thought with us being partners with the Scaglias, it would have discouraged any kind of reaction like this. But I was wrong, the Big Swede is obviously not afraid of them. To be honest, I'm surprised Jack hasn't retaliated yet."

"I am, too," Granny Suzy said. "I was for sure when they first blew up the truck on Little John and Joey that they would do something."

"Me, too. Maybe they're not as tough as everyone thinks," Anthony said.

"No, that's not it," John said. "I really do think Jack is trying to keep our partnership as legitimate as he can. I believe him when he says they're trying to get out of that world. But, when you sleep with pigs, you're going to get muddy. I understood that when we agreed to become partners with them, that the day would come when we would be presented with a scenario where we would have to decide if there was a line we were willing to cross.

"I'm an honest, God-fearing man, but I also have my limits. You can only spit in my face so many times before I'm going to react."

The kitchen table was silent for a moment before Little John heard Anthony start laughing.

"What did I say that was funny, Anthony?"

"I can't believe you'd let someone spit in your face more than once." That brought laughter from both Big John and Granny Suzy.

"So, little brother, what are you going to do?"

"I'm going to go talk to Anders tomorrow, try to reason with him," John said, weighing his words carefully. "If that doesn't work, if he's still going to take a hardline about this, then..." he trailed off then, going silent.

"Then what?" Suzy asked. "Are you going to kill him, John? Are you going to lose your soul over business?"

"If I have to, yes."

"Oh, Marone!" Suzy said, exasperated. "That's not you, Johnny. You're no gangster, no killer. You're not the Scaglias." "They blew up the truck my son was riding in, Ma," John answered back, angrily. "What kind of man am I if I let that slide? They're threatening my family, your family. Am I supposed to just let that go?"

"It's not worth throwing your life away over." "That's where you're wrong, Ma. It is."

"Anthony, say something to your younger brother. Tell him he can't do this."

The room was silent for a beat, and then Little John could barely hear his uncle say, "I think he's right, Ma."

"Oh, Marone," Suzy exclaimed again. "Not you, too."

"If he won't listen to reason, then I'll help you do it, John," Anthony said. "You won't have to do it alone."

"You don't have to do that, Anthony. I can handle it."

"No. We'll do it together."

"I'm not listening to this," Suzy said. "You two are being stunads. I don't want to hear this. Get out of my house."

"Ma..." John started.

"No, get out. Now."

Little John could hear the chairs scrape on the floor as his dad and uncle pushed back from the table. Not wanting to be caught listening in, he quickly but quietly made his way up the driveway to the Continental and kneeled down to try to shield himself.

Little John watched as his dad and uncle stepped from the side of the house and paused under the big oak tree in Suzy's backyard.

"If it comes down to it, I want you to let me do it," Anthony said.

John looked at his brother, and he shook his head. "No, Anthony. This is my idea. I'll do it."

John started to walk away but Anthony grabbed him by the shoulder and spun him around. It was the most forceful thing Little John had ever seen his uncle do.

Anthony put his hands on both of his brother's shoulders and looked at him square in the face.

"Listen to me, John, and don't say a word. Capisce?" John nodded his head. "You're my little brother, and I love you. I've always appreciated you taking the lead on all of this. You're more of a leader than I am, and people follow you. But you're still my younger brother. So, you have to listen to what I say.

"If Anders doesn't compromise, if we have to take this to a different level, I have to be the one to do it. Capisce? You can help, and I want you to help, but I have to be the one to do it."

"You really don't have to do this," John said. "I can handle it myself."

"This isn't a negotiation. Understand? This is the way it has to be."

"No, Tony. It was my idea, I should..."

Anthony shook his younger brother violently. "Stop. I'm going to be the one. I've been thinking about this for a while now. I already have a gun."

"You have a gun?"

"Yeah, I have a gun. It's in a coffee can, wrapped in rags, behind my toolbox in the garage. I've had it there for a while now. Ever since Ma told us about what Anders tried to do that day in the office. Just in case something like this came up. So, stop negotiating with me. This is the way it's going to be."

John stared at his older brother for a moment, before finally nodding his head.

"Good. Now if it comes down to it, I need you to help plan it, so I don't end up in jail, or dead. Got it?"

"Okay," John nodded. "Okay."

Anthony finally let go of his brother's shoulders, and then took a step back. He looked up at the sky, which was colored with streaks of orange as the sun settled in for the night. "What a beautiful evening it is, no? Look at that sky."

John took a look up as well, and barely noticed as Anthony stumbled back a half-step, putting his hand out to steady himself against the trunk of the tree.

"Anthony, are you okay?" John asked as all of the color drained from his brother's face.

"I'm fine," Anthony said as he slumped further into the tree. "I'm just tired. Maybe need a drink of water."

"I'll get the hose, Stay right there." John said. "Do you smell that?" Anthony asked.

"Smell what."

"That smell. It smells like burning hair."

"What are you talking about."

"You can't smell that? Huh," Anthony again looked at the sky. What was left of the day's sunlight seemed to illuminate his face. Without taking his eyes off the sky, Anthony reached out and grabbed his brother's forearm, keeping him close. "Listen Johnny, can you hear it?"

"Hear what, Anthony? I don't hear anything."

"You can't hear the angels playing the trumpets? It's so beautiful," Anthony finally lowered his eyes, meeting his brothers. "Life is so beautiful."

With that, Anthony Donato felt a hammer hit him in the chest as he pitched forward, landing at the base of the tree he had helped his father plant 30 years earlier.

CHAPTER 5

The days leading up to Anthony Donato's funeral were a nightmare, but they paled in comparison to the event itself.

Anthony was dead by the time he hit the ground at the base of the big oak tree, his heart exploding inside of his chest. The paramedics didn't even bother trying to revive him when they arrived, instead, just helping the coroner load up the body and take it away. And that wasn't the easiest of tasks, as his newly widowed wife Mary Ann held tight to his lifeless body, her wails of agony heard blocks away.

A heavy cloud of sadness and misery hung over the Donato compound as arrangements were made to put the beloved son, husband, brother and father to rest. Mary Ann was inconsolable, refusing to leave her bedroom, the bedroom until recently she had shared with her Anthony for more than 25 years, not even to eat. Jimmy, her oldest son who had recently moved into his own apartment in nearby Westminster, returned to run the household and he was the only one she allowed to see her.

Grandma Suzy was also nearly catatonic with grief. She didn't even have the energy to cook for the visitors that came to share in the mourning; that task fell mainly to Suzy's daughter Lucille and Big John's wife Milly.

John Donato did his best to lead the family during this time, making all the arrangements and greeting the guests. But it was easy for his son, Little John, to see his father wasn't right. Little John thought that it was more than just mourning for his older brother; it also had to do with the other situation, what to do about Anders Lindgren. The final conversation that Anthony and Big John had was about doing something drastic – Little John had no doubt they were talking about killing Lindgren, at the very least putting the fear of God into him.

But Little John could see that his father was having trouble getting through normal day-to-day functions. The idea that he could do something like take on Lindgren seemed ridiculous. Big John Donato was in no shape to do any such thing; he would end up in the ground of Crown Hill Cemetary next to his brother.

Anthony Donato's rosary and funeral mass was held at The Nativity of the Blessed Mother Church and the interment at Crown Hill. The Donato plot of graves was just south of where Charlie Salardino's ceremony was held nearly 20 years earlier. While this didn't match the pomp and circumstances of Salardino's, it was still an impressive affair with dozens of beautiful floral arrangements and nearly 100 mourners gathered graveside. Father Aldo Leopore officiated, delivering remarks that brought tears to even the most hardened men in the crowd, a crowd that included Raffaele, Jack and Tano Scaglia.

It didn't go unnoticed that the largest arrangement was sent by Anders Lindgren and the "CWF Family."

After the graveside ceremony and following the procession of mourners throwing roses and dirt on top of the casket, as the workers prepared to lower Anthony into the ground, Mary Anne flung herself on top of her husband's casket, pounding the polished mahogany while screaming at the top of her lungs, cursing God because he took her husband.

This went on for several minutes, with Jimmy Donato unable to calm his mother down. Finally, Jimmy turned to his cousins Joey Carabetta and Little John Donato and asked for their help, the three of them lifting Mary Anne off the casket and carrying her into a nearby car before the procession headed back to the Donato compound for the final gathering of mourners.

Mary Anne, who was given a valium that she washed down with half a bottle of vodka in the car, slept through the ensuing gathering, which everyone agreed was one of the finest wakes they had ever attended. Granny Suzy had recovered enough to oversee the preparation of the food for the event as steaming platters of cavatelli in red sauce, sausage and meatballs and farm-fresh vegetables, crusty bread and trays and trays of canoli, sfogliatella and other sweets were served nonstop for more than four hours.

Little John Donato felt like he was sleepwalking through the proceedings; to be honest he had felt like that ever since he watched his uncle collapse at the base of the big oak tree. It was all too surreal. Death was something new to him. Little John believed in God and the afterlife, and he was sure his uncle was in Heaven. Which was great for him. But the people Uncle Anthony had left behind were in misery. Aunt Mary Anne was a crazy person, and he wouldn't be surprised if she would have to be committed at some point. His cousin Jimmy, his closest friend in the world, was a shell of himself, the usual confidence he exuded was completely absent. They had barely spoken since Anthony's death, his usually exuberant cousin unable to mutter but a few words here and there. Little John was glad to see that Jimmy had stepped up and taken control as the head of his immediate family, but he was worried the fire, the spark that had defined who Jimmy was, may have been extinguished.

And then there was his father, Big John Donato. Little John was most worried about him. Although Big John had done everything that was required of him as the patriarch of the Donato clan and the unquestioned, even if it was unnamed, leader of the Italian growers, the toll that Anthony's death had exacted from him was almost incalculable. Most of Big John's hair had turned white overnight, and he had easily lost 20 pounds and looked extremely pale. He barely spoke at home, and Little John was sure his father hadn't slept since that horrible day when he watched his brother drop dead in front of him.

And, there was still the Anders Lindgren problem. Little John was the only one, outside of Granny Suzy, Big John and the recently deceased Anthony, who knew what had been discussed, and decided, that fateful day. In the state he was in, there was no way his father could take on a field mouse, much less the monster Anders Lindgren appeared to be.

Not to mention, Little John didn't want his father to do that anyway and possibly face eternal damnation. As much as Little John believed in the glory of Heaven, he also feared the thought of Hell. Murder was a mortal sin, one that condemned you to an afterlife absent God. The Church preached about forgiveness of sins, but Little John wasn't sure that worked all the time. How could you be forgiven if you knew you were committing a sin and did it anyway? Little John didn't necessarily buy that, in that case you could simply be forgiven if you ask.

But Little John also understood why his father had reached the conclusion he had. Family's livelihoods, families that they loved and cared for, were at risk. People's lives were at risk. Although Anders Lindgren hadn't done the deed himself, Little John was convinced the Big Swede had caused the death of his uncle.

These thoughts weighed on him heavily as he grabbed a folding chair and made his way to sit by Father Leopore, who was sitting by himself under the shade of the big oak tree.

"Hello, John. How are you doing?" the father asked as he finished off the final bites of a pistachio cannoli, wiping his hands on his black pants.

"I'm okay, Father. Just sad."

"It's okay to be sad, son. Losing someone you love is hard, even if you believe they are in a better place," Leopore said. "Death is always hardest on the ones left behind."

Little John nodded, and then put his head down. Father Leopore let the young man sit there in silence, putting his hand on his back in comfort. After a short while, the Father noticed big tears dropping out of Little John's eyes into the dirt at the base of the tree.

The two sat there like that for several minutes, until Little John raised his head, wiped his eyes and looked at the priest.

"Can I ask you something, Father?"

"Of course, my son, you can ask me anything."

Little John looked back at the ground of a second before seemingly gathering himself, and then looked at the priest directly in his eyes.

"Is it okay, in God's eyes, to do something wrong, if it's for a good reason?"

This question caught the priest by surprise. He was expecting a question about the afterlife, or Heaven, or something along those lines. This question about morality, from someone so young, caught him off guard.

"What do you mean?"

"I mean, is it okay to do something you know is wrong, a sin even, if it's for the greater good?"

Father Leopore looked at Little John, trying to read his face. "What are you thinking of doing?"

Little John shook his head. "No. Nothing. I'm just asking. You always preach that God is forgiving, that all you have to do is ask and your sins will be forgiven. Is that true? What if you know what you are doing is wrong, and you do it anyway? Will you still be forgiven?"

Leopore leaned back and thought for a moment before answering.

"That's not an easy question. The Bible tells us in Hebrews that if we sin willfully, knowing the truth, then there no longer remains a sacrifice for sins, and we can expect to be judged with 'fiery indignation.' Some would argue that means that if you know something is a sin, and you do it anyway, you lose the right to be forgiven," Father Leopore paused here. "But others argue that isn't exactly correct. What it means is if you continually sin, knowing it is wrong, then you endanger your ability to be forgiven. That goes against a basic principle of the church, the forgiveness of sin. You can argue that all sin, to a degree, is willful sin.

"Like I said, there's not an easy answer."

John took that in and seemed to think about it for a moment. "I don't know what that means." He shook his head before meeting the priest's eyes again. "What do you think, Father?"

Father Leopore blew out his breath before answering.

"What do I believe? Well, I believe the most basic principle of a good Christian moral life is that we are all made in the image of God. And He is all that is good. But God also gave us free will, which is a wonderful gift. But by giving us free will, humans often do what is wrong, even if they know it's wrong. Is there ever a good reason to do something wrong? I think you have to ask yourself, 'Is what I'm going to do a moral act?' In other words, do the ends justify the means? An act can be wrong, but can also be morally good if the intention, or final result, is good. For an act to be morally good, one's intention must be good.

"So yes, I think it is possible to be forgiven for doing something bad, or wrong, if your intention is good."

That answer seemed to take a weight off the young man, who visibly relaxed. "Thank you, Father."

"Now listen, John, that doesn't mean you can just go do whatever you want and you will be forgiven if you ask. Do you understand that?"

"Yes, father. I understand." John rose from his chair and embraced the priest. "Thank you again."

Father Leopore watched as John walked away and a sense of dread overcame him. He truly believed what he had told him. But he wondered, what had he just given the young man permission to do?

CHAPTER 6

Joey Carabetta watched as his young cousin spoke with the priest and was troubled. It appeared to be a serious conversation, with Little John carrying the weight of the world on his shoulders. Joey didn't like the priest; he was either a closet fanook or a liar, using his collar to get close to all the young girls in some kind of perverted game. But Joey knew Little John looked up to the priest, and wasn't surprised that he sought out his counsel.

It had been an interesting couple of months for Joey Cars. After having the situation in Grand Junction, when someone – who's he kidding? He knew who did it, that fat ass half albino Swede Lindgren - blew up his delivery truck, Joey was upset. He couldn't stop thinking that if they hadn't lingered a bit over their breakfast, he and Little John could have been in the truck when it exploded.

The night of the explosion he was sitting at Nettie's Place, drinking anisette and plotting revenge when Gaetano Scaglia sat down on the stool next to him. Joey didn't look up at him, but the older man leaned in close enough that he could smell his aftershave.

"Hey kid, how you doing?" Tano asked, gesturing to the bartender who brought him over a whiskey in a short glass.

Joey had been around Tano a bit since becoming a driver for Bel Fiore but had never really had a conversation with him before. Tano hung out a lot at Nettie's, overseeing a barbooth game they ran most nights. Plus, Joey thought he might be sleeping with Nettie's daughter Simona.

"I'm fine," Joey said under his breath, his eyes never leaving the bottom of the shot glass in front of him. "Never better."

"Ha," Tano laughed and slapped him on his shoulders. "Everyone in this room can see how pissed off you are, and for good reason. You almost got your greasy ass cooked this morning."

Joey Cars finally looked up at Tano, jaw clenched. "I said I'm fine."

"Easy kid," Tano said, a big smile on his face. "What are you drinking, anisette? Eww, get rid of that crap. Let me get you a whiskey."

"You don't have to do that. Nettie never charges me."

"I know. She don't charge me neither. Look, I wanna talk to you. I know what you're thinking; you're thinking about getting revenge on Lindgren for what he did. And you should be wanting to get payback. You wouldn't be Sicilian if you wasn't. But I'm telling you now, you ain't going to do that."

"And why not?"

"Because that's not what we want you to do," Tano said, knocking back the rest of his whiskey while gesturing for two more. "Look, kid, we've got plans for Lindgren, and for CWF itself. You think we're going to let that fantasma get away with doing something like that? You stunad?"

Joey shook his head.

"No, you're not stunad," Tano said. "I've been watching you. I like what you're made up of. I want you to stick close to me moving forward, okay? Does that work for you?"

Over the next couple of weeks Joey spent more and more time with Tano, who was always on the move. When Joey would get done with his job driving the delivery truck during the day, he would go home and shower, and then meet up with Tano either at Nettie's or Danilo's. Most of the time he would stay in the background, only making his presence known when Tano would call on him for something, whether it was getting him some cigarettes or fetching drinks.

Eventually, Tano had Joey stop working the delivery trucks all together and he became Tano's personal driver on a full-time basis. That suited Joey just fine, who was bringing in twice as much scharole doing that than he had with his day job. And Joey really liked Tano. The big man treated him well and was very charismatic. Everyone wanted to be around him. Despite the smushed nose, which was hardly noticeable after the surgery, Tano was very handsome and women threw themselves at him. Joey was happy to get the residuals.

But he also saw Tano's dark side. Joey often drove him to do collections, and he quickly learned it wasn't wise to owe Tano money. At first Joey just drove and observed on these collections, but eventually Tano had Joey participate as well. And at some point, Joey took over the job of being the muscle on these errands, with Tano sitting back and watching. It turned out Joey was naturally inclined to this task, and he was gaining a reputation as someone to be feared.

His relationship with Tano also allowed Joey to observe the rest of the Scaglias as well. The father, Raffaele, still commanded a ton of respect but it was obvious that he was slipping, often forgetting simple things. Joe, the youngest, wasn't around much, living in California for much of the time. He came in for one weekend and seemed to be a person of no consequence. He carried no real weight in the family, spending most of his time as his father's handmaid. There was concern that the youngest Scaglia was an addict, something that was infamnia in Italian families.

There was no question that Jack Scaglia was the ruler of the family. The eldest of the Scaglia boys, Jack had a presence that preceded him wherever he went. He still showed the proper respect to his father, but all decision making fell to Jack.

Joey thought Tano might harbor a tinge of jealousy toward his older brother, but he definitely looked up to Jack and showed him the proper respect.

And Jack had the respect, or maybe it was fear, of the neighborhood. On the nights when Joey and Tano spent their time at Danilo's, there was a steady procession of people coming in and out to see Jack, whether it was on business or just to pay respect. Neighbors, local businessmen, politicians, police and firemen, religious leaders all wanted to have an audience with Jack Scaglia. And Jack Scaglia welcomed them all. He was especially attentive to the people from the surrounding community. The working men who needed a little extra to pay rent this month, or the widows who were having trouble keeping their heat on. Jack welcomed them all, and they all left knowing their place in the neighborhood was safe, at least until next month's bill showed up.

One night, Danilo's even hosted Frank Sinatra, who was in town to perform a concert in Denver. They sat Sinatra at the big booth in the back, away from the star-struck patrons. Sinatra, who had a pair of beautiful showgirls with him, one for each arm, insisted that Jack join him for dinner. For the next couple of hours the men shared stories and plates of cavatelli and calamari, along with several jugs of homemade red wine. By the time they were done Sinatra could barely stand, and Jack had Joey drive the singer and his companions to the hotel they were staying in downtown. After helping Frank to his room, a sloppy Sinatra offered Joey an opportunity to spend some time with one of the girls.

Joey was tempted, and who wouldn't be? The girl was gorgeous, with platinum blonde hair and a body that defied nature. The pope himself would be tempted. And Joey's biggest weakness was women, always had been and always would be. But Joey felt like taking Sinatra up on the offer would somehow be a violation of the job the Scaglia's had given him. He didn't want to disappoint them, especially Jack, who had asked him personally to drive Mr. Sinatra to the hotel.

Joey took one final look at the showgirl, who was sprawled on a couch in the suite's sitting room, already half out of her sparkly dress. One of the straps had fallen off her shoulder, exposing a beautiful breast with a button-shaped pink nipple. "I'm sorry Mr. Sinatra, but I'm going to have to pass."

"Suit yourself. You're missing out," Sinatra said, draping a heavy arm over

Joey's shoulders while stuffing a couple hundred-dollar bills into his jacket pocket. "Tell Jack I had a great time tonight, and if he ever needs anything, just have him reach out."

The drive back to Danilo's that night was a difficult one, not because of traffic or drink or anything like that. Joey was lamenting the opportunity he passed up, but as soon as he walked back in the doors of the restaurant, he knew he had made the right choice. Jack, who was sitting at the end of the bar next to his father, saw Joey come in and gave him a slight nod. Jack then called over Tano, who was holding court at a nearby booth, and whispered something in his younger brother's ear. They both looked up at Joey and seemed to assess him, before Tano straightened up and returned to his audience.

No one said anything to Joey for the rest of the night, but he knew he had passed a big test. He was treated with a lot more respect, and trust, moving forward.

Now, he watched as his cousin stood and embraced the priest he had been having a conversation with. Little John grabbed the folding chair he had been sitting on and headed toward the working garage behind the houses, Granny Suzy's two dogs, Lady and Tramp, following behind him, their tails swinging lazily in the afternoon sun. Joey Cars also followed behind but at a distance, careful to make sure his cousin didn't see him.

Little John went through the big rolling door at the front of the garage and placed his chair in the spot where the rest would be stacked up following the end of the wake. He bent down and scratched each dog behind their ears in turn, receiving appreciative face licks for the effort. Little John filled a large bowl with water from the sink in the garage and placed it on the floor for the dogs, who greedily buried their noses to get a drink.

Little John took a look around the garage, which was closer to a utility building than an actual garage, but they all called it the garage. There were several cars in various states of repair, along with an Allis-Chalmers tractor that had both of its back wheels off in the rear of the building. It smelled like motor oil and grease, and Little John spent a great deal of time working on various projects here. There were several rolling toolboxes throughout, and a huge metal shelving unit on the back wall that had all sorts of different tools and parts and what not located on it. Uncle Anthony's personal toolbox was also on that shelving, three shelves up just above waist level.

Joey Cars watched from the shadows just outside the garage as Little John went to the toolbox and opened the various drawers, looking for a specific tool but not appearing to find it. He appeared to get frustrated and slammed the main drawer closed with such force that the heavy toolbox actually moved a bit, knocking over a couple of coffee cans that were next to it. The contents of those cans, various nuts and bolts and nails and whatnot, spilled onto the ground and Johnny turned and threw one of the cans as hard as he could against a nearby wall. Little John slumped down to the ground, breaking down in tears.

He sat that way for several minutes before picking himself up, wiping his eyes and retrieving the coffee can and putting the contents on the floor back in it. Little John went to place the can back next to the toolbox, when something caught his eye. He reached behind the tool box, bringing out another coffee can. Joey Cars watched as his cousin reached his hand in the can, pulling out a wad of shop rags that were obviously wrapped around something. Little John unfolded the rags, exposing a small, short-nosed pistol, dark and ominous looking. Little John stared at it for a good minute, before taking the gun and shoving it in his pants behind his back and making sure it was covered by his shirt. He then put the rags back in the coffee can and put the can back behind the toolbox. Little John turned and took a look around, not noticing Joey Cars who had moved back even deeper in the shadows.

CHAPTER 7

Big John Donato watched the last visitor drive away, the wake for his big brother Anthony finally coming to an end. The sun was just starting to set, leaving the late fall sky a combination of dark and light; a brilliant orange horizon broken by a line of purple clouds, the color of an angry bruise on an otherwise flawless canvas. He found that appropriate, for all the beauty and wonder that this world possessed it was still full of pain that you couldn't get away from.

John Donato had always shouldered a lot of responsibility during his relatively short life. The death of his father when he was just a child forced him to grow up early, and while Anthony was always by his side, his older brother seemed to defer to John in many ways. He would make the hard decisions, always with Anthony's support, but still, it was his call. Even in the move away from CWF to Belle Fiore, it was John who took the reins. The majority of the Italian group wouldn't have left without his leadership, so he felt particularly responsible for what was happening. Now, there were two of them six feet in the ground – Enzo Losasso and his brother Anthony.

John blamed Anders Lindgren for both of their deaths. There was no doubt that Lindgren's men were behind the beating that left Enzo Losasso mortally wounded; they had laid a bouquet of carnations next to his battered body after delivering the beating that the cops were calling a mugging, even though Enzo still had his wallet on him. And John blamed Lindgren for Anthony's death the same as if he had pulled a trigger himself. The stress that Anthony felt was like a ticking time bomb in his chest; it was only a matter of time before it did him in.

That's not even taking into account that Lindgren's actions had put his son, Little John, in danger when he blew up their delivery truck in Grand Junction at the start of all of this. That should have been enough to spur John into action, but he had waited, hoping he was wrong and hoping that things would get better. Or, if he was completely honest, he was hoping that the gangsters he had crawled into bed with would take care of it.

With the departure of all the mourners, the Donato homestead was eerily quiet. Anthony's widow, Mary Ann, was well sedated and resting in her home, Jimmy and the rest of Anthony's kids looking after her. John's mom, Suzy, had also retired to her home, finally allowing herself time to grieve the loss of her oldest child. John's family was safe in their home; last he had checked his wife Milly was taking a bath and Bella was fast asleep surrounded by an army of her favorite stuffed animals. Dominic actually had asked to go home with his Aunt Lucille and Uncle Paskey, which they had allowed. John was a little surprised that Johnny wasn't around and he wasn't sure where his oldest son was, but he was kind of glad he wasn't. What Big John was planning on doing wasn't something Little John should see.

John gathered up the remaining folding chairs and tables and stored them in the garage and then took a cold beer out of the refrigerator near its office. John popped the top and then sat down on one of the chairs in the break area, taking a long swig as he contemplated what he was going to do next.

Anders Lindgren had to be stopped. John was convinced now that the Big Swede wasn't going to quit until he destroyed Bell Fiore and all of its families. And John knew there was only one way to stop Lindgren. It was a big step up, what John was contemplating, but he didn't see any way around it. And because of what Lindgren had done to his immediate family, John felt that it fell to him now. He had never done anything even remotely close to what he was contemplating, but he also knew he could do it.

John finished off the beer in a one giant swallow, stood up and tossed the bottle in the trash and then walked over to the far wall of the garage where Anthony kept his toolbox. He reached behind it, feeling for the coffee can his brother said was hidden behind there. For a moment John thought it was missing; it had been pushed well behind the toolbox and he barely grazed it with his fingers. But the can was there, and John was able to grab it and bring it out. He reached in and pulled out the rags, expecting to find the gun underneath them. But the gun was missing.

Maybe it's the wrong can, John thought, and he moved the toolbox to the side to get a better look if there was anything else behind it, but there wasn't. There was another coffee can off to the side a bit, but it was filled with random screws and nails and such. John went back to the rags he had taken out of the first can and shook them, thinking maybe the gun had become entangled in them and he had just missed it, but he knew that wasn't the case. The rags weren't heavy enough to be hiding a firearm.

"Huh," John thought. "That's strange." He couldn't imagine where the gun had gone to; no one was supposed to know about its existence except for him and Anthony. John moved the toolbox back into place and then looked around, wondering if he had overlooked something.

Maybe this was God's way of stopping John Donato doing the thing he didn't want to do.

John shut the lights off and closed the door to the garage, wondering what to do now. Maybe Anthony had misspoke; maybe the toolbox the gun was hidden behind wasn't one in the main garage, maybe it was in the garage of his home. John walked over to Anthony's house, which was eerily silent and felt like it wasn't whole. He opened the door to the attached two car garage and went in, looking around for a toolbox, or a coffee can, or even a gun that was somehow left out. But he didn't see anything like that. Besides the two family cars, the only other things in the garage was the kids bikes, some yard equipment and a little plastic pool. That made sense; Anthony did all of the work on his cars in the main garage.

John left Anthony's house and then made his way to Suzy's, even though he knew that would be a futile effort. There was no toolbox in him mom's single car garage, and there definitely wasn't a gun. But he checked anyway, opening the door and flicking on the light. Everything appeared to be in its proper place. Everything, that was, except for his mom's Lincoln. Which was missing.

That was when he knew exactly where the gun was, and why he hadn't seen Little John recently.

CHAPTER 8

Anders Lindgren waited patiently as his standard poodle, Axel, lifted its leg and pissed on the wrought iron fence that surrounded the three-story red brick house at the southeast corner of 8th Avenue and Logan Street, and he laughed to himself. It was as if his beloved dog knew who resided behind the fence in the late Georgian Revival-style home with the two-story Roman Ionic colonnade topped by a widow's walk that was the envy of Denver's high society. Lindgren wondered if Colorado Governor Stephen McNichols was watching as he encouraged his other poodle, Freja, to follow the example of her brother and do her business on the corner of the property, but she just sniffed at it before pulling on her lead, anxious to return to her own nearby home.

Lindgren loved those two dogs, born from the same litter three years prior. They were magnificent creatures, black as the night and unbelievably intelligent. He kept them in a fancy cut that required weekly trips to the groomer, but he felt like it was worth it. At 65 years old, Lindgren had made more than a small fortune, and if he wanted to spoil his dogs, then he would.

When the dogs were done, Lindgren headed back to his residence a few blocks to the west of the Governor's mansion. He had moved into the Cheesman Park neighborhood in the mid 1940s, partly because of his love of the home now occupied by the Governor. Back then it was owned by the Boettcher family, which had built a financial empire around the turn of the century, and Lindgren felt like it was the finest house in all of the Rocky Mountains. Lindgren wanted to be as close to it as possible. His home, a two-story Queen Anne-style mansion, wasn't quite as elaborate, but was still one envied by many members of Denver's high society, even if that society never fully embraced Lindgren himself.

Lindgren used these nightly walks to clear his head and contemplate the moves he was going to make next. Lindgren had proven to be a shrewd, if not brutal, businessman during his life. His parents had run a successful flower shop back in their native Bunkeflostrand before immigrating to the states when Anders was a newborn just before the turn of the century. They settled in Longmont, Colorado, to be near his mother's family, and they opened up another flower shop, which Anders worked in from the time he was old enough to walk.

And while the family's shop was successful, Anders saw from an early age how people took advantage of his father, who was a gentle man. Anders vowed to never let that happen to him. He grew big and strong. It wasn't long until Anders hooked up with Glenn McGregor's crew, which terrorized Boulder County, performing petty crimes. Lindgren worked as McGregor's muscle, his main enforcer. Lindgren liked to hurt people, and he was good at it.

When prohibition took effect and McGregor started bootlegging, Anders was heavily involved. They made a lot of money in a short amount of time, and Anders took his share and invested a portion of it back in the family's flower business, which grew almost as quickly as the bootlegging operation. Anders and his father formed Colorado Wholesale Florists in 1925 and used many of the same tactics he used to push liquor to push his carnations.

When Anders felt that McGregor became a liability, he got rid of him. When a rival florist stood in his way of his plans, he got rid of them as well, usually not as permanently as what happened to Glenn McGregor, but it did happen on occasion. Prohibition ended but Lindgren's involvement in the criminal underworld didn't, as he ran loansharking and brothels throughout Boulder County.

CWF, meanwhile, continued to expand and became one of the top floral distribution centers in the entire west. At some point CWF got involved with the group of Italian florists, and Lindgren was more than happy to take them in. He didn't feel like they were the smartest group, so his arrangement with them, like it was with most of the growers that Lindgren utilized, was heavily one sided. He made sure everyone made just enough so that they wouldn't complain, but he was still taking advantage of them any way he could.

Then those pain-in-the-ass Donatos came along, the two sons and their spitfire mother. Lindgren actually admired the woman – she was tough as nails and attractive to boot. He tried to fuck her one time, but she resisted, and Lindgren shook it off. What did he care? He had plenty of whores who he could use anytime he wanted.

Then the Donatos came and tried to work out a better deal for themselves and the rest of the dagos and Lindgren wasn't going to have anything to do with that. Where were they going to go? CWF ruled the flower industry in the Rocky Mountains. If they left, he would crush them and take back whatever was left at a more advantageous rate than before. But then the Scaglias got involved and that really pissed Lindgren off. He still held a grudge against them from back in the prohibition days when they ripped off his stash but instead of going to war with them, McGregor went into business with them. Now they wanted to get involved in flowers? Fuck them. Lindgren took that personally and decided he was going to wipe them out, no matter what it took. Lindgren recruited some of his muscle from the criminal part of his empire to help out, blowing up a truck here and there, destroying some property when needed and even giving a beating to one of the troublemakers. After decades of relatively conflict free living, Lindgren was enjoying the action. He wasn't going to rest until the Italian florists were crushed, and he now was determined to destroy the Scaglias as well.

Lindgren was planning on ramping up his attack, and was helped along by the weak heart of the oldest Donato brother, who recently dropped dead just like his father. His death left the Italian growers in tatters and Lindgren felt like it wouldn't take much to put an end to them in short order. The easiest path to that was to take out the other brother as well and Lindgren had just decided, while his dog was pissing on the Governor's fence, that was going to be his next move. Tomorrow morning he would summon his top enforcer and give him the task of killing John Donato.

Happy with the decision he had come to, Lindgren picked up his pace and hurried toward his house, spurring his dogs along. Two blocks away from home, though, something didn't feel right to Lindgren and he slowed down. Lindgren had learned to trust his feelings, and he was always hyper aware of his surroundings, and something was off about the neighborhood that evening. He couldn't put his finger exactly on it, but he could feel it. It was quiet at that time of the evening, but that wasn't unusual. Two blocks from his home he saw a vehicle that seemed out of place – a bright blue Lincoln Continental under a huge Elm tree, but it was unoccupied at the moment. Lindgren took another look up and down his block, but outside of the unfamiliar car, he didn't see anything that should raise an alarm.

"Come on Anders," he said to himself. "Now is no time to get paranoid."

Lindgren resumed walking, his dogs practically pulling him toward his front door.

CHAPTER 9

Little John Donato watched from the shadows under a group of Colorado Blue Spruce trees on the northeast edge of Cheesman Park as Anders Lindgren made his way up 8th avenue. The Big Swede was hard to miss, a 6-foot-3 phantom walking a pair of huge, black poodles. It was pretty well known that Lindgren lived in one of the huge mansions across the street from the park on 8th, but Little John had no idea which house it was when he had first driven over there earlier that evening. Little John had parked a couple of blocks east of the park, in an alley between Grant and Lincoln Streets, and then walked to Broadway before heading into the park. It was pretty quiet at this time of the night, with most of the families already having packed up and headed home. Little John was happy for the solitude, as it gave him an opportunity to think about what he was doing. When he had left the Donato family compound, there was no doubt in his mind he was going to kill Anders Lindgren. But by the time he had driven to Lindgren's neighborhood, he had calmed down a bit.

As he walked up 8th Avenue, looking for Lindgren's home, he realized he didn't have a real plan. Was he going to go door to door until he found the right one? That didn't seem practical, and someone would probably call the cops on him before he ever found Lindgren. And what was he going to do if he found the right home? Ask to come in, or just shoot Lindgren on his doorstep? Instead, Little John decided to walk over to the park where he saw a bench under a group of big Spruce trees to sit down to think about what he was doing.

Little John was about to give up and head back home when he spotted someone walking west on 8th in the distance. As the person moved closer, Little John realized it was Lindgren. When he spotted the Big Swede, Little John reached down and felt the weight of the pistol in his pocket. He still wasn't sure what he was going to do when Lindgren stopped near the alley where Granny Suzy's Lincoln was parked. Lindgren looked down the alley at the car, and then appeared to survey the surrounding area. Lindgren was acting like he was looking for something specific but not seeing it. After a good minute or two, he shrugged his shoulders and started moving again, crossing the intersection of 8th and Broadway, less than 30 yards from where Little John was sitting in the shadows.

As Little John watched, Lindgren went to a home in the middle of the street, easily the nicest one on the block, and headed up the entry way. Something in the way the man walked, with the arrogance of someone with great power, and those two ridiculous looking dogs, set Little John off again. All of the anger that he had felt towards Lindgren returned. Knowing his Uncle Anthony was dead because of this man, that his own father was on the verge of a heart attack himself because of this man, that Jimmy and his other cousins lost a father because of this man, that his aunt Mary Anne was now a widow because of this man, that his Granny Suzy was heartbroken because of this man...the fire that had driven Johnny to first search out his uncle's gun was back. Little John stood up, took the gun out of his pocket and headed toward the house where Lindgren was just now closing the front door.

Little John didn't even get 10 feet before someone big and strong grabbed him, slamming him down to the ground while saying "What do you think you're doing, kid?"

CHAPTER 10

The air rushed out of the lungs of Little John Donato as he hit the ground hard, the snub-nosed pistol skittering from his hand. The impact was so great that Little John saw stars, but he didn't black out. When he was able to focus, he was peering up into the face of Gaetano Scaglia, flush red with anger, his surgically repaired nose just inches from Little John's own.

"What the fuck is wrong with you?" Tano barked, spittle flying from his mouth and hitting Little John in the face. "You're going to get yourself killed."

"Get off me!" Little John struggled to try to break free from Tano's grasp, but the mobster had a death grip on him. Little John was younger and bigger, but Scaglia was surprisingly powerful.

"Settle the fuck down before I knock your dumb ass out," Tano said. When Little John finally stopped struggling, Tano picked him off the ground and roughly dragged him to the nearby park bench, throwing him onto the seat.

"Don't you fucking move a muscle," Tano pointed a big meaty finger at him before walking over and retrieving the gun, tucking it into his waistband. He then joined Little John on the bench, grabbing him by the shoulder and again asking him "What the fuck is wrong with you?"

"I'm going to kill that bastard," Little John snarled, looking hard at the front door of the house Lindgren had entered. "He's destroying my family. I'm not going to let that happen."

Tano sighed and loosened his grip. "That's not going to happen, kid. Your family is too strong for that. But you getting sent to jail for killing him, or worse yet, you getting killed yourself isn't going to help."

"Well, you guys aren't helping any," Little John sneered at Tano. "Big, tough gangster family getting beaten by a Swede. I thought you Scaglias were supposed to be tough."

Tano slapped him, hard, and Little John saw stars again and slumped to the ground.

"You shut your mouth, kid," Tano said, before picking Little John up and putting him back on the bench. "We're going to handle it."

"Why should I believe you? You guys haven't done shit yet."

Tano looked at the kid and had to admit he had a point. As soon as the first Bel Fiore truck was blown up, Tano had went to Jack wanting to take Lindgren out. But Jack preached patience; he wanted his relationship with the Italian growers to be as above board as possible. Tano understood Jack's position, even if he disagreed with it. For the past half-dozen years Jack had been making moves to make sure the family was as legitimate as possible. Tano didn't really care if they were legitimate or not; he enjoyed being a gangster and thrived on the action. Jack had other plans and wanted to carry the family in that direction. They had interests in greyhound racing, in restaurants and night clubs and in real estate that were as clean as they could be. The flower business was going to be another one of them. But that pale motherfucker Lindgren wouldn't let that happen.

After Enzo Losasso died, however, Jack changed his mind. He finally agreed that the Big Swede needed to be taken care of, and gave his brother the go-ahead. Tano immediately had put things in motion to get it done, but it didn't happen quick enough as the Scaglias were informed about Anthony Donato's death the same evening they had made the decision to move on Lindgren.

Tano didn't blame Little John Donato for being angry; in fact, he totally understood it. He would have reacted the exact same way. He had grown to admire the Donatos during his time working with them. They had an innate toughness in them that he could recognize, both families coming from Potenza like they did. And he knew the Scaglias owed them a debt, from back in his grandfather's day, even if no one would tell them why.

He also really liked the cousin, Joey Cars, and was grooming him to be his right-hand man. That kid was cunning and hard as granite and had shown a knack for the "life." Tano knew Joey really admired his two cousins, Jimmy and Little John, but he didn't see either of them going down a similar path. Jimmy was too clever for his own good, and Little John was too pure of heart, even if he was just planning on killing someone less than five minutes ago.

It was Joey Cars who, after watching Little John retrieve the gun from the garage following Anthony's wake, alerted Tano to the current situation. Joey was currently behind the wheel of Tano's car, two blocks to the north on Broadway.

"Look, kid, you really don't want to do this. Leave this to us, okay? You have my word that we'll take care of it."

Little John looked in his eyes and knew he was telling the truth.

"You better."

Tano had to give it to the kid, he stood his ground. Most kids his age would have broken down by now, the tears streaming down their face. But not Little John Donato – Tano thought his eyes were as dry as an old lady's cunt.

"Quindi, se cerca di convincerti," Tano said. "You've got some balls on you."

At that moment a Packard station wagon came barreling down the street, screeching to a halt in front of the park at 8th and Broadway. Big John Donato jumped out of the driver's side door while Jimmy Donato popped out of the passenger side. They were both frantically looking around, trying to find Little John before he did something he'd regret. Big John started to head up the street toward Lindgren's house when Jimmy turned toward the park and saw Tano waving at him from a park bench, Little John sitting next to him.

Big John looked like he was about to start running when he heard Jimmy say, "Unk." Big John turned back to Jimmy, who nodded toward Little John and Tano. Big John did start running at this point, and when he got to the bench he took his eldest son into his arms.

After a short but intense embrace, Big John stepped back and took a look at his son. Beside a bright red welt on his left cheek, he seemed fine.

"Are you okay?"

"I'm fine, Pop."

"Did you...?" Big John was afraid to ask the question because he didn't really want to know the answer. He figured they had reached his son in time; the street seemed too calm for a murder to have just taken place there. But still...

"No," was all Little John said.

Big John looked over at Tano Scaglia, their eyes meeting. Big John didn't necessarily like the other man; he thought he was uncouth and kind of a thug. But at that moment he knew Scaglia had stopped his son from doing something that he never would have recovered from. He had a new-found respect for the man and mouthed a silent "thank you" to him.

Scaglia silently nodded his head before turning to Jimmy. "I was sorry to hear about your dad. He seemed like a good man when I met him."

"Thank you," Jimmy said quietly, shaking the hand Tano offered to him. Jimmy was surprised to feel something in Tano's hand when he took it, but then realized he was giving him the gun that Little John had brought to the park. Jimmy silently slipped it into his pocket as Tano turned and shook hands with Big John. He then addressed Little John.

"Sorry about the smack, kid," he said, lightly touching the check he had hit just a short time ago. "You've got a lot of heart, more than most people have. Don't let the world take that away from you."

CHAPTER 11

Little John Donato rested his head against the window in the backseat of his dad's station wagon, watching the world go by outside of it without really registering what he was seeing. His mind was racing, going over and over the last couple of hours. Had he really come down to Cheesman Park to kill a man? Would he have actually gone through with it if Tano Scaglia hadn't shown up?

And what to think of Tano Scaglia, the big, bad mobster that everyone was afraid of? Little John admitted he was initially terrified when he looked up and saw that it was Tano who had slammed him to the ground, but anger quickly overcame any fear he may have been feeling. Tano had provided the voice of reason then and, Little John thought, some measure of compassion.

Neither Jimmy nor his father had said anything since they got back in the car and headed back home, both of them silently staring forward through the front windshield. Jimmy, usually always so put together, looked terrible, his hair unkempt and giant bags under his eyes. Johnny's father didn't look much better.

"Hey Pops?"

"Yeah Johnny?"

"I bet you're pretty sore at me right now, aren't you?"

Big John hesitated a bit before answering, concentrating on the road in front of him. LIttle John started to think he actually wasn't going to answer, before his father finally started to reply.

"I'm not, actually. Sure, I'm upset that you would do something so stupid and put yourself in danger. But I understand why you did it. You thought you were doing the best thing for the family, and I can't fault that."

Little John felt an enormous sense of relief hearing his father say that. He was worried that their relationship was forever going to be damaged, but now he understood that wouldn't be the case. It may have changed because of what had occurred, but the love between the two would always be there.

"I have to ask, though, what made you think killing Anders Lindgren was a good idea?" Big John asked as he deftly swerved to miss a sedan that had broken down in the middle of the road.

Little John thought for a second about what he should say, whether he should tell his father that he knew Uncle Anthony was planning on killing Lindgren before he had a heart attack. If he should say that in front of Jimmy, who may have had no idea what his father was contemplating. But Little John decided right then and there that he would be completely honest with not only his father, but Jimmy as well, from this point forward. They were the two men he loved more than any others in this world and he was not going to keep secrets from them. So, Johnny told them about how he listened at Granny Suzy's window that day, overhearing their conversation about what to do with Anders Lindgren, and their plan to take him out. And that, when Uncle Anthony passed away, seeing how it affected Big John, he was worried he was going to have a heart attack himself.

At first, Little John said, he was surprised to hear Big John and Uncle Anthony talk like that. They were two of the most decent men he knew, even more honorable than most priests. To hear them talk about murdering someone was shocking. But the more Little John thought about it, the more he understood it. From the time he was a little boy, back when he was in short pants, he had been taught there was nothing more important than family. Your family was everything, and if you didn't have family, you didn't have anything. The church taught you God came first, but Little John grew to understand that wasn't exactly true; that God should guide you in everything you do, but that sometimes family came before God. God would understand that, and God would always be there. The same couldn't be said for family if someone took that away from you. So, sometimes you put family ahead of God.

And Anders Lindgren was a threat to the Donato family. There was no doubt in Little John's mind that Lindgren was the reason his Uncle had a heart attack, and looking at his dad, he wasn't far behind. Little John said he felt like he had to do something, even if it was as horrible as murder.

God would understand.

"Seeing what this was doing to you, and what it did to Uncle Anthony...I don't know. I had to do something," Little John said softly. "This was all Anders Lindgren's fault. He didn't have to do what he did. If he had just been fair from the beginning, we wouldn't be in this spot.

"I know the church teaches you not to hate, but I hate him. And I wanted to see him pay. I wanted to see him dead."

Big John drove along in silence for a long stretch, thinking about what his son had just told him. The fact that his 16-year-old son felt this way was distressing. That the only solution he could find was to kill someone. What had he done wrong as a father that his son was willing to take another man's life, even if that man was evil, and was a threat to the family. But hadn't he and his brother come to the same conclusion? Why was their decision to take out Lindgren justified, but Johnny's similar thought so wrong?

The drive continued in silence until they made their way back to the Donato compound. It was dark by the time Big John pulled around behind the houses to the utility garage, the sun setting in a brilliant collision of purple and orange that mellowed into a calm, cloudless night where you could see every star in the heavens. Big John turned the car off, telling Jimmy and Johnny to wait while he went into the garage and came back out with three folding chairs, three bottles of Royal Crown and a small hand lantern. He led them to the big oak tree behind Granny Suzy's house, unfolding the chairs and indicating for them to sit down as he used a bottle opener to take the caps off of the RCs.

"Sit down. I want to have a talk with you guys."

Little John and Jimmy took a seat, not sure what to expect. Big John Donato wasn't prone to having talks like this with his children, much less with a nephew like Jimmy. There was no question that Big John loved his family and was a good parent, but he led by example, not through words.

Big John sat himself, taking a big swallow from his cola before starting. The lantern threw shadows across his face, adding to the surreal feel to the whole thing for Little John, who had no idea what his father was about to say.

"I don't have a lot of memories of my father, James," John started as he looked out at the horizon, his eyes not really focused on anything. "He died when I was really young, I think seven or eight. I can remember he had really rough, strong hands from working at the farm. I used to like to put my hand flat into his palm, to measure my hand next to his and I was always amazed at how much bigger his hand was than mine. And I remember he used to let me sit on his lap and act like I was steering the trucks and tractors on the farm. He always used to laugh when we did that, and he had a loud, deep laugh you could hear all over the farm. And he used to sing songs from the old country in a really deep voice that always made me laugh. I can remember him singing to mom, Granny Suzy, and trying to dance with her in our small kitchen."

John smiled at this memory, obviously going back in time in his mind.

"Like I said, I don't remember a lot about him. But I do remember he loved to go fishing in that little creek behind the farm there, you know the one on the north end?" Little John and Jimmy knew exactly what creek he was talking about, fishing and swimming there many times themselves through the years.

"My last memory of him was going fishing with him there, this was maybe a week or two before he died. One of his cousins who also worked at the farm, Mariano Minella, was also there. You know, Old Man Minella? Well, Mariano would say a little prayer every time just before he cast. He would say the prayer, and then just sit there waiting for the fish to bite. Daddy, meanwhile, would work at it, moving up and down the edge of the creek, trying different positions. And on that day, Mariano couldn't pull a fish to save his life. Daddy, meanwhile, had caught three or four in just a short amount of time.

"Mariano was getting more and more frustrated as the day wore on. Finally, after Daddy had pulled out a particularly large fish, Mariano looked up at the sky and cursed God, throwing his pole into the creek before heading back to the farm. This caused Daddy to laugh so hard he almost lost his own pole."

John paused, taking another drink from his soda. "I was mortified. The things Mariano had said, if he had said those same things in church the walls would have come down on top of him. I told Daddy that Mariano shouldn't have said those things about God, but Daddy just shook his head while he continued laughing. He said to me, 'Look, God is great, I love God and praise him every day. He gave us this wonderful world we live in. And he brought your lovely mother to me, and then blessed us with you and your brother and sisters. But you can't expect God to do everything for you. If you expect God just to provide without putting in work yourself, you're going to go hungry.'"

Little John had never heard this story about his grandfather; in fact, he had hardly heard anything about Grandpa James at all, except when Granny Suzy would talk about how he was the most handsome and kindest man she had ever know. Little John had broken out in gooseflesh while listening to the story, and he wasn't sure if it was because the temperature had dropped significantly as the sun had gone down for the night, or if it was because he was hearing about a man who until then had just existed as a photo on Granny Suzy's mantle.

"I'm not sure why I told you guys that story, but it popped into my head as we were sitting here," Big John said. "I know he died well before either of you were ever born. He must seem to you the same way my Grandpa Rocco seems to me, just a memory for other people to have. But what Daddy said that day, about how if you expect God to just provide for you, you were going to be disappointed, always stuck with me."

Granny Suzy opened her back door then, letting Lady and Tramp out to do their business one final time before bedtime. She looked exhausted, the events of the past several weeks catching up with her. She looked over at the group gathered under the big oak tree, putting her hand to her heart.

"My men," she said softly, her eyes moist in the night air. "John, va tutte bene?"

"Si, Mama. Si," Big John answered. "I'm just having a talk with the boys."

Suzy nodded, ushering her dogs back into the house. "It's a beautiful night, but don't stay up too late."

They all wished her goodnight as she went back in the house, and Big John waited until she had turned out the light in the kitchen before beginning again.

"Johnny, I'm sorry I put you in a position where you thought you had to do what you went to do this evening. That was unfair to you and I should never have let it happen. That was a failure on my part as your father."

Little John started to protest, wanting to absolve his father of the guilt he was feeling, but Big John put his hand up to stop him.

"No. It was. But that's not to say I don't understand it. After all, that was the same decision I had come to with my brother." John looked over at Jimmy, who hadn't said anything outside of wishing his grandmother a good nigh,t for several hours.

"And Jimmy, I am so sorry for what you are going through. I can't imagine. Even though I also lost my dad, I was so young when it happened…it's a totally different situation than what you are going through. I want you to know, we are here for you, no matter what you need. You've always treated Johnny like he was your brother, so you are a son to me as much as he is."

A single tear rolled down Jimmy's cheek as he nodded to his uncle. "Thank you," was all he could say.

"Now, back to what happened earlier and the whole Anders Lindgren situation," he turned back to Little John as he said this part. "It is not your place to handle this. I don't care if you think you are doing something to protect the family, or to protect me, it is not your place as long as I'm still here. Do you understand?"

"Yeah, but…" Johnny started, and his dad cut him off again.

"No buts. You two," Big John pointed at his son and Jimmy, "are the future of this family, but for right now, I am the head of it. And you need to respect that. Capisce?"

They both nodded but that wasn't enough. "I want to hear you say it." They both said yes.

"Good. That's settled." Big John sat back in his chair, finishing off his soda. The group sat there for a beat, listening to the crickets play their symphony. It truly was a beautiful night, one that seemed to be in abundance during the fall in Colorado. It was cool out, but pleasant, and Big John felt like he could almost forget the troubles that still faced his family. But before he could, his son reminded him.

"So Pop, what are you going to do about Anders Lindgren?"

That was the question, wasn't it? What to do about Anders Lindgren now? He had made the decision not even two weeks ago to take Lindgren out. But that was before Anthony had died, and his son had gone to kill the man himself. Things had changed since that fateful day and Big John wasn't sure what to do. Big John Donato wasn't a killer; that wasn't his nature at all. But he had no doubt that he could do that, if the future of his family came down to that.

"I'm not sure, son. I'm not sure what the right thing to do is. But, I will do what I have to, to protect this family, to protect the two of you," John said. "I don't think Anders Lindgren is going to stop until he destroys us. That's not the type of man he is. He's made his way in this world taking advantage of others. And that's not right. And I won't allow him to do that to us.

"I'm not a man like Lindgren, someone who takes advantage of people. But I'm also not a pushover, someone you can just bully. I'm stronger than that; our family is stronger than that. I will not allow him to destroy us, and he's mistaken if he thinks he can. What does that mean? I don't know. But like what my Daddy told Mariano Minella all those years ago, that if you wait around for God to provide, you will end up disappointed."

CHAPTER 12

Dressed in fine silk pajamas, Anders Lindgren had started to nod off while watching the Tonight Show with Jack Paar, Axel and Freja already asleep at his feet. The show that evening featured a young comedy duo, Burns and Carlin, doing a bit where David Brinkley was interviewing John F. Kennedy. It was funny, Anders had actually laughed out loud a couple of times, but he was having trouble keeping his eyes open. Although the sofa he was sitting on, a French provincial style three-person seater with lavender cushions, was expensive, it wasn't very comfortable, unlike the big four poster bed Lindgren had upstairs. In fact, his back was sore from sitting on the sofa, so he went through a rather loud and obnoxious stretching routine when he got to his feet.

The noises he made while stretching out his back awoke the dogs, who now were sticking their snouts in his face as he bent over, coming as close to touching his toes as his rather large belly would allow him.

"Yes, yes. You're good dogs. Daddy loves you too."

Lindgren straightened up, going over to the television and clicking the unit off. He then went through the kitchen to the backdoor, the dogs at his feet. He let them out one last time before they would retire to bed, closing the door behind him as the dogs raced into the fenced off backyard. He would give them as much time as they needed to sniff around and pee one final time – they were trained enough to only do their other business on one of the three walks he took them on each day. When they were ready to come in, they would return to the door, scratching at it to let him know they were there.

Lindgren went over to the icebox and took a bottle of vodka out, getting a tumbler from a nearby cabinet and filling it a third of the way. He downed it in one swallow, the ice-cold liquid warming him as it went down. The final drink of the night would help him sleep for a bit; not that he slept much these days anyway. As much as he loved this big house, it was lonely at night. His wife, Juni, had passed away three years ago and, while he didn't necessarily miss her, the house did feel empty without her. He never brought the women he slept with to his home, and rarely did he have one of his men stay the night. He didn't feel the need for bodyguards. Almost all of the illicit activity he was involved in was in Boulder County, and there wasn't any real opposition to his dealings there anyway.

No, the dogs were his only constant companions at home. Maybe he would think about bringing in a new wife. There was the one lady at CWF who worked in accounting who was always friendly towards him, and the dogs liked her when he brought them in the office. She was nice to look at and seemed pleasant. She was probably 35 years younger than him, but he did not care what anyone thought. Yes, he decided, he will ask her to dinner the next time he saw her. A young wife might be good. He had grown stale over the last decade, Lindgren thought. But this business with the Donatos and the Scaglias had reignited something in him.

Uncharacteristically, Lindgren poured himself another drink, downing it quickly before returning the bottle to the icebox. The dogs had not returned to the back door yet, which was surprising. Usually, they quickly peed and then were ready to come back in and go to bed at this point of the night.

Lindgren opened the back door, flicking on the porch light as he stepped out. It was a large backyard, fenced in with a detached two-car garage that opened into the alley in the back right corner. The light at the back door only illuminated the porch, so most of the yard was still enveloped in darkness. There was a motion light on the side of the garage, but it wasn't illuminated.

"Freja? Axel?" Lindgren called out, surprised the dogs didn't immediately come when he flicked on the patio light. "Where are you, pups?"

Lindgren walked to the edge of the porch, peering into the darkness, calling for his dogs again. It was not like them to not come when called; they were well trained and usually completely in sync with Lindgren's commands.

Lindgren took a couple of tentative steps off the porch, calling for the dogs again. The night air was still, and he could hear the traffic on nearby Broadway. He could also faintly hear the sound of a struggle toward the back of his property along the fence line, and maybe a whimper?

Lindgren took another couple of steps into the yard, his eyes adjusting enough so that he could see that the gate next to the garage that opened into the alley was ajar.

That gate was never open. You could only open it from this side of the fence, and he knew he hadn't opened it, so that was odd. He scanned the entire yard and nothing else seemed out of place. The night was still and chilly; Lindgren didn't think it would be long before the first snow started to fall.

"Freja, Axel, come," Lindgren called, but there was still no sign of the dogs. Lindgren didn't see them anywhere in the yard, and he was pretty sure they must have gotten out of the gate. Which was also surprising, because they were so well disciplined that he never worried about them leaving the yard, even with the open gate, unless he commanded them to.

Lindgren shivered in the night air, not sure if it was because of the falling temperature or because of the dawning sense of dread he was feeling. There was definitely some kind of commotion going on just outside of his gate.

"What's out there, huh pups? Something out there?"

Lindgren took a couple of hesitant steps further into the yard, now on alert. "Is someone there? Hello?"

Something crashed hard on the alley side of the fence, causing Lindgren to retreat quickly to the kitchen, grabbing a pistol that he kept in a drawer next to the icebox. He then headed back out into the yard. "If there's someone out there, I want you to know I have a gun and I will use it." He could hear the rising fear in his voice, and he cursed himself for it.

About five feet from the open gate, Anders' feet went out from under him as he slipped on something wet on the grass. He hit the ground hard, but he was able to hold on to the pistol thankfully. Lindgren laid flat on his back for a moment, catching his breath before pushing his way up to a sitting position. There was something viscous and warm covering the grass here, and it appeared almost black when Lindgren dipped his fingers in it before bringing it up to his face.

"Oh no, no, no, no," Lindgren cried as he scrambled to his feet. The dark liquid was blood, and there was a lot of it. "Axel? Freja? Where are you?"

Lindgren rushed through the gate into the alley and found himself in the middle of a bloodbath. The two poodles were in the middle of the alley, playing tug of war with the lifeless body of a big gray rabbit. There was at least three other dead rabbits strewn around the dogs, their dark fur caked with blood.

"What the fuck is this?" Lindgren watched as his dogs ripped the rabbit in half, Axel with its head in his mouth while Freja tossed the hindquarters high into the air. He was relieved that his dogs appeared unharmed but was confused by the scene in front of him. Where did the rabbits come from, and how did they get into his yard? And how did the gate get opened?

"What are you dogs doing?" Lindgren was angry now, the dogs not heeding his call and appearing out of control. Freja had moved on to one of the other rabbits, flinging its dead body high in the air, watching it hit the ground before pouncing on it with her two front feet. Axel, meanwhile, looked right at Lindgren before swallowing the top half of the rabbit he had been wrestling Freja for moments earlier.

This doesn't make sense, Lindgren thought, raising his pistol while surveying the scene in the alley. Although it was dark, everything appeared normal, the streetlights on nearby Broadway casting strange shadows. All of the homes on this alley had detached garages that bordered their properties, but they all appeared closed and undisturbed.

"Is someone there? Hello? If you're there, be aware I have a gun." Lindgren pointed the gun out ahead of him. "If there's someone there, you better show yourself."

Lindgren waited for close to a minute before finally lowering his gun. "Hmph. You are getting paranoid, Anders," he said to himself before turning back to the dogs, wondering how he was going to get them back into his yard.

"Axel, Freja, home," Lindgren hissed, putting gravity in his voice. That seemed to snap the dogs out of their frenzy, as they both quickly went through the fence before sitting at attention just inside the gate.

"Good dogs," Lindgren said, taking one last look around the alley. As he did, Joey Carabetta emerged from the shadows of the garage across the way from Lindgren's property, a nasty looking gun at the end of his extended right hand. Surprise filled Lindgren's face as Joey quickly closed the distance between them, firing the gun when he was about two paces away from the Big Swede.

The explosion of the gun destroyed the silence of the night, the blast catching Lindgren in his right shoulder. Lindgren stumbled backward to the opening in his fence, trying to understand what had just happened. The dogs, Axel and Freja, were growling loudly, but their training had kicked in and they remained frozen in place, waiting for the next command from Lindgren.

Lindgren looked up at his assailant, recognizing the face of a son of one of those dago growers that were a thorn in his side. Lindgren was using his left hand to hold himself erect while trying to raise the gun in his right hand, but it refused to work, his shoulder destroyed by the gunshot. Blood had started to pour freely from his wound, drenching the front of his silk pajamas.

Joey fired his second bullet into Lindgren's substantial gut, and the Big Swede fell to his knees. He let out a groan that was almost subhuman; a guttural sound that silenced the barking of Axel and Freja, who now took a couple of nervous steps backward, whimpering.

Lindgren let out several of these groans; Joey Cars remembered hearing two or three more of them before he put the gun against Lindgren's temple and fired into his brain. The Big Swede collapsed, his torso falling into his yard where his dogs quickly stood over him, their protection coming too late.

The whole thing took less than five seconds, but Joey Cars felt like he had been exposed in the alley for a long time, and the gun blasts had been surprisingly loud. He was anxious to get out of there. Neighbors were beginning to open their windows and back doors to see what was going on in the alley. Joey Cars pulled the collar of his coat up high and his hat down low, hoping the shadows in the alley prevented him from being identified. He dropped the gun next to Lindgren's lifeless body and then sprinted down the alley toward Broadway, where he jumped into the passenger side of a waiting car that sped away, well ahead of the sirens that he could just now hear in the distance.

CHAPTER 13

Raffaele Scaglia escorted the final customers of the night, a young man from the neighborhood and his pretty date, out the front door of Danilo's, waving goodbye and telling them to come back soon before locking the door behind them. The dining room was empty now except for a couple of busboys who were cleaning up, and Jack Scaglia, who sat at the corner of the bar, nursing an amaretto sour, going over the next day's racing form for the Rocky Mountain Kennel Club. The Scaglias had recently been approached about investing in the business, and Jack had discovered he really enjoyed betting on greyhound racing. He was planning on going out to the track in Commerce City for a matinee performance the next afternoon.

It had been a busy night in the restaurant as they served a little more than 200 customers, including a couple of VIPs in a player from the Denver Bears and the mayor of nearby Aurora and his mistress. Ralph patted Jack on the shoulder as he passed him on the way back to the kitchen, telling the busboys they could go home, that he would finish cleaning up. He emerged a short time later with a couple of plates of pappardelle with a Bolognese of pork and beef and a basket of crusty bread, taking a seat in the booth at the front of the restaurant.

Jack grabbed a jug of red wine from behind the bar and joined his father in the booth and the two ate in silence, a Lou Monte song on the radio the only sound in the place. A short time later they heard the back door open as Gaetano Scaglia and Joey Carabetta returned to the restaurant. Tano directed Joey Cars to a seat at the end of the bar, and then went around and grabbed a couple of tumblers and a bottle of scotch. He poured each of them a few fingers of the liquor, telling Joey "Here kid, drink this," as he slammed back his own glass. He then poured them both another, as Ralph got up and headed back into the kitchen, coming back out with another couple of plates of pasta. Tano put the bottle next to Joey, telling him to have as much as he wanted, and then he grabbed his plate of pasta and joined his father and brother in the booth at the other end of the restaurant.

Jack and Ralph waited as Tano dove into the dish, inhaling the pasta while mopping up the sauce with hunks of bread. When he finally finished, he took a deep breath, leaned back and loosened his tie.

"How did he do?" Jack asked while nodding in the direction of Joey Carabetta.

"Great," Tano said while filling up his glass from the jug of wine. "I couldn't have done better myself."

"Good. It's good to finally have this business behind us."

Tano and Ralph nodded in agreement, with Ralph saying, "That Swede was always a pain in the ass. I know when we first partnered with McGregor back when we were running booze with Charlie, he was always causing problems. Hot-headed and always prone to violence. I'm surprised it took this long to come to a head."

"Well, we don't have to worry about him anymore," Jack said.

"No, we don't," Tano agreed as he poured them all another glass of wine. "So, what's next for Bel Fiore, and the Donatos? The rest of the flower growers?"

Jack shrugged his shoulders. "We absorb what we can from CWF, and we move forward. Run the business legitimately. There's no reason for any part of other things we do to touch it. We'll step back, let John Donato run it, and take our piece when there's a profit.

"This is our future, the future of our family. In ten years, fifteen years, we can be completely legitimate if we want to be. This is the path forward."

That was Jack's dream, that by the time he had grandchildren that were old enough to understand things, that the Scaglia family would be completely legitimate. He had no qualms about what his family had done to gain their power and wealth, what he had done himself. His father had done what he had to do for the family. Jack didn't know a man more worthy of respect than Raffaele Scaglia. He was a good father, a good husband and a good friend to people who weren't as fortunate in life. He definitely was not a man to be crossed, but that didn't concern Jack as his son. Sometimes as a man you had to do things that were not so nice, so proper.

Even the Donatos, who at times Jack could admit seemed a little too self-righteous, had a line you did not cross. So yes, the Scaglias had done some horrible things in the advancement of their family. So be it. Jack would not apologize for that. But he didn't want his children, or his grandchildren, to have to make similar choices.

Jack knew that Raffaele was on board with the plan to take the family legitimate; in fact, he was helping steer the family in that direction. He also knew that Gaetano would push back against it. Tano enjoyed being a gangster, and he was good at it. But that's not a way to live a long life. You either end up laying in the morgue, riddled with bullet holes, or in jail, where one night they find you hanging in your cell when they come to do a body count.

No, the Scaglias needed to go legit, and Bel Fiore Flowers was one step in that direction.

But until then, there was still work to be done. Dangerous work. Some of their partners would not agree with the move to legitimacy and would fight to keep what they had and take what the Scaglias had as well.

"So, do you think he has what it takes?" Jack asked Tano, nodding toward Joe Carabetta at the end of the bar.

"Joey Cars? For sure," Tano smiled. "There's no question."

"Good. Keep him close to you, okay?"

"Definitely," Tano said. "You know, he's not the only one in his family that is promising. His younger cousin, Little John Donato..."

"No!" Raffaele said, angrily. "You keep that boy out of it."

"Okay, pops. I was just saying he's a tough kid, he has a lot of grit. I wouldn't be surprised..."

Again, Raffaele cut him off. "No. And that's an order. The Donatos have suffered enough."

"Jeez, I get it," Tano relented, throwing up his hands. "I wish I knew what the Donatos have over us that we have to be so careful around them."

"Yeah, Pop," Jack agreed. "I've been wondering the same thing. You won't ever talk about it. Why are the Donatos so special."

Raffaele looked at his two sons and decided it was finally time to tell them the story. He put his hands flat on the table, smoothing the tablecloth, wiping some crumbs onto the floor.

"Okay, I'll tell you. But it doesn't leave this table, capisce?" Raffaele said, looking for agreement. He wouldn't continue until both Jack and Tano agreed.

"When I tell you the story, you'll understand," Raffaele said. He poured each of his sons another glass of wine and raised his glass in salute. When they all had taken a drink, he began.

"My mother told me shortly after your grandfather died. He had sworn her to secrecy as well, but she wanted to unburden herself, and make sure I would look out for Rocco Donato and his family if I could."

Jack and Tano were both enraptured, happy to finally hear the story of why the Scaglias and Donatos were tied together.

"It happened back in Potenza, when your grandfather Danilo was just a boy..."

ABOUT THE AUTHOR

Sons of Potenza is the debut novel by John Rosa, a Colorado native who grew up in a large and loud Italian American family that grew carnations and gathered every week for Sunday pasta. He spent more than two decades working in journalism before evil hedge funds took over and he made the move to join the public sector as a communication specialist for the State of Colorado. He lives in Littleton Colorado with his beautiful wife Julie, who comes from an even larger and louder Sicilian American family, and their myriad dogs. Father to Brittany, Robert, Megan and Nico, and Papa to little Gio, John hopes to one day retire to Italy where he can take long walks with his great love Julie. And the dogs, of course.